MORE THAN
A GAME

More Than A Game

TERENCE O'LEARY

Swan
Creek
Press

Swan
Creek
↶*Press*
Toledo, Ohio

Copyright © 2004 by Terence O'Leary

First Swan Creek Press Edition 2004
ISBN 0-9753216-0-9
Library of Congress Control Number: 2004092195

For information on ordering additional
copies and quantity discounts contact
www.swancreekpress.com
Phone: (419) 381-0115
Fax: (419) 381-8696
Email: swancreekpress@buckeye-express.com

For my children, Brittany & Brian
and
For Karen, always . . .

Acknowledgment

All stories have a turning point. I met Jane Bradley at a writer's conference. After reading the first draft of *More Than a Game*, Jane convinced me that I didn't have a novel but the seeds of one. Four rewrites later, here we are. I am forever indebted to Jane for her critiques and encouragement.

Every person I have known has shaped this novel

Prologue

Chosin Reservoir, North Korea

November 1950

Marty stumbled. The heel of his boot snagged the sharp edge of the crevice, and he slid, his face diving into the dry white snow as his helmet snapped against the back of his neck. An icy fog whooshed from his chest as he fell on his M-1 carbine. Quickly rolling on his side, he heard the staccato burst of gunfire muffled by the snow jammed between his ear and helmet. His uncontrolled slide continued, his backpack plowing the dry snow in front, slowing his descent until finally jamming against a rocky outcrop coated with gleaming ice. Marty shook his head then quickly scanned the ridgeline of the Taebaek Mountains. The gunfire from the North Koreans looked like showers of sparks against the white mountainside.

He searched for Sergeant Garrity, the sergeant's screams still ringing in his ears, "GET DOWN THE MOUNTAIN! GO! GO!" Garrity swung the BAR around and laid down a stream of covering fire for his retreating squad. Rapid bursts of bullets echoed off the mountains. Marty cringed seeing his sergeant illuminated by a bright red-orange flash of light, as one, then another grenade exploded. A sheet of ivory snow broke loose from the edge of the ridgeline. Marty rolled onto his stomach, locked his hands behind his helmet and pressed his cheek against the stinging whiteness. He squeezed his eyes shut as the cascading snow hit him like an ocean wave and pinned him against the rocks. The light vanished.

Hyperventilating in the darkness, he couldn't control the fear that he was buried alive. His hands clawed the snow. He screamed, "My God, My God. Don't do this to me". His fingers broke through the crust of ice. A shaft of light streaked down his arm as frigid air filled his lungs and tears brimmed his eyes. He felt the butt of his rifle jammed into his ribcage.

Sporadic bursts of gunfire echoed into his chamber. The shots tapered off. The screams began. Marty knew he wasn't shaking from the cold.

Marty lost track of time. His body was still encased in the snow, but his mind had slipped away. He was home walking across a baseball field to a girl sitting in the bleachers. A shadow fell across his white cocoon. Marty burrowed his fingers through the snow. As his hand broke through to the surface, Marty felt the wind, an icy blast of Siberian wind pressing against his hand like a block of ice. Marty jerked his hand back and blew on his fingertips sticking out from his cut-down gloves. He stared through the white tunnel his hand had made through the compacted snow. He saw the mountainside covered with snow, so white, so pure. His fingertips crept up through the tunnel again and enlarged his viewing hole to reveal the top of the Taebaek Mountains, then sky, startlingly blue with a wisp of snow blowing like sand across a dry baseball diamond.

It was an uncontrollable urge to pee that forced him to move. He shifted to his side and carefully widened his viewing tunnel by pushing the snow patiently to the outside. An icy blast caught the rim and careened down the tunnel, so cold it burned his lungs as he breathed. He pulled his hand back, curled and pressed his fingers against his chest. He could see the ridgeline, the blackened snow where he last saw Sergeant

Garrity. He thought he saw clumps of dirt or were they uniforms? With measured breaths he waited and waited but there was no movement in his field of vision.

The sun slipped below the tip of the mountain peaks turning the snow from gleaming white to dull ivory. As his ice tunnel darkened, panic returned. Feeling the walls closing in on him, he thought there is no way he could stay there in the dark. Rolling onto his stomach he pushed up on his forearms then wedged his knees under his chest. His left hand blindly searched the ground until his fingers felt and wrapped around the butt of his carbine. Marty took a deep breath then arched his back and pushed up with his arms. As his helmet broke the surface, he swung his M-1 to his chest. Still covered in snow, he knelt, lifted his rifle to his shoulder and aimed at the ridgeline. The wind froze the hair in his nostrils and seared his exposed fingertip to the metal trigger. As he sighted down his carbine, his left hand quivered then began to shake. The stock of his rifle rattled against his cheekbone. He cradled the carbine in his arms, fell forward onto the snow, and then crawled on his elbows and knees up the ridge.

Carefully peering over the edge he saw the bodies. It was incomprehensible. Why would they be naked? Marty remembered the screams. Sutton and Forester. Frozen. Sutton was curled into a ball, his arms wrapped around his knees pressed to his chest. Marty couldn't see Suttons' face because it was buried into Sutton's knees. Marty forced his eyes away from the frozen ball and quickly scanned the ridge. He swung his gaze back and slowly crawled forward to the second corpse. Forester was stretched out on his back, his right foot under his left knee as if he were sliding into base. The corporal's arms were extended from his body, his fingers curled into claws as if he were trying to grab the life escaping. Marty inched closer. The blowing snow filled the cracks under the bodies and swirled into their crevices. Forester's piercing black eyes stared blankly at the mountaintop. Marty's shaking fingertips reached out to close Forester's eyes. Touching the brittle, frozen eyelashes, his fingers recoiled as the lashes snapped. He swallowed and sank back into the snow kneeling on his boots. His right hand traced the sign of the cross. He jammed the butt of his M-1 against the frozen ledge and pushed up. Hunched over, he forced one foot and then the other to where he had last seen his sergeant.

It took Marty a second to realize the next body wasn't his sergeant but Private Cummings. As a kid he remembered his uncle's outside faucet, the dripping water forming an icicle hanging from the rim. Cumming's icicle was bright red. It protruded through the pant leg of his right thigh. The soldier lay on his stomach. The metal of Cumming's carbine was frozen to his cheekbone. Marty's hand brushed Cumming's shoulder as he moved on.

Are they all dead? Marty wondered as he stumbled along the ridge. He stopped seeing the charred stumps. Mary tried to pull them together in his mind. As he saw Sergeant Garrity's blackened head, "All the King's horses and all the King's men couldn't put Humpty Dumpty together again," kept spinning through his mind. His knees buckled. Collapsing he saw the furrow in the snow then heard the shot. The next furrow was by his right hand. Marty rolled to his left falling into the crater carved into the icy ledge by the grenades that killed Garrity. He made himself as small as he could. A burst of shots burrowed into the ledge behind covering Marty with shards of ice and stone. He looked down at the wristwatch still ticking on Garrity's charred stump of an arm. Marty gagged then forced the rising bile back into his stomach.

Peering up the mountaintop he saw flashes by the ledge where the foot trail curved around the ridge. The bullets thumped behind him. Frigid winds gusted down the mountains swirling clouds of snow. The North Koreans on the ledge vanished in a white fog. Without thinking, Marty's boots dug a foothold. He scrambled up and rolled out of the crater. His boots slipped as he half-ran, half-slid down the sloped icy path. His labored breathing billowed icy vapors.

Too fast. He struggled to bring his racing feet back under his chest. As he saw the path curve and the drop-off over the edge of the mountain, Marty fell on his back. Digging the butt of his carbine into the snow to break his slide, his left boot slid over the mountainside. He leaned to his right, his backpack hung over the edge, as his body careened around the bend. The rifle butt jammed against an upraised rock. His arms felt like they were torn from their sockets. The sudden stop yanked Marty onto his stomach. Quickly he looked up at the swirling snow. The North Korean's hold was blocked from view by the twist in the path. He couldn't see them. He gulped frigid air. They couldn't see him.

Searing pain traveled from his shoulder joints and down his arms as he pulled his carbine back to his chest. He rolled to a sitting position cradling his rifle in his lap. Looking down the mountainside, he tried to follow the downward serpentine path cut through the stark gleaming cliffs. He knew if he followed the path that eventually he would stumble across his retreating army column, the army column whose flank his squad was supposed to be protecting. As he stared at the darkening cliffs, a wave of panic washed over him. He glanced at his watch. He'd never get down in the dark. Shadows crept across the bottom cliffs. Marty forced himself to his feet, took a quick glance back then carefully started down the footpath.

Marty froze in midstep as he rounded the cliff, his eyes staring at the end of the barrel protruding from the top of the boulder, waiting for the bullet's impact to tear through his chest. As he sucked in a breath, he could barely see the helmet covered in snow behind the rifle. He wondered if he would hear the shot. The white-silhouetted figure shifted and smashed the rifle against the rock.

"Friggin' A, Marty! I would have shot you. The frigging gun's frozen." He slammed the rifle again on top of the boulder.

"CRACK!" The shot sounded like the snap of a whip by Marty's ear. Marty found himself on the ground.

"MARTY!"

In a daze Marty watched the soldier lurch from behind the boulder, dragging his left leg.

"MARTY!" The soldier collapsed by Marty's side. "Are you hit? Jesus Christ, Marty. The frigging gun. Where're you hit, Marty? Where're you hit?" The soldier roughly rolled Marty over and his hands began pawing Marty's chest.

"Henry," Marty grabbed the soldier's ice-cold, bare hands and held them to his chest. "Where're your gloves?"

"You're not hit." Henry pulled his hands back and jammed them under his armpits. He knelt on his right knee with his left leg stiffly protruding to the side. He glanced to his carbine lying on top of the boulder. "Frigging gun. I couldn't get my finger on the trigger with those damn mittens. I yanked them off when we got hit, when Garrity said go." Henry shrugged his shoulders. "They're still up there somewhere."

Marty sat up studying Henry's gaunt pale face, his cheeks covered with stubble that looked like smeared brown dirt under dark eyebrows crusted with ice. As their eyes met, Henry looked away and wiped the frozen snot from the end of his nose.

"Where's your pack?" Marty asked.

Henry shifted and sat back on his right haunch. He grimaced as he grabbed his left leg and pulled it in front. "I ditched it."

"You what?"

Henry looked up the mountain. "It got hung up on one of those ledges." His eyes went wild. "They were shooting at me.

I didn't have time. I just unsnapped it and ran." Henry looked
from the mountain to Marty. "You got a cigarette?"

Marty unzipped his coat and reached into his shirt pocket.
He pulled out a crushed pack of Chesterfields. Henry's shaking
fingers clutched the end of the cigarette then slid it between his
chattering teeth. Marty lifted the pack to his mouth and bit
down on the end of a cigarette. He slid the pack inside his coat
then pulled his Zippo lighter from an inside pocket. Henry
cupped his hands around Marty's hand and bent his face to the
lighter. After Henry got his cigarette lit, he kept his hands
around Marty's lighter while Marty bent to light his own.
Marty deeply inhaled, letting the smoke warm his lungs. He
tilted his head back and exhaled a stream of smoke into the
falling snow.

Henry grunted as he shifted his leg on top of the snow.
Marty noticed the grimace cross Henry's face.

"You okay?" asked Marty.

Henry snorted a puff of smoke. "I think I got shot in the
ass."

"What?" Marty quickly glanced at Henry's leg.

"When I took off it felt like a wasp stung me in the ass. I
don't know . . ." Henry laughed, "It's not like I can see it."

Marty shouted, "Turn over."

"Forget it."

Marty grabbed Henry's shoulder and yanked him onto his
stomach.

Henry screamed, "Easy! Marty!"

Henry's left pant leg was smeared in blood. Marty slid his
knife from his belt. "Stay still." He traced the knife's point up
the smear to the jagged hole in the back of Henry's pants.
Marty sliced a flap through coarse fabric and underpants then
pulled it open. He could see the purple pucker in the meaty
flesh covered with a paste of frozen blood. Marty said, "Well,
you got your purple heart, Henry."

"Great!" Henry said as he looked over his shoulder at

Marty. "Just what I want to tell my folks: 'Got shot in the ass while running away from the frigging Chinese army.'"

"Chinese?"

"Hell, Marty? You think they were North Koreans? Didn't you see the uniforms? We got the whole frigging Chinese army coming down the mountain."

Marty quickly snatched his carbine and scanned the upper mountainside. He tried to peer through the lengthening shadows on the cliffs. He looked back to Henry and then at his wound. "It's stopped bleeding." Marty shuddered. "It's too cold even for warm blood to flow."

Henry rolled to his side and used his arms to push himself onto his right haunch. Marty stared at the path leading down the mountain disappearing into the twilight. A gust of icy wind swirled off the cliffs. Henry locked his hands under his armpits. "Going to be dark soon, Marty." Henry waited until Marty looked at him. "You better get going." He nodded to his carbine on the boulder. "I'll cover your back."

Marty slowly stood and took a few steps towards the edge of the cliff. He watched the approaching shadows like long fingers of dark fog rolling up the mountainside. He looked at his wristwatch then at the descending trail. He could make it. It wouldn't be easy but if he could stay on the path, he could make it down. But what about Henry? The wind pelted his face with what felt like thousands of pinpricks. He turned and looked at Henry propped on his elbow lying on the snow.

Henry met his stare then looked down the steep twisting path. "Go, Marty." Henry hit his fist against his leg. "There's no way we can both make it down in time."

Marty didn't want to die. Staring at Henry, he brought his hands next to his face and blew on his frozen fingertips. He knew if he left Henry behind, he would leave a part of himself on the mountain that he would never get back. Making his decision, Marty tugged his coat collar tighter around his neck.

"It's the wind that'll kill us. We got to get out of this wind." He bent over, set his rifle on the ground, grabbed the top of Henry's coat and yanked him to his feet. "We'll wait until first light, then we'll get off this frigging mountain."

As Henry stood Marty bent down and picked up his M-1. Henry put his hand on Marty's shoulder, turned him around to face him and shouted above the rising wind, "Go, there's still enough light for you to make it down."

Marty moved closer and searching Henry's face asked, "Would you abandon me, Henry?"

Henry recoiled as if Marty had slapped him.

"I didn't think so." Marty slid his hand under Henry's arm and led him back towards the boulder.

Henry stood leaning against the boulder, shaking uncontrollably. The rapidly falling snow covered his carbine. Using his rifle as a makeshift shovel, Marty grunted trying to dig frozen snow out of the fissure between the boulder and the cliff face.

"Henry," Marty motioned towards the crevice. Marty stepped to the side and squeezed Henry through the narrow gap. Where the boulder had split from the cliffs was a small natural cave. Marty pushed Henry into the darkness.

Marty unsnapped his knapsack and tossed it into the cave. He crawled in behind it. Kneeling, he used his rifle to scoop the snow into a wall at the fissure's opening. He could hear Henry's chattering teeth behind him. He left a small aperture at the top to let in the feeble moonlight. He sank back against the wall next to Henry's shoulder. Marty dug a cigarette from his inside pocket. He lit it and held it out. Henry lifted his shaking hand and tried to take the cigarette. He stared at his hand in disbelief.

"I can't feel my fingers." He sank back against the wall. Marty leaned forward and placed the cigarette between Henry's swollen chapped lips.

Marty lifted his knapsack then smashed it on the cave's floor again and again. The packed sleet and ice broke loose from the canvas. His cold fingers fumbled with the buckles. He finally opened the knapsack and blindly searched inside until he felt the rolled woolen socks. He took the Chesterfield from Henry's lips and took a long drag then slid it back between Henry's teeth.

Marty unrolled the woolen socks then carefully slid them onto Henry's rough hands. He began massaging Henry's thick fingers.

A long ash broke off from the cigarette and fell on Henry's chest as he asked despondently, "We going to make it, Marty?"

Marty looked at Henry's ashen face illuminated by the fiery glow of the cigarette. He kept massaging Henry's fingers. "First light . . . first light we head down. Once we get back to the road, we'll hook up with the column. They'll be there. Hell, they're spread all the way back to the reservoir." Marty tried to bend the tips of Henry's fingers. "We'll make it, Henry."

Marty could feel his own fingers warming as he kneaded the wool covering Henry's hands. As he shifted his knees his foot hit the knapsack and knocked it over. Henry stared vacantly at the open mouth of the knapsack.

Marty stopped, his fingers just too tired to keep massaging Henry's hands. He pulled another Chesterfield from the pack. As the Zippo illuminated their cave, Henry laughed. "Marty!" He laughed again. "Christ, I don't believe it. You kept the frigging mitt."

Marty followed Henry's gaze to the knapsack.

Henry pointed his sock covered hand. "You weren't supposed to keep it."

Marty quickly lit a cigarette. Darkness enveloped the cave except for the glow from the cigarette. He took a drag then slid the cigarette between Henry's lips. He scooted away from Henry and picked up the baseball mitt, the leather cold and stiff in his hands. He kneaded the leather just as he had kneaded Henry's hands. He slid his left hand inside the mitt. He formed his right hand into a fist, like a baseball, and wrapped the mitt around his fist. The embers of the cigarette dimmed then died leaving the cave dark. Marty moved. He edged along the cave wall until his shoulder pressed against Henry's shaking body. He looked to the opening at the top of the wall of snow. Holding the mitt against his chest he let the mitt carry him home as he waited for first light.

Chapter 1

"Come on, Brian! Get out here!" Kevin screamed from outside.

Brian cringed. He quickly glanced away from the monitor. As he looked out his upstairs bedroom window, he saw his dad standing in the driveway with a bucket of white, golf-sized, plastic balls at his feet. His dad was tossing one of the whiffle balls that he used for batting practice in the air and then catching it with his baseball mitt.

A starburst of purple light brought his attention back to the screen. Brian jerked as if he was slapped. His fingers danced across the keyboard powering up his life shield as the trolls surrounded and trampled his online character, the wizard Merlwy. Quickly checking his available spells, he keyed his invisibility cloak then sent a help message to other members of his group in the role-playing game. As two friendly Viking warriors raced into his realm through the portal from the next level, Merlwy uncloaked and swirled a quarter staff at the back of one of the trolls.

"Brian!"

Brian screamed, 'Not Now!' in his head but called out, "I'm coming!" The troll collapsed under Merlwy's staff, but three more trolls rushed to take his place. Brian could see his Viking allies coming to his aid. He darted a glance out the window, knowing the price he would have to pay if his dad shouted his name again.

He checked Merlwy's life shield that held the menacing trolls at bay. He drummed his fingers on top of his keyboard wrist support while waiting for the Vikings to get in position behind the trolls. The Vikings seemed to take forever as he watched his life shield weaken. Too slow. Too slow, he thought watching the approaching Vikings while his whole body tensed waiting to hear his father scream his name. He mumbled, "I can't wait." He threw his stun spell then ran Merlwy headfirst towards the middle troll, his quarter staff whirling. The other two trolls came up behind Merlwy as the wizard tried to drive the center troll back towards the Vikings. He felt as if the trolls' mace and hammers were pounding his own back as Merlwy's lifeline darkened. He tried to have Merlwy push the troll back, but with each step Merlwy's staff slowed. Brian's character stumbled then disappeared under the onslaught from the trolls. Brian watched his fellow RPG Vikings stop and then retreat to the portal. He threw his hands up in frustration and stared at the screen as Merlwy was crushed under the trolls.

"Brian!" The small plastic golf ball bounced off his bedroom window.

He pounded his hands on the keyboard as he muttered, "It's not fair. We would have won. I just needed more time." He glared out his window and quickly glanced away when he saw his dad staring up at his room. Brian punched the escape key. He grabbed his baseball cap from the desk then raced downstairs.

The white whiffle ball bounced off the garage door and rolled down the black sloping driveway to his dad.

Brian tapped the end of his bat on the blacktop as he stood at the top of the driveway with the closed garage door behind him trying to clear the image of the trolls pummeling Merlwy.

"You never could hit my curve ball," his dad said as he bent and snatched another plastic ball from the pail by his feet. Kevin wiped the sweat from his forehead onto his arm then rubbed the ball on his shorts. God, how many years, he thought? How many pitches? He high-stepped his front leg and let her fly. He watched as the white ball blended with the white garage door. He saw the sun's flash on the aluminum bat and heard the *thwack*. He turned and watched the golf ball fall like a chip shot on his neighbor's grass across the street.

Kevin snatched another ball from the pail, stared at his son and shook his head as if he were calling off signs from an imaginary catcher. But he wasn't shaking off signs, only images of Brian going all the way back to kindergarten. The memory of the skinny, six-year old kid with the oversized, orange plastic bat swinging wildly at balls merged into the image of the eighteen-year old youth dressed in a St. Pat's High School baseball uniform, white with green trim. His son Brian, two inches taller than his own five feet ten inches, made him an even six feet but fifty pounds lighter. Brian, with the wiry, muscled body of a gymnast or track sprinter, squinted into the harsh sunlight with his piercing blue eyes. What did his wife Karen say? "Eyes like Steve McQueen or was it Paul Newman?" Well, he got the eyes from me, thought Kevin, but he got the looks from his mom. Sometimes Kevin felt his son was just too good-looking. He needed to be more rugged to give pitchers the stone stare.

"Come on, Dad," Brian said with an edge to his voice. "You going to pitch or not? The game starts in an hour."

Thwack! Kevin palmed the line drive and in one fluid motion tossed the ball from his glove to his free hand and pitched again. Brian bunted, driving the ball back to his dad's feet.

Two hundred pitches a day: Summertime outside against the garage door, wintertime inside the garage. Since first grade, not using a baseball, but a much harder to hit small plastic whiffle ball, two hundred pitches a day. I should do the math, thought Kevin going into his wind-up. Two hundred pitches a day, three hundred sixty-five days a year, for what, twelve years. *Thwack!* Kevin didn't bother to turn and look. He knew if it were a league ball, it would have cleared the fence. He was into his rhythm now, just him and Brian. Just pitch and catch.

Kevin laughed as Brian spun like a top. Brian just managed to dig the top edge of the bat against the driveway to keep from falling. Kevin laughed again. "That change-up gets you every time, Brian." Kevin picked another ball from the pail, tossed it in the air and caught it with his mitt. Studying his son, he let the laughter fade from his voice as he said, "You've got to look for it, Brian. How many times have I told you? A good pitcher will set you up with his fast ball then slide his change-up by you every time."

Brian looked down at the driveway and tapped the tip of his bat against the blacktop. He felt like he was under siege from the trolls.

"You ready?" asked Kevin.

Brian bided his time still tapping the bat on the driveway. He reached up and lowered his cap on his forehead.

"Brian."

Finally, he looked up. The plastic ball became a rock hurled from a troll. He snapped the bat like Merlwy's quarter staff. The ball streaked towards Kevin's head.

"Shit," yelled Kevin.

Brian dropped his bat and raced to his father. "You okay, Dad?"

Kevin rubbed his left cheekbone. "Damn, that stings."

"I didn't . . . mean it." Brian lifted his hand towards his father's cheek thinking if he could touch the bruise he could take it away.

Kevin caught his son's hand and pushed it away.

Brian retreated then guiltily offered, "Let me get you some ice."

"I don't need any damn ice."

Brian straightened and looked up at his father. "If it happened to me you'd say ice it before it starts swelling." He met and held his father's gaze. "I'll be right back." Brian trotted up the porch steps and into the house.

Feeling his cheek go numb from the cold, Kevin said, "I don't know if your forty-five year old Dad is getting too slow or if you're getting too fast."

"Dad, no pitcher stands just twenty feet from the batter."

Kevin pulled the ice bag from his cheek and snapped, "That's where I've always stood."

Brian shook his head. " Dad, in case you haven't noticed, I'm not playing little league ball."

Kevin looked up to meet his son's blue eyes. He relaxed and smiled. "Next time I'll duck."

Brian laughed. "How 'bout I get you one of those hockey face masks?"

"How about," Kevin replied, "you get your stuff together and we hit the road."

"You think the scouts will be there, Dad?" asked Brian.

"Probably a whole pack of them," Kevin said. "Brian, they can be worse than hyenas. Don't talk to them. Don't let them distract you. If they start hounding you, just tell them to come see me." Kevin pushed his son towards the house. "Grab your bat bag and let's head over to the field. We got a game to play."

Even if he were blind, Kevin would know it was spring baseball. He inhaled the scent of freshly cut, damp grass. After the wettest month of May in the last decade the outfields were a lush green. Kevin looked over the field as if he were looking at his own backyard. He saw the grass sticking in clumps to the bottom of kids' cleats. One of the outfielders slid to catch a practice fly ball. He stood up, laughed, and tried to rub out the streak of green on the bottom of his pants.

Kevin leaned against the chain link fence in his 'no mans land,' an area he carved out between the dugout and the

bleachers. He wasn't a coach. The last time he coached Brian
was at St. John's grade school when his eighth graders took the
city championship. But he stayed close enough to the dugout
to hear the same dumb jokes from the kids, and if Coach
Macerak wanted, he could wander down to the fence and he
and Kevin would go over the lineup. During the four years that
Brian played for St. Pat's, Kevin and Coach Macerak developed
quite a series of signals. When Coach Macerak scratched his
left ear it meant, I'm going to pull the pitcher. A corresponding
scratch to Kevin's left ear meant, good idea; the right ear
meant, better wait.

Brian watched his dad pace back and forth between the
bleachers and the dugout. Kevin's hands were stuffed deep into
his back pockets; his Hens baseball cap shielded his eyes from
the late afternoon sun. Brian didn't have to look at the scoreboard; he knew how close the game was by his father's pace, fast
or slow. Kevin almost reached the bleachers, whipped his head
around, pivoted on his toes and paced quickly back towards the
dugout. He cocked his head and his gaze swept the baseball
field.

It felt like a wave of reassurance as his father's eyes passed
over him. In his entire life Brian could never remember playing a game alone. His dad was always with him, either in the
dugout or pacing the sidelines. The feeling was as familiar and
comforting as the well-worn glove on his hand. Brian nodded
to his father then shifted into his defensive crouch at second
base. He bent his knees; the tip of his open glove on his left
hand almost touched the dirt. He bounced on the balls of his
feet, like a jaguar ready to spring.

"Settle down, Chris, come on settle down. You got this
guy," Brian said to the pitcher. As the curve ball faded out of the
strike zone the umpire shouted, "Ball four!"

Now the fun begins, thought Brian, eyeing the runner on
first as the base runner took his leadoff moving closer to second. The runner and Brian both moved with the pitch. The

batter smacked a line drive up the middle. Brian dove but couldn't quite reach the streaking ball. The tip of his glove caught just enough to knock the ball down. Brian scrambled on his hand and knees, snatched the ball with his open right hand and tossed it to Trevor, the shortstop covering second. Trevor threw the ball to first completing the double play. Brian stood up and scraped the damp dirt from his knees. He smacked the loose dirt from his glove on his thigh then flashed a thumps-up to Trevor.

How are they going to pitch you today, thought Kevin. He rested his hands on top of the fence and watched Brian take his practice swings. He shifted his gaze from Brian to the Start High School baseball coach talking with his pitcher on the mound. That was one conversation he sure didn't miss. You don't want to give him anything to hit; but you don't want to walk the lead-off batter, especially, when that lead-off batter holds the high school city record for the most stolen bases in a season. Kevin chuckled as he remembered Coach Macerak say he was going to stir up the hornets' nest. He initially had Brian batting either third or fourth, but if St. Pat's got a runner on base he couldn't really use Brian's speed. He moved Brian to the lead-off spot and never looked back.

"Ball four. Take your base," the umpire said.

Brian mentally counted the four step lead-off he took from first base then settled his weight fifty-fifty ready to race to second or dive back to first. "What are you going to do, John?" Brian smiled and called out to the pitcher who had played on Brian's grade school team but was now a starting pitcher for the opposing high school. "Come on, John, catch me if you can, come on." Brian faked as if he were hustling for second, watching the pitcher as the pitcher pretended to ignore him. "I'm going, John, soon as that ball leaves your hand, I'm gone."

The catcher slid to the side away from the plate and batter. He took the pitch out and reared up ready to throw to the second baseman. He saw Brian still standing four steps away from first base.

Brian nonchalantly walked back and tagged up at first. "Now why did I think you were going to do that, John," teased Brian. He settled back into his lead-off. "This time, I'm really going, John."

Pitch out. Brian took a quick step to second then froze. The pitcher ducked as the catcher threw a strike to the second baseman. Brian skipped back to first base.

"Wow, John, that catcher's got a good arm," laughed Brian. "Maybe he should be pitching instead of you." Brian tagged up on first then eased away from the bag.

Kevin watched Brian's feet. It's the little things, he thought. It's always the little things that give you away. Brian's weight was fifty-fifty, both feet pointed straight ahead as the pitcher went into his wind-up. "He's going," muttered Kevin as he watched Brian's back foot pivot and turn towards second. The batter swung and missed at a high curve ball giving Brian an extra split second. As he slid into second, he heard the ball thump into the second baseman's mitt. Brian popped up on the base like a jack-in-the-box, signaled with his hands and yelled, "Time, ump." He started brushing the dirt from his pants. He didn't look at the pitcher but smiled at the catcher. The catcher just shrugged his shoulders and walked behind the batter.

"Yeah, that's right," said Kevin to himself. "Give him your four thousand dollar smile." It was one of their jokes. Kevin paid four thousand dollars and Brian wore the braces for three years.

"Ball four," said the umpire.

Brian stayed at second as Trevor trotted to first. Coach Macerak took off his baseball cap and wiped his forearm along his forehead.

Kevin read the hand signal from Coach Macerak. "So you want a double steal," Kevin said. "I don't know. That catcher has got a rocket for an arm. Ah, what the hell, it's early." Kevin took off his cap and swept his hand over the top of his brown hair signaling his okay.

Brian did a double take as he took the signal from the third base coach. "All right," he grinned to himself. He nodded to Trevor at first then stepped away from second base. He eased into his zone, the zone he found on the track field, the only other sport he lettered in. A sprinter, fast but not fast enough to be a record breaker. What Brian had was a first step. No one could touch him coming out of the blocks; a few could catch him and pass him but not in the first thirty yards. Second to third was ninety feet. There was no conscious thought to steal. His eyes focused on the pitch, and without thinking his feet started moving. The throw from the catcher was high. By the time the third baseman caught the ball and brought it down, Brian easily slid under the tag. Trevor on second called for time out.

"How you been, Colin?" Brian asked the third baseman.

"Okay, Brian. How about you?"

"Good. I've been good, Colin."

Colin glanced to the bleachers. "See all those scouts in the stands."

Brian said, "They're all here to see you, Colin."

"Yeah, right!" "You're not going to try and steal home are you, Brian?"

"Come on, Colin. It's the first inning. We've got runners on second and third with no outs. The coach would kill me if I tried to steal home."

Brian dove back to third. Colin took the throw from the pitcher and went through the motion of sweeping his mitt down for the tag.

Kevin studied the infield. The third and second basemen were playing close to the bags to hold the runners so they wouldn't try to steal. The first baseman was out of position. He was playing back trying to cover the opening between first and second instead of playing up to guard against a bunt. Kevin waited until Coach Macerak looked in his direction then took off his sunglasses and slid one of the stems into the top of his shirt so they hung from his top collar. Coach Macerak did a double take, then looked at Brian on third base and Trevor on second. He looked back at Kevin and nodded his head, then turned and relayed the signal to the third base coach.

Brian picked up the sign from the third base Coach. As the pitcher went into his stretch wind-up, Brian said, "See you around, Colin."

The batter pivoted and squared the bat. The bunt rolled down the first base line. The first baseman scrambled and frantically ran towards the bunt. Looking like a crab, the catcher scuttled forward after the ball as Brian raced home across the plate.

Kevin leaned against the fence watching the two teams slap hands after the game. He saw the Start high school coach call Brian aside, and he wondered what the coach was saying. He heard the familiar, approaching clicks of high heels on the tarmac. He turned as he felt her hand slightly brush his shoulder.

"Don't tell me you ran into a door."

Kevin rubbed his hand across his face trying to hide the bruise from his wife.

She lifted her hand and pushed Kevin's hand away then gently placed her palm under Kevin's cheek and swung his face back towards the sunlight. "What happened?" She softly rubbed the skin on his cheekbone. Suddenly, she burst out laughing. "Brian got you didn't he? He whacked you with one of those plastic balls."

Kevin brushed her hand way. "It's not that bad." He couldn't help smiling at his wife. He looked into what he called her cat eyes, deep brown eyes with specs of green. Her smile spread from her eyes to her high cheekbones and to her narrow lips.

"Wait until tomorrow when it changes color."

"Karen," Kevin said while giving her a look that said enough is enough.

"Okay, okay." She stood next to her husband by the fence and watched the St. Pat's boys gather their equipment. "How did Brian play today? I only caught the last inning."

"They walked him three times."

"I betcha' he's happy about that."

Kevin shrugged. "He got three stolen bases and he made a great leaping catch in the third inning."

As Karen scanned the St. Pat's uniforms, she suddenly said, "Where's Brian?"

"Over there."

Karen followed his gaze to the bleachers by the third base dugout.

"That's Start's coach," said Karen, "but who are those men waiting behind him?"

"Scouts." Kevin turned and leaned against the fence. "I wasn't sure if they'd show up here. I expected them to wait for the state finals in Columbus." He put his wrap-around sun-glasses on and squinted to make out the distant figures. "I think the one on the right is Jacobs from Arizona State. I heard he was making a quick tour through the Midwest. The other one might be Baxter from Miami. I'm not sure about the third one."

"But I'm sure he's from another baseball college," Karen said with a rising edge to her voice.

Kevin twisted his head towards his wife. He opened his mouth but stopped the words before they sprang from his lips. He drew a deep breath. He didn't want to go into another round of their seemingly endless fight over Brian's future education. He swallowed and said quietly, "They're good schools, Karen."

Karen couldn't leave it alone. "Athletic scholarships. Brian can get an academic scholarship. He's been . . ." She suddenly stopped then waved her hand in dismissal.

Kevin stared at his wife until she looked back at the bleachers. He noticed the gleam of perspiration on her upper lip. "That suit, you must be burning up in this heat."

Karen's face relaxed as she felt the tension fade away. Her right hand clutched and fanned the bottom of her black skirt. "It's not the suit; it's the pantyhose. It feels like they're taped to my legs."

Kevin cocked his head towards the parking lot. "Head home. I'll get Brian and be right behind you."

Karen shook her head and moved closer to her husband. She clutched his arm. "I need to stop and see my dad."

Kevin looked at Karen and waited.

Karen continued, "He had another chemo session this afternoon. When I talked to Mom—" She leaned her head against Kevin's shoulder and whispered, as if whispering could hide the words, "It's not working."

Kevin's palm cradled Karen's black hair as she sagged against him. She took a deep breath then pulled away. "I better go." Her hand slipped down Kevin's arm to his hand.

Kevin held tight. "Tell Marty," he searched for words then helplessly shrugged his shoulders.

"I know," Karen squeezed his hand, "I'll tell him."

Kevin sat in his car, his mind swinging like a pendulum between his father-in-law, Marty, and his son, Brian, who was walking from the dugout. He had the windows down and a slight breeze evaporated the sweat from his skin. He popped the inside trunk release as he saw Brian walk across the parking lot. Brian tossed his bat bag into the trunk and slammed the lid.

Three boys sped across the parking lot on twenty-inch bikes. The lead boy slammed on his brakes. The back wheel shrieked and spun in an arc on the pavement. The boy planted his foot on the ground and shouted, "Brian!" Almost colliding, his two young friends slid to a halt next to Kyle's bike.

"Kyle. What's up?" asked Brian, smiling at his eleven-year old cousin.

Kyle pointed to the black kid on the bike next to him, "This is my friend, Stanley. He just moved here from South Carolina. They're living where the Millers used to live."

Brian nodded and said, "How's it going?"

Stanley looked from Brian to Kyle as if seeking confirmation as he uttered, "Kyle, said you're the wizard Merlwy."

The red haired, fair skinned, freckled boy on the other bike said, "He is Merlwy." He looked away from Stanley dismissing the question and asked, "You going to be online tonight, Brian?"

Kyle cut in, staring at Stanley, "I told you he's Merlwy. You ever get trapped by the gnomes or crushed by the trolls, you just call Merlwy. He's got a spell to get you out of anything."

"Not only that," added Red, "you get hurt, the trolls crush your leg or slice off your arm, you call Merlwy and he'll make you good as new." Red looked at Brian with admiration. "He knows magic spells that no one else does."

Feeling his father's eyes, Brian glanced over his shoulder. He quickly turned back to the boys and said, "I got to go."

Straddling his bike, Kyle scooted forward to the driver's door.

"Hi, Uncle Kevin."

Kevin looked at his nephew with short curly hair and the thick long eye lashes that all the girls envied. "Where've you been, Kyle? I haven't seen you for a while."

"I don't know." Kyle looked down and snapped the top of his foot against the pedal, spinning it. "I've just been around."

Kevin turned, reached into the unused ashtray and pulled out a pack of Wrigley's gum.

Kyle took one piece and popped it in his mouth. Kevin held the pack out and motioned to Kyle's friends. Kyle took two more sticks of gum.

Kevin said, "Ask your Mom if she wants to come over for a cookout on Sunday."

"Okay." Kyle wheeled his bike to his friends and shared the gum. He gave a quick wave then the three riders sped across the lot.

Kevin swung his right arm up on the seat and faced Brian. "Merlin?"

Brian's face reddened, "Merlwy." He turned away from his father and looked out the passenger window." He shifted uncomfortably in his seat as he said, "It's just a game, Dad."

Kevin started the car. "What'd Start's coach have to say?"

Brian took off his St. Pat's cap and wiped his forearm across his forehead. He reached to turn on the AC.

Kevin said, "No. You'll stiffen up."

Brian shook his head in frustration. "I'm burning up."

Kevin shifted the car in gear and pulled out of the parking lot. "It'll cool off in a minute."

Brian felt his shirt stick to his back as he leaned forward. He thought, why can't I ever just do what I want.

"Well?"

Brian asked annoyed, "Well, what?"

"Start's coach."

"Oh," Brian turned and watched the baseball field shrink behind them. "He saw the scouts and wanted to know if I decided . . . you know . . ." Brian shrugged. "Did you talk to the scouts?" Brian laughed, "Were they impressed with my three walks?"

Kevin tightened his lips and glanced at his son. "I told them we weren't making any decisions until after the state finals."

Brian sank into his seat and chewed his lower lip, the word *we* rocking through his mind.

"We're in the driver's seat, Brian. After the finals we'll take a tour of some of the campuses. I've got it pretty well narrowed down to five. See . . ." Kevin glanced at his son and waited until Brian turned and made eye contact. "At any of these schools I figure you can go right to the pros. That's what Dave Winfield did. He was drafted by the San Diego Padres right out of college. He never played in the minor leagues. You've got the talent, Brian. You can do the same. Hell, playing for Arizona State or Miami is just like playing in the minors anyways." Kevin noticed the distant look on Brian's face. "Tell you what, let's save this discussion till after the finals."

Brian spun in his seat.

"Dad . . ." He wanted to scream, 'No, that's not what I want. I want to go to college at UW. I want to go there because then I can . . .' Looking into his dad's eyes he felt like a little kid again. "Nothing." He shrunk down in the car seat and stared vacantly out the front window. "Nothing, Dad."

Chapter 2

Every time Brian walked into Mr. Thayer's office he thought the high-tech computer seemed out of place on his counselor's desk. Brian wrinkled his nose against the musty odor that drifted off the hundreds of books that lined the floor to ceiling bookshelves. A number of books came from the original downtown high school that was built in 1876. Mr. Thayer looked as if he came from the original St. Pat's. Although he was only fifty-two, his white hair, granny glasses and blue, wide lapel suit made him appear much older. Brian glanced past Mr. Thayer to the window. The large statue of St. Patrick dominated the front lawn of this suburban school that was built in the early seventy's. Brian unconsciously pressed his hand against his churning stomach. He knew why Mr. Thayer called him to his office. He knew he didn't have the answer Mr. Thayer wanted to hear.

Mr. Thayer glanced at Brian then motioned with the tip of his pen to the high-backed leather chair in front of his desk. The guidance counselor/academic dean looked down and started reviewing the pages of Brian's folder.

Brian drummed his fingers on the armrest, but stopped and clenched the chair as Mr. Thayer looked at him. When Mr. Thayer looked back at the paperwork Brian's feet started tapping on the wooden floor.

Mr. Thayer pointed his pen at the top sheet and said, "Nanotechnology." He adjusted his glasses as he studied Brian.

"I would assume that nano comes from the Greek nannos meaning dwarf." He waited for Brian's reply.

Brian's feet stopped tapping as he leaned forward in the chair. "Dwarf . . . small . . . actually it refers to a billionth of a meter which would be about the width of four or five atoms." Brian's light blonde eyebrows arched as he smiled. "Dwarf if you consider that four atoms side by side are about . . ." Brian rubbed his hand on his forearm then pinched and pulled a single hair. He held it up between himself and Mr. Thayer and said, "Four atoms side by side are one thousand times smaller than this hair."

Mr. Thayer took off his glasses and held them by the stem in front of his face.

Brian flicked his fingers and tossed the hair away. "Nanotechnology is the building of machines or . . ." Brian pointed his hand around the room, "new materials . . . one atom at a time."

Mr. Thayer tapped his glasses on Brian's folder. "Your senior project was titled *Nanotechnology and Medicine*."

"Nanotechnology will affect all aspects of human life, but I think the greatest advancements will come in medicine. We can create these extremely small machines and insert them into the bloodstream." Brian turned his hand palm up and traced his finger along the veins in his wrist. "You know it's sort of like that old movie *Fantastic Voyage*. These machines can search out and destroy cancer cells at the same time they clean the arteries." Brian held up his hand and looked at his fingers." If you lose your fingertips to frostbite we will be able to regenerate them." Brian leaned back in the chair and rested his chin on his palm.

Mr. Thayer slipped his glasses back on. "This . . . nanotechnology exists?"

Brian slowly shook his head. "In theory." Brian saw Mr. Thayer's look of skepticism. "Nanotechnology doesn't go against the laws of physics." He leaned forward, pressed his elbows on his knees and clasped his hands together, wanting desperately for Mr. Thayer to understand. "Just because we don't have the technology now to create these machines doesn't mean it can't be done." Brian pointed at Mr. Thayer. "Someday these machines will be built."

Mr. Thayer stared at Brian's finger.

Surprised by his own intensity, Brian dropped his hand and sank back into his chair.

Mr. Thayer shuffled Brian's folder. "This university . . . where did I put it? Here." He pulled the paper to the top. "UW."

Brian nodded. "They're the best. They were the first university to offer a doctoral program in nanotechnology." Brian stood up and walked to the window. He looked down at the statue of St. Patrick. "They have the computers. They have the people." Brian pictured himself in a lab at UW. He continued talking as if he were at the university. "It'll take breakthroughs in a number of different sciences; bioengineering, molecular biotechnology, physics, chemical engineering, physiology plus computers have to get faster. But they're all there at UW. They have everything. They can pull everything together." He shook his head. "Imagine being part of the research. Look at everything we have today that came from the research when scientists put the first man in space and on the moon. If we can enter this miniature world, think of what we can create. Think of the lives we can change." Brian turned. He saw his reflection in the window and then pictured his grandfather and how much his grandfather had changed in just the last month. "Imagine being able to say, 'Here, Grandpa, we're going to inject this machine into your bloodstream and it will kill the cancer cells. You'll get better, Grandpa.'"

Mr. Thayer stared at Brian's back then shuffled the papers in Brian's folder. "I'm a little confused. Help me out here, Brian."

Brian turned from the window and looked at Mr. Thayer.

"For the last year," Mr. Thayer continued, "our goal was to have you accepted at UW." He held up a sheet of paper. "This is a copy of the acceptance letter they sent to you." He set the letter aside and searched through the file for another form. "Financials, between government grants and the Mosebly scholarship." He traced his finger down the paper. "Your family income." He looked up at Brian. "What am I missing here, Brian?" He held up a single sheet of paper. "Why did the university call me yesterday and say they still have not received your signed acceptance."

Brian leaned against the windowsill and stared at the floor.

Mr. Thayer took off his glasses and pointed one of the stems at Brian. "There are eight hundred boys here at St. Pat's. Ninety-eight percent will go on to college, but the vast majority will not go to the college of their first choice, either because of academics or finances. You have the chance to pursue your dream. What are we waiting for?"

Brian pressed his palms against the sides of his head. He wanted to scream, IT'S NOT THAT SIMPLE! He took one deep breath and then another. As he calmed, still looking at the floor he said, "My Dad wants me to go to a college . . ." He shook his head and laughed at the irony. "Where you major in baseball."

From across the room Mr. Thayer could feel the frustration consuming the young student. He waited until Brian looked up then gestured to the chair in front of him.

"Brian, I've been at St. Pat's for over twenty years. I can't even count how many young men like you have sat across from my desk and pondered their future. A number of boys have felt pushed to follow in their parent's footsteps, to go to this university and become a doctor because his father is a doctor, or a funeral director to inherit the family business, or a lawyer to become Smith and Son. I've stayed in touch with a number of them, others I've run across at social functions." Mr. Thayer looked directly into Brian's startlingly blue eyes. "There are a lot of unfulfilled men out there, Brian. A lot of carbon copies. Men who will never realize their own potential, men who will go through an entire lifetime without a sense of their own self worth."

Brian felt his cheeks flush. He looked away from Mr. Thayer.

"Nanotechnology, it sounds like science fiction to me." Mr. Thayer swiveled his chair and grabbed a book from one of the shelves then tossed it on his desk in front of Brian. "But if I would have been his contemporary I would have said the same thing."

Brian looked at the book by Jules Verne.

The bell clanged signaling the change of classes. Mr. Thayer lifted the acceptance letter for UW. He scanned the sheet then keyed his computer. "The deadline is Friday the fifteenth. After that they open your spot to another student." Mr. Thayer rubbed the bridge of his nose. "Brian, how old are you?"

Surprised by the question Brian answered, "Eighteen."

"You are an adult." Mr. Thayer waved the acceptance letter at Brian. "This is your decision." Mr. Thayer set the paper on his desk then hooked his glasses behind his ears. He closed Brian's file and took another file from beneath.

Brian felt the dismissal. He stepped quietly across the wooden floor. His hand touched the doorknob. He wanted to turn, run across the room and snatch the acceptance sheet from UW and sign his name. He squeezed the doorknob. He felt as if his Dad were on the other side of the door trying to pull him out into the corridor. He jumped as the doorknob turned. He caught his breath as another student opened the door and entered the room. Without looking back Brian fled down the hallway.

Chapter 3

Brian sat on the bottom row of bleachers next to the baseball diamond at St. Pat's High School. He was hunched over on the aluminum bench, his face cradled between his two palms. He stared at the sun burnt grass trampled by countless feet on the ground before him. His empty stomach rumbled, but he had no appetite. He could suddenly smell her perfume, a scent of lilacs. Her feet slowly crept into his field of vision, open toe sandals, toe nails painted a dark red that looked almost purple, thin ankles, ballerina calves.

A soft voice said, "If you want to be alone, I'll leave."

He quickly lifted his hands and squeezed his baseball cap visor. "No, Ali. Don't go." Brian pulled the visor lower on his forehead. He didn't want her to see his face, to see how weak and confused he felt.

She sat next to him on the bench. Brian shifted uncomfortably. His body betrayed his mind as he became aroused, just being next to her stirred him.

"What's wrong?" she asked.

Not trusting his voice, Brian didn't answer as he just shook his head and stared at the ground. He felt fingers gently massage the back of his neck. Her fingers didn't relax him. They made him more tense.

"Don't close me out, Brian." She slid her hand from his neck to his chin and slowly turned his face to her. "Talk to me." She waited. Brian finally looked at her.

"No," Brian said as he saw his own confusion reflected in her emerald eyes. He sprang from the bench and walked to the infield grass.

"Brian!" Ali jumped off the bench following him, put her hands on Brian's shoulders and shook him. "Talk to me!"

"Ali, I don't know how to tell my dad. This," Brian pointed to the St. Pat's diamond, "is as much him as me." Brian shook his head and wandered to the bleachers. "You know my dad played Triple A ball. He was a pitcher. I don't know . . . he played three or four seasons. At least that's what I can tell by going through old scrapbooks. He doesn't talk about it. You know my dad; he hardly talks at all. Especially, lately, with the team going to the state finals, I keep getting the feeling that . . ." Brian rubbed his hand through his short blonde hair. "that he is reliving his life through me." Brian flung his hands in the air. "I keep thinking I'm supposed to go to the pros because he never did. Ali, you've been to my house. You've seen the pictures on the walls in his study."

Ali nodded as she walked over and sat on the bench. She motioned Brian to sit next to her.

Brian felt anger coming to the surface. "I'm in every one of those damn pictures but." He shook his finger at her. "They all have something to do with baseball." He bit his lower lip and shook his head. "Every one of those pictures is about baseball. I'm swinging a bat or sliding into base. He has team pictures going all the way back to kindergarten. If he is sitting at his desk, you can't help but notice the eighth-grade city championship picture behind him. I'm standing there with this stupid grin on my face and he has his arm around my shoulder."

Brian stood and shoved his hands into his back pockets. He stared at the empty diamond. He kicked the chalk line leading to third base. "But part of me believes it. Part of me believes I'm going to play for the Tigers." He spun around and looked at Ali on the bench. "I'm good, Ali. I know I can play pro ball. How much is me and how much is what Dad taught me?" Brian shook his head. "I don't know." Brian waved his hand at the baseball diamond. "This is my home, Ali; I know this field better than my bedroom. I can run those bases with my eyes closed."

He walked back and sat on the bench facing Ali. She shifted her upper body to face him.

"I can see the rotations, Ali." Seeing that she didn't understand Brian continued. "Most players are lucky if they can just see a ball coming at them. I can see the stitches on the ball spinning." He waited to see if she understood. He saw the question in her emerald eyes. Lifting his hand he rubbed the freckles on her ivory cheek, then entwined his fingers in her long, wavy, reddish-blonde hair. "If you can see the rotations you'll know where the ball will go, whether it's going to curve, or slide or drop." He let his fingers slip from her hair as he stared at her. "I know where the ball is going, Ali. That's why I can hit it."

Brian swung his legs around and set his feet on the ground. "They say the hardest thing to do in professional sports is to hit a baseball." He leaned forward and let his hands hang over his knees. "It's not hard for me, Ali." He lifted his right hand and rested his chin on his palm, his elbow pressing into his knee.

"Do you love it?" asked Ali.

Brian laughed, "What?"

"Baseball. Do you love playing baseball?"

Brian laughed again and looked at Ali. He stopped laughing when he saw she was serious.

"I don't know."

"Come on, Brian."

"I . . . I don't . . . It's part of my life, Ali. It's always been part of my life. I can't remember a day I haven't played baseball." He looked at Ali. "It'd be like reading a book for you. You're always reading books, but does that mean you love reading books?"

"I do."

Brian laughed as he saw Ali smile. "You're not fair."

"Yes, I am."

Brian clapped his hands together. "Okay. Okay, in some ways I love playing baseball. You hit a home run. It's . . . it's a charge. Not even so much hitting it as watching it." Brian lifted his right hand and flicked his fingers towards the centerfield fence. "Just like a meteor streaking out. And." He glanced at first base. "Stealing. But only against a good pitcher." Brian nodded as if he just realized something for the first time. "Someone who makes it a real challenge." He swept his hand to the bleachers. "The cheers. You hit the game winner and the cheers stay with you. They're in my ears when I fall asleep and when I wake up in the morning. You walk through the school hall and you're Brian McBride, the baseball player." Brian turned to Ali. "You know I designed the web page for St. Pat's. One kid, Alan, said I did a good job. I hit the grand slam against Rodgers and everyone stopped me in the hall and slapped my back."

Brian looked at the dugout. "To my dad, college is just one more step to the pros. UW . . ." Brian shook his head, "No way! For him only a school like Arizona or Cal State, a team that regularly competes in the College World Series is acceptable. When I tell him I want to go to UW . . . Wow! No way, Ali!"

Ali asked, "Are you scared of your dad?"

"What do you mean?" Brian snapped. "Like he's going to hit me or something." Brian shook his head, "My dad never hit me; well, when I was little, I remember him smacking my butt, but I'm sure I deserved it. I'm not . . ."

He paused as he felt Ali's eyes searching his face. Brian tried to sort through all his conflicting feelings. "I'm not scared of him, Ali." He leaned forward on the bench, clenched his hands and knocked his fists together. "My dad . . . he'll be mad if I go to UW. That I can handle." Brian squeezed his fists together. "But I also know he'll be disappointed in me." Brian's fists turned white. "And I don't know how either of us will handle that."

Brian opened his fists and stared at the ground. He raised and squeezed the rim of his St. Pat's baseball cap.

Ali didn't say anything. She slid closer and let her cheek rest against his shoulder.

Chapter 4

Brian looked at his plate and rolled a meatball through his spaghetti. His stomach twisted into a knot and just looking at the spaghetti made him nauseous. He wanted to be anywhere but here, sitting at the kitchen table between his mother and father. He couldn't believe his mother was telling his father about the scholarship to UW. He had planned to tell his dad, later. So what that tomorrow was Friday the fifteenth, the day he had to commit or lose admittance to UW. He would have eventually told his dad. No. He wouldn't. He couldn't. And somehow his mother realized this and forced the issue.

"Kevin," said Karen, "If he doesn't commit by tomorrow they'll give his spot to another student."

Kevin clanged his silverware against his plate. "So, give his spot to another student."

"Forget it!" shouted Brian. "Just forget it!" He kicked his chair back and fled to his bedroom.

Kevin spun to his wife. "What the hell's going on?"

She shouted, "You don't have a clue do you, Kevin?"

Kevin glared at his wife. He grabbed his beer and pushed away from the table.

In his study Kevin leaned back in his chair and set his feet on his desktop. He cradled a beer and stared at the photo display. As usual he started with the center photo, Brian with the large oversized, yellow plastic bat, his eyes focused on the ball off camera. Kevin glanced at the other photos drifting back through the years. He always lingered on Brian's eighth-grade championship photo, the one with his arm draped around his son's shoulder, both smiling for the camera.

It seemed the whole season was a prelude to that game. Crossgates was the powerhouse, winning the league championship four out of the last five years. Their coach, Steve Tasker, a science teacher at Crossgates, once pitched a no-hitter for Ohio State. It was rumored the kids practiced all year long in a pole barn Tasker's dad had in Neapolis.

It was the end of July, a hot day with no wind. School had been out for seven weeks, but it seemed the whole eighth grade class and a lot of the student body filled the bleachers. Smiling, he remembered the cheerleaders. The only sport they cheered for was football, but they decided to show up for the championship baseball game. Decked out in green and gold uniforms, they led the student body with choruses of "push 'em back, push 'em back, push 'em way back." He remembered his team laughing, the kids shouting, "Hey, this is baseball not football." But the cheerleaders probably did more for that victory than anyone else. They kept the boys loose.

Defense, as it had all season, kept them in the game. Brian turned two double plays that cut off Crossgate rallies. St. John's was down 3-2 in the bottom of the ninth. Trevor took a close, inside fastball for ball four then ambled to first base.

Kevin stopped Brian before he went to the on-deck circle. He watched Coach Tasker talk with his pitcher on the mound. "He's going to brush you back," Kevin said. "He's going to throw his fastball, high and inside. You've got to look for it and move—fast."

"You sure?" asked Brian looking at Coach Tasker and the pitcher on the mound.

"It's a pitcher's move. It's what I'd do. He'll brush you back with his first pitch to get you off balance. Then he'll come back with his pitch, his curve ball. He'll throw it low to catch the outside corner of the plate." Kevin stared at Tasker still talking to his pitcher. "After the brush back, when you get back into the box, stand away from the plate. Let him think he got to you. Wait till he takes the signal from the catcher and goes into his wind-up then move back to the plate, tight then . . ."

"I know, Dad," said Brian. "The first swing's mine. After that I just try to put the ball in play."

The crowd gasped as Brian hit the dirt.

Brian brushed the dust from his uniform pants. He glared at the pitcher, then turned and looked at his dad. He smiled. Keeping his back to the pitcher, he gave a quick nod. Slowly he went into the batter's box.

Kevin watched the arc of the ball streaking towards the fence. He knew it was one of the few moments that life gives you. For a short time you are unbearably happy, and more than that, it's a moment you share with your son. A moment that will always be entwined in both your lives. In that instant, watching the ball like a comet crossing the heavens, Kevin wanted that moment to never end as he saw Brian mobbed by the screaming, hysterical team of St. John's eighth grade baseball champions. The students poured from the bleachers. He watched his son hoisted on Mike and Colin's shoulders as he came out of the dugout.

Carried by his teammates, Brian pumped his fist into the air. He searched for his father. He caught his dad's eyes, laughed and waved.

Kevin held up his hand and tried to save the moment.

Now Kevin crushed the empty beer can and tossed it into the trashcan by the side of his desk. He felt betrayed by the two people he loved most. All the hours, all the years he and Brian spent together to create a life that most kids could only dream about, to play pro-baseball with all the money and all the glory. It was there for Brian. All his son had to do was reach out and grab it.

As Karen walked into the office she saw the rebuke on her husband's face.

"I'm trying, Karen. I am trying to understand how I got ambushed by this. You always run interference for him. You had to know about this for months. If Brian didn't tell me, why didn't you?"

Karen leaned on the edge of Kevin's desk feeling the weight of his reproach. "Brian kept saying he was going to tell you. So, I kept waiting." She met Kevin's stare. "Tonight, at the table I realized he wouldn't tell you about UW." She brushed her black hair from the side of her face. "I also realized that if he wouldn't tell you about UW that he would go to any university you picked for him."

Kevin slammed his hand on the desk. "Karen! I've got a dozen scouts and recruiters from some of the top colleges in the nation knocking on our door waving letters of intent with full scholarships. Granted, they're baseball scholarships, but he would go to one of the best universities in the United States." Kevin lifted his hands and pointed them at Karen. "You want him to go to college; I want him to go to college. So, he's going to college, and." The look on Kevin's face said this is so simple anyone could understand. "We don't have to pay anything."

Karen couldn't help but see Brian's baseball pictures behind Kevin. She shook her head in exasperation. "Maybe it is my fault, Kevin." She started to leave the office but stopped and sat in a chair to the side of Kevin's desk. She took a deep breath while resting her arm on the desk.

"It started back in kindergarten. Anything to do with sports you were always there for him. Baseball, soccer, basketball, play with him, practice with him, teach him. You were there, Kevin. But anything academic." Karen stressed the word, "Homework! It was always, go see your mom."

Kevin jabbed his finger at her. "You're the one with the college degree."

"Come on, Kevin, it doesn't take a college degree to check a first grader's homework." Karen held her hands palm up in front of Kevin. "And somehow it evolved from there. Anything about schoolwork Brian would come to me; anything with sports he would go to you." As the realization sunk in Karen pulled away from Kevin. "It is my fault," She shook her head. "Because I see both sides of Brian and you don't, Kevin. You see the ballplayer, that's all." Karen tapped her fingernails on the desk. "So your choice of colleges is based on which has the best baseball team." Karen's cheeks flushed as her voice rose. "I was right. You don't have a clue. You have no idea what your son wants."

Kevin shouted, "That's not fair."

"Fair," Karen shouted back. She slapped her hand on his desk. "What's nanotechnology?"

"I don't know!" Kevin slid his chair back.

"What do you two talk about?" She pointed at the baseball photos. "Do you talk about anything besides baseball?" Karen flung her hand as if knocking away the pictures. "It's a game, Kevin! Brian doesn't want to go to college to just play a game. He wants to go to college to learn. It's his life, Kevin, not . . ." Stopping, afraid if she didn't, she could never take back her words. Her pulse racing, her cheeks crimson, she stared at Kevin.

"He's a ballplayer, Karen."

She was surprised by his calm, steady voice.

"He's the most gifted ballplayer I've ever seen." Kevin swiveled in his chair and looked at the photo array. "He's going to play baseball, Karen."

Karen watched her husband stare at Brian's photos and shook her head. She stood and walked out of his office.

Chapter 5

Brian heard the muffled shouts of his arguing parents through his closed bedroom door. He turned the volume way up on his computer to drown out their voices. Clangs of Viking swords and the thumps of Trolls' heavy, wooden maces echoed off the walls of his bedroom. He tried to make his fingers dance across the keyboard, but instead of seeing the Trolls and Vikings he saw images of his mother and father flailing away at each other. He wanted Merlwy to cast his invisibility cloak and make them all disappear. The thumping grew louder. He suddenly realized the knocking wasn't coming from his speaker but from his bedroom door. "What?" he shouted.

He saw his mother tentatively open the door. Ignoring her, he turned back to the monitor.

Karen walked over and started making Brian's bed. It was a fight she long ago gave up on. Especially before the computer, his room would look like someone turned it upside down and shook it. Books, notebooks, magazines, papers, rulers, paperclips were scattered all over the floor. Going across the room was like jumping from one ice floe to another, trying to find the one open piece of carpet. But at least some of that changed with the computer. Now, she thought, the only books are his schoolbooks on his desk and the only paper sits in the printer's tray. She fluffed the pillows then set them on top of his blankets.

As Brian watched his mother rearrange his books on his desk, he shouted, "Just leave them alone!"

"Brian, turn off the computer."

"I can't stop now. I'm right in the middle of a battle."

"Brian!"

He pounded his keyboard and his screen saver, the image of the double helix of DNA, floated across the monitor.

"Mr. Thayer said he needs to know tomorrow, right?" asked Karen.

Brian kept staring at the screen saver. Feeling overwhelmed he said, "It doesn't matter, Mom, I'll just tell them no."

"You've got to think about this, Brian. You tell them no; they won't give you a second chance."

"So, I'll go to another college. I can always major in chemistry or . . ." Feeling defeated his voice trailed off.

Karen sat on the bed. "Brian." She patted the blanket and said softly, "Come here."

Brian reluctantly left his computer and sat next to her.

"I never told you." Karen waited until her son looked at her before she continued. "When I was a senior in high school, I applied for and was accepted at Northwestern. I was into drama. I had the lead in our senior production of *Anne Frank*."

Brian tried to recall the pictures of his mother taken twenty-five years ago when she was eighteen.

"When I opened the acceptance letter I threw my arms around my Mom. I didn't know how happy I was until I realized I was crying. I wanted so badly to be an actress. I'd sit for hours in front of my mirror reciting lines, over and over, each time changing my expression until I thought I had it just right."

Brian was stunned. He couldn't imagine his mother, the actress, on stage in high school.

"That night your grandfather, my dad, drove me to Baskin Robbins to get ice cream and bring it back for the family. I thought we were going to have a celebration party for my acceptance at Northwestern. I should have known something was wrong because Dad barely said a word all the way there. On the way home your grandfather told me that next year your Uncle Mark would be a senior at Central Catholic, Uncle Matt would be a junior at Central Catholic, and your Aunt Patty would be a freshman at McCauley. I sat there wondering why he was telling me what I already knew. Your grandfather wouldn't look at me but kept staring straight at the road as we drove home. It got very quiet in the car."

As he saw her face change, Brian reached over and held his mother's hand.

"I remember how cold the bag of ice cream felt in my lap. And then my dad said he had enough money to send me to Northwestern or my two brothers and sister to Catholic high schools, but he didn't have enough money to do both. If I went to Northwestern, Mark, Matt and Patty would have to switch and go to public high schools."

Brian felt her squeeze his hand.

"At that moment I hated my dad! And I hated him for a long time. I didn't go to Northwestern. That one sentence from your grandfather changed my whole life."

Brian felt his mother's hand relax as she took a deep breath. He waited for her to continue.

"I worked that summer at a flower shop then went to UT in the fall. Four years later your Aunt Patty graduated from McCauley and I graduated from UT. We had a double graduation party. Your grandfather got drunk and passed out halfway through the party. That night after everyone left I sat on the front porch. Your grandmother came outside and sat next to me. All she said, "I don't think he will ever forgive himself for not being able to give you Northwestern."

Brian sought, somehow, to comfort her as he saw the tears in his mother's eyes.

"It took me a long time to realize that on that one night we both lost our dreams." Karen wiped the tears from the corners of her eyes. She straightened and squeezed Brian's hand and stared into his blue eyes. "Mr. Thayer needs to know tomorrow." She shook her head. "You tell him yes!"

Brian watched his mother gently close the door behind her. He didn't know what to think. He never thought about the choices his parents made for their lives. For as long as he could remember his mother always worked. She never talked about her job, never seemed happy or unhappy with it, until today. And what about his dad? He was a ball player. Why didn't he go to the pros? Was it his choice?

Brian lay on his bed cupping his hands behind his head wondering what he was going to do.

Chapter 6

Brian stood in front of his locker in the hallway of St. Pat's High School. He stared blankly at the books in his hand, stood oblivious to the male students jostling along the hallway. The light punch on his shoulder almost knocked the books loose from his hand. He tightened his grip and turned.

"You doing drugs, Brian?" laughed Chris, St. Pat's starting pitcher. "Didn't you hear me call you?"

"Hey, Chris."

Chris studied Brian's pale face. "You feeling okay?"

Brian shrugged his shoulders, "I'm fine."

Chris moved closer to Brian and lowered his voice. "You've been acting pretty, well, I don't know," Chris arched his eyebrows, "weird these last couple of days. You getting uptight about the state finals?"

Brian took the top book from his pile and exchanged it for another on the shelf. "Chris, have you ever known me to get uptight about baseball?"

"Well, no, but this is the state championship."

"And to quote my dad, 'it's still nine guys playing nine guys'."

"Yeah, that's cool. Hey, I gotta catch my bus. See you at practice."

Brian watched Chris disappear into the throng of students carrying backpacks and heading to buses or cars for the ride home and the start of the weekend. He stared at the slowly

moving second hand on the large clock on the wall. He tried to
swallow, but his mouth felt too dry. He loosened his tie and
unbuttoned the top of his shirt. He found himself reviewing
the same arguments in his head that had kept him awake all
night. He stuffed his books into his backpack then slammed his
locker door. He spun the lock then wandered down the hallway
following his feet to Mr. Thayer's office.

Brian swung his backpack to the floor and sat in one of the
hall monitor's chairs. He stretched his legs out, crossed his feet
at the ankles and folded his arms across his chest. Staring across
the corridor at the door to Mr. Thayer's office, he felt like he
was physically being torn in half. His mother was yanking on
one arm and his father on the other and the ripping pain was
shooting down the center of his chest. He felt dizzy as the same
repeating arguments swirled through his brain. He didn't think
he was capable of getting up from the chair and crossing the
hallway to the counselor's office.

As he sat there he suddenly realized that not making a decision was really making a decision. If he didn't cross the hallway
he would be letting his father shape his future.

In complete frustration he said, "Why can't I just be home
playing my role playing games on my computer?" He wondered what Merlwy would do? The answer startled him-
Merlwy does whatever I want him to do.

Brian fidgeted with his feet. *What do I want to do?* He took
a breath and held it trying to think of nothing else but that simple question which would determine his fate. Sitting in the
chair talking to himself he snapped, *Come on, Brian, what do you
want to do with your life?* And suddenly he knew. All the day-
dreams came into focus. *I want to be part of discovering a new
world.* The pain eased in his chest and his mind cleared. He
sprang from the chair forgetting his backpack. He raced across
the hallway.

Locked. His knuckles turned white from gripping the
doorknob so tightly. "No!" He pounded on the door, rattling

the glass window frame at the top of the door afraid that Mr. Thayer had already left for the day. He shook the doorknob. "Mr. Thayer!"

"Brian?"

He whipped around at the sound of his name seeing the guidance counselor coming down the hallway.

"What is the matter, Brian?"

"Mr. Thayer," Brian quickly drew in a breath. "I thought you had left."

"No. I was in a meeting with the principal. It seems one of our student's, oh well, never mind that." He took his keys from his pocket and fiddled with one trying to insert it into the lock. "I hope you didn't break it."

"I'm going to UW."

Mr. Thayer jerked his head up and studied the young student's face. "Great! I had almost given up on you, Brian."

"I . . ." Brian looked away and shrugged his shoulders as his voice trailed off.

Mr. Thayer opened the door and motioned Brian inside. "It's the decision that matters not how you arrive there." Mr. Thayer walked to his desk and began sorting through piles of folders. "Well, I know it's here somewhere."

"Here it is." Mr. Thayer flourished the paper. "Now." He picked up a Bic pen from his desk. "No, this won't do." He dropped the ballpoint pen back on the desk, reached into his sport coat and pulled out his Mont Blanc fountain pen. He unscrewed the top and smiling handed it to Brian.

Brian grabbed the pen and signed his name at the bottom of the acceptance letter.

"Well, this is a new one for me," said Mr. Thayer accepting the pen back from Brian. "You're the first student I've had to major in nanotechnology." Mr. Thayer slid the pen into his inside pocket then extended his hand.

Brian returned the firm handshake.

Mr. Thayer nodded. "Off you go, then."

"Thanks, Mr. Thayer." Brian released the guidance counselor's hand and slowly turned to the door.

"Oh, Brian."

Brian turned sideways and looked at Mr. Thayer.

"If you have the chance, Brian, visit me on Christmas break." With his index finger, Mr. Thayer pushed his glasses higher on his nose. "Keep me updated on this nanotechnology; after all, I can't have the students think I'm turning into an old fogy.

Brian laughed, "You'll never be an old fogy, Mr. Thayer."

Brian walked down the hallway with a bounce to his step. For the first time in weeks he felt his muscles unwind. He suddenly realized that he was hungry. He couldn't remember the last time he ate. Stopping, he snapped his fingers. He pivoted and ran down the hallway to grab his backpack.

Chapter 7

Duck Creek Metro Park meandered through small, rolling hills in northwestern Ohio. During spring thaw the creek was really a river, sometimes overflowing its banks with melting snow. Now in late May it lived up to its name, a creek slowly flowing through the forest. The jogging path ran alongside the twisting creek. Brian was on the homeward stretch of his five-mile run. He was approaching what his dad always called the swinging bridge, a cable suspension bridge with wooden slats, which doubled back over the widest section of the creek. A father with his young son stood on the bridge. The toddler peered over the side as he held one of the suspension cables. He pointed at the driftwood floating with the current under the bridge. Slowing to a walk Brian smiled at the boy. He remembered standing at the same spot with his own father at about the same age. On that day a runner came down the path and jogged across the bridge. As the runner came closer to the middle of the bridge, it sprang up and down like a trampoline. Brian could remember laughing as he bounced higher and higher until his dad grabbed his arm. He couldn't remember what his dad shouted at the jogger, but he remembered the words were loud.

As he left the bridge, Brian's breath quickened as the path curved upwards away from the floodplains. He broke out from under the canopy of leaves into the sunlit fields. He sprinted the last quarter mile, sucking air through his nose and out through his mouth. Slowing he hooked his hands behind his head. His chest heaved. He looked across the field to the parking lot. Ali sauntered across the field. Lowering his hands to his hips Brian stood quietly watching her. If someone asked him how he felt, he couldn't say. He always felt awkward around girls. All of his time was spent with baseball or behind a computer monitor. He met Ali when they literally bumped into each other at a science fair at McCauley, a parochial girls' high school. That night while immersed in his role-playing game on the computer an instant message popped up from Ali.

Ali's reddish-blonde hair was pulled back in a ponytail and held in place with a green scrunchie. Her ivory cheeks had a slight flush as if she had just finished running. She wore black shorts over a black leotard. Brian couldn't say what he felt because he never felt this way looking at anyone else. All of these new feelings completely flustered him. As she stepped from the grass to the gravel, Ali's eyes smiled at Brian.

Brian searched for words and finally stammered, "How was your class?"

Ali stood on her toes and performed a pirouette.

Laughing, Brian asked, "Walk with me?"

They fell into a matching rhythm walking side by side. Brian tried to dry his hand on his tank top. Hesitantly he reached for Ali's hand.

"I'm all sweaty," apologized Brian.

Ali took his hand. "Me, too."

Brian brought her hand to his lips and kissed her knuckles.

They left the gravel path and wandered to a side trail. As they entered the woods the high, green leaves blocked out the sun. Brian felt a brief chill as the cool air evaporated his perspiration.

Brian had explored all the trails during his so called "Indian scout days." With his friend Sean they would ride their bikes the mile or so from their homes, lock the bikes by the ranger

station, and go "Indian scouting." Sean swore the Battle of
Fallen Timbers was fought in these woods and any small trian-
gular stone immediately became an arrowhead.

Veering from the trail, Brian led Ali into the thick brush. As
the path narrowed, Brian walked in front of Ali still holding her
hand.

"Stay close and don't touch anything. There's a lot of poison ivy off the path here," said Brian.

"Poison ivy," shrieked Ali as she bumped into him from
behind.

"Just stay on the path; you'll be fine."

"Path?" asked Ali incredulously. "Where do you see a
path?"

"Actually, it's a deer trail. The deer follow it down to the
water."

"Yeah, and how do you know that?"

Looking over his shoulder Brian smiled and said, "Boy
Scouts."

The promontory jutted out about a hundred yards above
Duck Creek. Brian always felt like he was walking into a theater. The sides of the theater were formed by thick brush to the
left and right. The canopy leaves of tall oak and sycamore trees
became a ceiling. Ahead of him the winding creek was the
screen. Crossing the small, open clearing, Brian sat on the
fallen tree trunk and pulled Ali next to him.

"It's so quiet," whispered Ali.

Whispering Brian said, "You don't have to whisper."

They both laughed. Ali looked from Brian then down to
the river. "Duck Creek?"

Brian followed her gaze. "Yep, they're definitely ducks."

"Did you talk to your Dad?" asked Ali.

Brian's face darkened. He reached down and peeled bark
from the tree stump. "Let's not talk about that now." He
glanced down to the creek. He swung his leg over the tree

stump and sat facing Ali. "Let's talk about you. It seems you know everything about me, but I know so little about you."

Ali kidded, "Well, we've only know each other for what, six weeks now?"

"Forty-four days," said Brian. "Actually." Brian glanced at his Timex wristwatch. "Closer to forty-four and one-half days."

Ali smiled and nodded her head. "I'm impressed." She moved closer to Brian on the log. "So what do you want to know?"

"You said you wanted to work with handicapped kids?"

Ali held her finger up and tapped Brian's chest. "Physically challenged, especially, hearing impaired."

Brian threw the bark strip on the ground. "Why?" He looked at her questioningly. "Why do you want to do that?"

Ali rose and walked to the edge of the promontory. She peered over the edge and watched the ducks paddle in lazy circles. She swung back to Brian. "My cousin Tiffany." She laughed just thinking of her. "We're best buds and she definitely wants to meet you. She's four months younger than me. We lived two blocks apart and we both went to St. Joan of Arc, kindergarten through eighth grade. About fourth grade is when it started. I knew something was wrong. On the playground I'd call her name and she just didn't hear me. It got progressively worse. Now she's legally deaf."

"That's . . ." started Brian.

Tossing her hair back from her shoulders Ali waved her hands. "Don't worry about Tiffany. She's fine, really. She started classes right away and somehow roped me into taking them with her. Kept telling me she needed someone to practice with and she wanted me. Actually the signing classes were pretty easy. Lip reading, now that's tough."

"Ali," Brian waited until Ali looked at him then mouthed, "You can read lips?"

"Only when they're moving." She smiled.

"So when do I meet Tiffany?" asked Brian.

"She's living up in Minneapolis. Tiffany jokes that her dad got transferred to Siberia." Brian could hear the smile in her voice as Ali said, "She's coming to visit this summer for two weeks."

"It's got to be hard. You can't talk with her."

"Brian," Ali laughed and shook her head. "Duh. You of all people, Internet, AOL, we chat everyday."

"So that's why I can't get through on the phone. Here I thought it was another guy."

Ali scrambled over and punched him on the arm. "Another guy. Yeah, right."

"Ouch," Brian rubbed his arm.

Ali laughed and walked back towards the creek. "Tiffany is amazing. You wouldn't know she's deaf and she talks like she always did."

Brian stood. "You know there are so many new programs that will be developed with nanotechnology, especially, for people who are," Brian looked at Ali, "physically challenged . . . hearing or sight impaired."

Ali chuckled and clapped her hands.

Brian continued, "This is close, Ali. I'm not talking decades but years. Some of the work is already being done with computers." Brian stood and started pacing. "Already, there are cochlear implants. I don't know if it would work in Tiffany's case, but there are new designs and advancements being made every day. Wow, Ali," said Brian getting more excited just thinking about the possibilities. "People have no idea how science will improve their lives." Brian quickly crossed the distance between them and grabbed both of Ali's hands. "Ali, think of how the world's going to change." Brian pulled her into his embrace. "Some day we are going to do away with the term physically challenged. To be part of that, Ali, to be part of making someone's life better." Brian pulled back from Ali and looked into her eyes. "Give me Tiffany's e-mail address. I'll hook her up to some web sites. Maybe they can even help her now."

Ali nodded. She leaned her face forward until their lips touched.

Brian couldn't remember how they both ended up entangled on the ground. He felt Ali's breasts rise under her leotard and press against his chest. Her warm tongue darted in and around, then filled his mouth. He rolled on top of her. He felt his heart beating against hers. She entwined her arms around Brian's back. She pressed him closer against her. She felt his hardness press against her leg. Ali's hands squeezed his back. Brian exhaled as he shuddered.

Embarrassed, Brian rolled off Ali. Feeling completely inadequate, he couldn't believe he came in his shorts. He turned and shielded his body from her. He tried to cover the stain on his shorts with the bottom of his tank top.

Ali placed her hand on Brian's shoulder. She tried to turn him back to her, but felt his resistance. "Hey." Ali put her hand on his cheek. Brian let her turn his face but wouldn't meet her eyes.

"I did, too," Ali said softly.

Brian's eyes slowly found hers. With a questioning look, Brian said, "I didn't mean to . . ."

Ali slid her palm then her fingertips over his lips. She pulled the scrunchie from her ponytail and hair tumbled to her shoulders. She tenderly tugged Brian down next to her. They lay side-by-side staring at the sunlight filtering through the green leaves of the forest. Their breathing slowed. Brian's fingers gently combed through Ali's hair like reddish, golden flax flowing across his fingertips. Ali turned her face towards Brian and closed her eyes. Her breath rippled on his neck. Brian's eyes closed as he breathed in the scent of her hair mixed with the forest.

The caw of a crow woke Brian. He opened his eyes and searched for the bird. He watched the crow emerge from the shadows, soar over their heads and fly towards the river.

Ali stirred as Brian tried to free his arm from under her neck. He flexed his hand, stinging needles surged throughout his arm. Ali stretched her long body then sat next to him.

Brian whispered, "Look." He pointed down to the river.

Ali spotted five deer at the creek's edge.

His mouth hovering near Ali's ear, "We must be downwind from them." As he spoke the largest, the buck, raised his antlered head and gazed up at the promontory.

Ali looked at Brian as he stared at the buck. He seemed hypnotized.

"You're staring at that deer like you know him," Ali whispered.

"Buck." Still staring, Brian continued, "I've seen him before."

The buck shook his head and the herd bounded across the creek and up through the woods.

Brian sprang to his feet and said, "Man, it's late. I got practice at five." Taking both her hands he pulled Ali up from the ground. He reached out and gently untangled a twig from her hair and led her back to the path. Stopping suddenly Brian spun around. "Ali, don't tell my dad!"

Astonished Ali said, "I'm going to tell your dad?"

"No," Brian grinned at the look on Ali's face. "Not about . . ." He laughed again. "I mean . . . that you can read lips. If he finds out, he'll make you come to every game. I can hear him now, "Okay, young lady, what's that coach saying to his pitcher. Believe me, Ali, don't. For both our sakes, don't let my dad know."

Chapter 8

It's just another game, Brian kept telling himself as he scanned the Ohio State baseball diamond. His father was still talking with Coach Macerak in the dugout. They were huddled together in the back of the bus for the long ride down to Columbus. Looking to the bleachers he saw his mother and Ali who had driven down with a caravan of St. Pat's cars, the windows decked out with gold and green banners. He let the thought linger in the back of his mind, win the game against St. Ignatius, then tomorrow play in the finals for the state championship. He'd been here before, two years ago as a sophomore, when Moeller trounced them 10-3 in the finals. Brian looked to the warm-up pen where his friend Chris was loosening his arm. They didn't have Chris for that game. Chris had been on the JV team, still looking for his fastball.

As he stood in the on deck circle, he felt the stare from the St. Ignatius pitcher. Looking at the pitcher he couldn't believe the intensity glowering in the pitcher's eyes. He smiled at the pitcher. God, lighten up. It's just a game. He ran his hand down the barrel of his bat searching for any irregularities. Batting was simply physics in motion, point A making contact with point B. He had compiled software and ran programs on his computer, point of impact, velocity, and trajectory. He stepped into the batter's box and tapped the end of the bat on home plate waiting for the familiar ping to shoot up his forearm.

Brian concentrated on the rotation of the stitches as the curve ball headed towards the plate. Leaning back from the plate he let the pitch pass close to his knees for a called ball. He stepped out of the batter's box and stretched the bat over his back while studying the outfielders. They had shifted, expecting him to pull the ball to left field. The third baseman played deep behind the bag. Brian saw the first baseman talking to his friend Colin, who stood on first base, but he couldn't hear what they were saying. As he stepped into the batter's box, Brian glanced at Coach Macerak. The Coach ran his hands up and down his arms and all over his upper body. When the coach tapped his belt buckle twice, Brian took the signal for the hit and run. Shifting in his stance Brian angled his body slightly towards first base. It was a high fastball. As Brian made contact he flicked his wrists driving the ball down. The ball bounced on top of first base then ricocheted like a cannonball down the right field line.

As Brian rounded first base he saw the right fielder dash after the streaking ball heading towards the right field corner. Brian searched for the third base coach as the ball of his foot lightly touched the top of second base.

The pitcher raced towards right field waving his glove to take the cut off throw from the right fielder.

Somehow Brian kicked it up another notch as he saw the coach waving him home. Out of the corner of his eye he saw the white shooting meteor impact in the catcher's mitt. He slid and felt his bones jar as he collided with the catcher. The catcher was on top of him then rolled to his side and kneeled next to Brian. Brian saw the ball clutched tightly in the catcher's mitt.

"YOU'RE OUT!!" screamed the umpire.

Slowly Brian rose. He wiped the dust from his uniform. The catcher stared in disbelief at the ball in his glove then looked up at Brian. Brian offered his hand. The catcher took it and Brian pulled him to his feet. They looked at each other, shrugged their shoulders and walked away.

"I can't believe they nailed me. I just can't believe it," Brian said to Coach Macerak. He took his helmet off as he stepped into the dugout.

"The pitcher went out and took the cut," explained Coach Macerak. "Man, that kid's got an arm. He threw a strike from right field. Hey," Coach Macerak patted Brian's shoulder. "You scored Colin." Coach Macerak turned to the rest of the St. Pat's team standing by the edge of the dugout. Raising his voice he said, "Okay, guys, it's really simple. We got ourselves a tied game with three innings to go. We win; tomorrow we're in the state finals. We lose; we go home. Enough said."

"Brian!" yelled Trevor, as he threw the warm-up toss to him before the start of the ninth inning. Brian, near second base, caught the ball and whipped it to Colin on first. Brian yanked his cap low on his forehead to shield his eyes from the sun. He settled into his defensive stance, rocking lightly on the balls of his feet. "Throw strikes, Chris," he shouted, "just throw strikes."

Spitting out sunflower shells, Kevin thought, how the hell could they be laughing at a time like this. Standing by the fence near the home teams' dugout, he watched Karen and Brian's girlfriend. He tried to think of her name. Ann, Angie, Alice, no. What was it? Ali, that's it, Ali. Karen and Ali were sitting in the bleachers laughing like a couple of teenagers. Kevin shook his head and mumbled to himself, "Jesus, we're deadlocked going into the ninth inning. How the hell can they be laughing? Okay, we got our ace pitcher Chris on the mound then Brian and the top of the order due up in the bottom of the ninth. We hold them; then we kick butt." He popped a couple more sunflower seeds into his mouth as he looked to the field. A gust of wind kicked up and blew off Trevor's cap. Trevor zigzagged across the infield, trying to catch what looked like a small green tumbleweed. Suddenly Kevin felt the chilly wind shear that brought tingles to his arms. His eyes tightened as he watched the squall line roll in behind centerfield.

Crack!! Damn it, that's gone, Kevin thought. The wind seemed to hold the ball then swirled and shifted. Brandon, the left fielder timed his leap. The ball brushed the tip of his glove then bounced off and over the fence. Brandon threw his glove to the ground as a flash of lightning split the sky behind him.

Between the shouts and screams of the St. Ignatius fans, Kevin heard the rumble of thunder.

From second base Brian saw the thunderheads roll in behind centerfield. He turned and saw a look of panic cross Chris' face as they both thought we're now down by one. If the umpire calls the game we lose. "We'll get it back, Chris," Brian said. "It's only one run. Throw strikes, Chris. Come on, just throw strikes."

"STRIKE THREE, YOU'RE OUT!!" yelled the umpire.

"Okay, Chris, just two more to go," shouted Brian.

Kevin's hands were white from gripping the top of the fence. He seemed mesmerized by the thunderheads rolling in behind Brandon. "NO, you can't do this," screamed Kevin. He shook his fist at the approaching black sky, "NO!!"

Hearing what sounded like a waterfall Brian turned. He saw Brandon engulfed by the torrential downpour. He stood completely numb as he heard the umpire shout behind him, "That's it, game's called!" Brian felt like a wave from the ocean had splashed on top of him. He turned and watched the spectators under the dark sky flee to the shelters or run to their cars. He saw the St. Ignatius players dancing and exchanging high-fives by their dugout. He fought to keep his balance against the wind and rain. He felt like he was trapped in a swirling river. Everything seemed to be in motion except the solitary figure standing by the fence staring at the baseball diamond.

Chapter 9

Kevin endured the long, quiet bus ride home from Columbus. He wasn't Coach Macerak. He didn't have the wherewithal to console the players. He sulked in the corner at the back of the bus. His damp clothes, like the other players' uniforms, never really dried. By the time the bus pulled into St. Pat's parking lot and opened its doors, the smell was like opening a gym bag that had sat in the bottom of a locker for a week.

Brian avoided his father. He couldn't bear to see the haunted look in Kevin's eyes. It wasn't as if he felt his father blamed him for the loss to St. Ignatius; it was much more than that. His father looked completely defeated, something Brian felt wouldn't change when his father woke up the next day.

On the bus ride back Brian sat next to Colin and stared at the rain beating against the window. Slowly he got over the shock of having a thunderstorm wash away St. Pat's chance for a state championship. He thought about tomorrow. The baseball season was finished. Baseball practices were over. He felt guilty because all of the sudden he felt relieved. Now he'd have time to study for his finals. And he'd have time to spend with Ali. He leaned his head against the cold, damp window and as his breath fogged the glass he traced Ali's name on the glass.

As the bus pulled up to St. Pat's, Brian turned and saw his father sitting alone on the last bench of the bus. His teammates slowly gathered their gear and made their way to the exit. After they left, Brian stood in the aisle and waited for his father. Kevin just sat hunched over staring at the floor. Brian wondered if he should go and talk to him and what would he say. He could still see his dad standing in the downpour by the fence. Brian took a step towards him then stopped. Feeling a wave of panic Brian turned and hurried off the bus leaving his dad alone.

As he jumped down from the bus, Brian saw his mother and Ali standing in the breezeway. Ali ran and threw her arms around him. Brian looked over Ali's shoulder to his mother. Karen looked at her son then shifted her eyes to the empty open door of the bus.

"Mom." Looking like he didn't know what to do Brian said, "Dad's still on the bus."

Reaching into her purse, Karen found her car keys and slipped them into Brian's hand.

"Why don't you drive Ali home," Karen said. "I'll get a ride with your dad."

Brian replied, "You sure, Mom?"

Karen nodded and looked back to the bus.

"Kevin," said Coach Macerak, "the bus driver wants to go home. I see Karen's over there waiting for you."

Seeming to take all of his energy, Kevin grabbed the seat in front of him and pulled himself up. "We would have beat them," Kevin said. "Chris would have shut them down then Trevor, Colin, and Brian . . . Brian would have beaten'em. These boys are state champs, Coach. They're the best team St. Pat's ever fielded. It can't end like this." Kevin slammed his hand down on the seat. "IT'S NOT RIGHT!!"

"Kevin." Coach Macerak just shook his head. He turned, walked down the aisle and off the bus.

Standing in the doorway of the bus Kevin saw Brian with his arm around Ali walking to the parking lot. Kevin stumbled down the steps then walked right past Karen. He didn't say a word. He wouldn't look at her. Karen opened her umbrella and followed Kevin into the dark drizzle.

When Kevin returned home the first thing he did was check the mail. Picking up the bills and flyers he walked back to the kitchen. He threw the mail onto the table then grabbed a beer from the refrigerator. Karen stood by the stove putting on a pot of water to boil for noodles. She glanced at the mail scattered across the table. Her heart skipped as she saw the letterhead for UW. Crossing to the table she quickly scooped the mail back into a pile.

"Let me see'em," mumbled Kevin.

He didn't notice the slight tremor in Karen's hand as he snatched the mail from her. Karen turned her back and walked to the cupboard to get a box of pasta.

Shuffling the mail Kevin stopped and read *TO THE PARENTS OF BRIAN MCBRIDE*. He saw the return letterhead for UW.

Karen saw the dark look cross Kevin's face as she snapped the dry pasta. Small broken pieces went flying across the stovetop. She dropped the pasta into the pot.

Kevin tore open the envelope and read: We are pleased that Brian McBride has accepted the Mosebly Foundation Scholarship to UW.

"WHAT THE HELL IS THIS!" screamed Kevin waving the letter at Karen? We didn't agree on this."

Keeping her back to him, Karen stirred the pasta in the boiling water.

Kevin yanked her shoulder and spun her around.

As she turned, Karen lifted the silver spoon as if to hit him. "DON'T!"

Kevin backed away and collapsed onto a kitchen chair.

Karen reeled from the stove and faced Kevin with the long, silver spoon held in her hand. "Brian's going to UW!" She looked at the spoon in her hand then threw it into the sink.

"That's where he wants to go and that's where I want him to go!" Karen charged forward and pushed her hands down on the kitchen table in front of Kevin. She screamed at him, "It's not your life, Kevin. You've had your chance!"

Kevin recoiled as if Karen had slapped him. He knocked his chair back from the table. The chair bounced off the wall. He crossed the kitchen, opened the top cupboard and grabbed the bottle of Jack Daniels.

Karen heard his office door slam shut. She slowly sank into the kitchen chair and mumbled, "Shit."

Chapter 10

"Is Dad working today?" asked Brian. He stood at the kitchen counter and slid two brown sugar Pop Tarts into the toaster.

Karen opened the cupboard and took out a travel mug. As she filled it with coffee she said, "I don't think so. I don't think he's feeling too good right now." She stirred cream into the mug. "In fact I wouldn't be surprised if he sleeps most of the day. Brian, listen." Karen snapped the lid on the mug and looked at Brian. "Your dad knows you accepted the scholarship to UW."

The Pop Tarts popped up in the toaster. Brian reacted like it was a gunshot. "You told him," Brian said incredulously.

"They sent an acceptance letter." Karen turned off the coffee maker. "It doesn't matter. What matters now," she looked at Brian, "is that the three of us need to sit down and talk."

"How mad is he?" asked Brian.

Karen shrugged her shoulders. She looked at the kitchen clock. "You've got five minutes. Got gas in your Jeep?"

"Mom, you don't have to keep asking me. I ran out of gas one time," said Brian returning his mother's stare.

Karen quickly crossed the room to Brian. "I've got to go, I'm late. Don't dawdle." Seeing his forlorn look, Karen gave her son a kiss on the cheek. "It's going to be okay, Brian."

As he heard his mother's car pull out from the garage, Brian slid the Pop Tarts onto a plate. He listened intently for any sounds in the quiet house. He did not want to see his father, especially, since he was alone. He jerked when he heard the toilet flush in his parent's bedroom. Brian quickly grabbed a napkin and wrapped it around the Pop Tarts. Carrying them in one hand, he snatched his keys from the counter and ran out the back door.

The house felt empty. Kevin rolled onto his side. He waited until the room stopped spinning then glanced at his bedside alarm clock, 1:30 P.M. His throat was so dry he couldn't swallow. He pushed himself up and stumbled to the bathroom. He opened the medicine cabinet then fought with the lid on the aspirin bottle. He shook four aspirins into his palm. As he went to toss them in his mouth, one of the aspirin fell to the floor. "Christ!" He held onto the sink and stared at his pale reflection in the mirror.

In the kitchen his hands shook. He splashed orange juice down the side of the glass and onto the newspaper's sports section headline lying on the table. *'ST. PAT'S LOSES HEARTBREAKER—ST. IGNATIUS ADVANCES TO STATE FINALS.'* He couldn't read the story. He collapsed onto a kitchen chair. He turned the pages of the newspaper and scanned the sports articles. Something clicked in the back of his mind. Kevin went back to the headline for the third feature, *'Jenkins out for season—to undergo reconstructive knee surgery today.'* While reading the story he sipped his orange juice. He read it twice. Kevin folded and tossed the paper on the table then headed to the shower.

Kevin stood motionless and looked out the plate glass window of the new downtown multi-million dollar baseball stadium.

"It's a damn shame, Kevin, damn shame. Your boy should be in the state finals," said Coach Bruno.

Coach Bruno, the Hens first black head coach, left his desk and stood next to him. Following Kevin's gaze, Coach Bruno shook his head and said, "I know; she sure ain't the old Rec Center. Hell, that was a ballpark. This," gesturing towards the field, "this is what they call family entertainment. Families come here to picnic and party. We've got playgrounds and fireworks, clowns, a state of the art music system that'll blast you out of your seat." Pointing, Coach Bruno continued, "We've even got our luxury booths, playpens for adults." Coach Bruno waved his hands as if dismissing the field. He returned to his desk and propped his feet on top of his desk as he slouched in the chair. He looked at Kevin while he chewed on the end of a toothpick. "What brings you, Kevin? I know it's not to talk about the good old days. 'Cause we both know they were never that good."

Kevin looked at the short stocky coach. "Jenkins."

Coach Bruno pulled the toothpick from beneath his thick, bushy, salt and pepper mustache. "What about him?"

Kevin said, "You need a second baseman."

"I got Smith."

Kevin laughed.

Coach Bruno joined the laughter. "Yeah, I do have a problem at second." Slowly it dawned on the Coach. He pulled the toothpick from his mouth and pointed it at Kevin. "Now, wait a minute, you're not thinking . . ."

"Brian's a lot better than Smith. You and I both know it."

"How old is your kid?"

"Eighteen."

"He's young, Kevin. I thought he'd be going on to college ball. I've heard he's been scouted, Stanford, Miami, Arizona. Hell, any of those schools would love to have him. Give him a couple of years in college ball, then bring him around."

Kevin turned and looked at the baseball diamond. "You need a second baseman, Coach. Brian's ready." Kevin stuffed his hands deep into his pockets as he stared out at the field. He swung around and faced Coach Bruno. "Give him a try out?"

Coach Bruno tried to read what was hidden behind Kevin's face. "What's going on, Kevin?"

Kevin shrugged his shoulders.

"Is your boy going to college?"

Avoiding the question Kevin said, "Brian's ready to play now, Coach. Give him a try out?" Kevin knew Coach Bruno detected the pleading in his voice.

Coach Bruno tossed the toothpick in the garbage can at the side of his desk. "Shit, Kevin, you're talking Brian, our home town boy. I've been scouting him myself since he was twelve. He's the complete package: hit, field and, man, can he run. He's damn good, Kevin. You sure this is what you want? You've been there. You know what Triple A ball is like."

Kevin made his right hand into a fist. He brought it in front of his mouth and blew on it. "Give him the chance, Coach."

Coach Bruno swung his feet off the desk. "Bring him around, Kevin. We'll go through the formality of a try out, but that's all it's going to be, just a formality. He wants second base, it's his."

"Coach . . ." Kevin was interrupted by a knock on the office door.

Coach Bruno shouted, "Yeah."

Assistant Coach Meyers stuck his head in the door.

"Come on in, Tony," said Coach Bruno. He pointed to Kevin. "Tony, this is Kevin McBride. Kevin played ball for me. When was it? Jesus, I can't believe it. It's got to be twenty years ago."

Kevin shook Tony's hand.

"Better get used to him, Tony," said Coach Bruno. I imagine you'll be seeing Kevin a lot. His son Brian is our new second baseman."

Assistant Coach Meyers closed the door as Kevin left. He turned, faced Coach Bruno and asked, "He played for you?"

"Two, maybe three years." Coach Bruno pinched another toothpick from the holder on his desk. "As a coach you couldn't ask for a better player. First one in the locker room, last one to leave. No one worked harder. He was a kid then. Shit, we all were, but he was a believer. He believed baseball was more than a game."

Coach Bruno took off his cap. He swiped his sparse, curly black hair streaked with gray back from his gleaming ebony forehead. "Kevin would have a couple of beers in the locker room after a game and start spouting off about how being part of the team was the best thing that ever happened to him. To hear him carry on you'd think we were the Knights of the Round Table. He'd get up on the mound and try to slay the fire breathing dragon." Coach Bruno put his cap back on and shook his head. "But it was never just him. It was him and the eight guys backing him up." Coach Bruno laughed. "He was contagious. When he was on the mound he had them playing as a team. I don't know how many times team defense bailed him out. How many double plays they turned to get him out of a jam. He made that team better than he ever was."

Coach Bruno stared out the window and drifted back through the years. The coach continued, "The best earned run average he ever had was 5.75. He had the heart. God, he had the heart. But his fastball barely hit 85.

Coach Bruno pulled the toothpick from his mouth and studied the chewed up end. Satisfied that it still had some life he stuck it in the side of his mouth. "It was pretty lean times back then. Word came down that I had to cut payroll. I had to let a pitcher go. It came down between McBride with an ERA of 5.75 and that cocky, son of a bitch Johnson with an ERA of 3.5. We still had a chance for the playoffs." A pained expression crossed Coach Bruno's face. "I'm the coach and I had to call him into my office and let him go. I had to look into his eyes . . ."

Coach Bruno stopped. He turned away from Meyers and stared out the window to the baseball diamond.

Meyers fidgeted in his chair. His eyes stayed on the Coach, waiting.

Coach Bruno heaved a sigh. "It crushed him. He never played ball again." He removed the toothpick from his mouth and held it between his thumb and index finger. He pointed the mashed toothpick at Meyers. "When he walked out of the locker room the spirit of that team walked out with him. I hated him because of what he made me see in myself."

Coach Bruno exhaled slowly. "Time heals all they say. But, shit, I still feel like it just happened yesterday." Coach Bruno stood up and moved to the window. He stared at his field. "Set up the try out, Tony."

Chapter 11

Karen sat on the porch swing one leg tucked under while the other pushed the swing back and forth. The trees in the front yard were in full bloom and as the wind stirred pink blossoms floated gently down to the grass. She had changed from work clothes into shorts and a tee shirt. Her coffee cup rested in her lap. She wondered where Kevin was. There was no note, no message, just an empty garage when she returned home. She thought about calling him on his cell phone, but what would she say? She looked up as Kevin's car turned into the drive then pulled into the attached garage. On the one hand she felt the relief of knowing he was safely home, but she also wondered what sort of mood he would be in. She heard him rummaging around in the house.

Twisting the cap off a bottle of water, Kevin walked onto the porch. He glanced at the space next to Karen on the porch swing then sat on one of the green plastic chairs. He took a deep drink of water while staring at the yard. The rhythmical clicking of the porch swing filled the silence between them.

Kevin blurted out, "I want him for the summer."

He quickly glanced at Karen, searched her eyes then looked back to the yard. "If he wants to go to UW in the fall . . ." Kevin took another sip of water. "If that's what he *really* wants to do, then that's what he'll do."

Karen untucked her leg and settled both feet on the ground. The swing lurched to a stop. Confused and suspicious she leaned towards Kevin. "What do you mean? You want him for the summer?"

"The Hens lost their second baseman for the season."

"Kevin!" Karen slammed her coffee cup on the swing's armrest.

"It's a summer job," snapped Kevin.

"It's not a job," retorted Karen.

Kevin took a breath to quell his rising anger. He lowered his voice and said, "Give him this chance, Karen. You want him to go to UW. You want him to have that opportunity. Fine! But you also got to give him this chance to play ball. Give him to me for the summer, Karen."

Sitting back in the swing, Karen brushed the hair from the side of her face. "Brian's just going to walk in from the street and become the second baseman for the Hens?"

"Yes."

Karen studied Kevin's face then said seriously, "You're not kidding."

"I'm not kidding."

Karen stood and leaned against the porch's wooden support beam. She gazed at her blossoming trees. The wind stirred and the pink petals fell like raindrops to the green spring grass. She held her hand out and caught a few of the falling pink blossoms in her palm. "They never last long enough." She turned and moved closer to Kevin. She said slowly, accentuating each word, "If he wants to play for the Hens this summer, if that's what he *really* wants to do, then that's what he'll do." Karen snatched her coffee cup from the swing and walked into the house.

Kevin was still staring at the front door as Brian's Jeep pulled into the driveway. Brian turned off the engine, sat in the Jeep and stared at his father sitting on the porch. He felt trapped. He couldn't leave, but he didn't want to confront his father knowing that he now knew Brian was going to UW. He wanted to put that conversation off forever. Brian realized that sitting in his Jeep was just making matters worse. He yanked the door handle then popped the door open with his elbow. He grabbed his book bag from the passenger seat and glumly looked at the concrete as he walked up the driveway.

"Why don't you grab your bat bag, Brian," said Kevin calmly. "Meet me in the car."

Brian was taken by surprise. That was the last thing he expected his father to say. He straightened and met his father's eyes. "Dad, it's over."

"There's something I want to show you."

They took the old four-lane Anthony Wayne Trail downtown. Brian was silent not wanting to start a conversation with his father. He glanced out the window trying to figure out where they could possibly be going.

Brian's blue eyes widened as they pulled into the parking lot of the Hens stadium. "What are we doing?"

Kevin turned off the engine, leaned over the steering wheel and peered at the logo above the gates of the stadium. "God, that is an ugly bird." He swiveled in his seat to face Brian. "Do you know how the Hens got their name?"

Brian looked around the near empty parking lot. "What are we doing here?"

Kevin ignored Brian's question. "The story I heard in the locker room is they coined the name. When was it? I think 1896. The team used to play at Bay View Park, right on the edge of Lake Erie. The baseball field was surrounded by marshes. If you hit a ball out of the field you'd see all these strange birds, with long legs and short wings scurry after the ball." Kevin motioned to the logo, "Hens."

"Dad, why are we here?"

"Jenkins is out for the season," said Kevin. "There's a spot open for a second baseman."

"You got to be kidding me," said Brian. "Like I'm going to just walk in there and play for the Hens."

Looking at Brian, Kevin smiled and shook his head. "You sound just like your mother." He pointed to the baseball field. "No, I'm not saying that. What you have is a chance to try out for second base. That's all!"

"Dad," exasperated Brian said, "We're just going to walk in there and they're going to give me a try out?"

Kevin looked at his son. "I know the coach." Kevin opened his door and got out.

Brian quickly followed and looked over the car's roof at his dad. He couldn't let it wait anymore. "What about UW?"

Kevin met Brian's stare and said, "What are you going to do with your summer?"

Brian felt the tug. He couldn't help it. He turned and looked at the stadium. He looked back to his dad then ducked into the car and picked up his bat bag.

Side by side they walked up the steps to the stadium's main gate.

"It doesn't matter." Kevin took off his Hens cap and held it as they walked through the main gate. "You're not good enough to play with these guys."

Brian stopped. The hair on the back of his neck stood then he laughed. "You know that used to work, Dad." He watched as his dad kept walking. "Back when I was in eighth grade. The old, get me mad, motivation speech." Brian shook his head. He could tell from the way his dad's shoulders were shaking that Kevin was laughing. As he ran to catch up, Brian said confidently, "Let's see if they're good enough to play with me."

Brian sat on a steel bench in the dugout. He saw his dad talking to one of the coaches by third base. He took his baseball cleats from his bat bag. The bottoms were still covered with mud from the rainout loss to St. Ignatius. He broke off a glob of dried mud and tossed it over the rail. He wished he had brought his baseball pants, but he had thrown his dirty uniform down the laundry chute. He thought, God, I'm going to look like a clown wearing jeans, an Old Navy tee shirt and, he pulled his St. Pat's green and gold baseball cap from his bag. He tossed his running shoes into his bat bag. It's just like his dad. Always got to do everything his way. Whatever he wants. If Kevin would have told him, he could at least look like a baseball player out there. He jammed the St. Pat's cap down on his forehead then picked up his well-worn Rawlings glove. He walked up the steps of the dugout and out to the field. As he moved towards second base there was no sense of awe or wonder at being in the Hens stadium. It was a baseball field. Granted, in a nice, state of the art, modern stadium but still just a baseball field, with the bases, like any other field, ninety feet apart. Just as he had done thousands of times before, he slid his glove on and went into his crouch by second base. He felt at home.

Kevin leaned against the wall that supported the box seats between home plate and first base. Tall, thin, assistant coach Meyers was in the batter's box smacking grounders and line drives to Brian near second base. As Brian warmed up, Coach Meyers extended the range, making Brian dive further and jump higher. Soon as Brian caught the balls, he would throw them to the first baseman.

Kevin looked across the diamond to the bullpen where Tim "the Cannon" Lipinski was warming up. Lipinski had spent the last two years with the Detroit Tigers but had shoulder surgery in the off-season. He was rehabbing with the Hens. Kevin, watching him throw, knew he would soon be moved back up to the Tigers.

Hearing chatter, Kevin glanced to the dugout. The word was out. A number of the Hens players lined the front row of the dugout. Watching them Kevin chuckled. Their heads swiveled like they were at a tennis match as they watched the balls streak from Coach Meyers to Brian to the first baseman. Coach Meyers picked up the tempo trying to get a ball past Brian. Before Brian finished his throw to first the coach would crack another grounder. Brian was able to stop the first couple, but the third darted by his outstretched glove as he crashed to the infield.

Brian spit out a mouthful of dust. He scrambled up from the dirt wiping the back of his hand across his mouth. He crouched, his elbows by his knees, the tip of his glove almost touching the ground. Bring it on, old man, he said to himself as he laughed. Come on, bring it on.

Coach Meyers waited as Brian dusted off his clothes and repositioned himself. When Brian smiled Coach Meyers shook his head and said, "He's sure one cocky son of a bitch." The coach switched to hard line drives watching Brian make not only the catch, but also the strong throw to first to pick off the runner before he could get back to first base. Coach Meyers hit the line drives harder and harder. One of the drives came off the top of the bat, high, heading for center field. Brian leaped. The force of the line drive locked the ball in the mitt's webbing. Brian pivoted in mid-air; opening his mitt he propelled the ball from his glove to his throwing hand. He threw. The ball smacked into the first baseman's mitt as Brian's feet landed on the ground.

Coach Meyers stared at Brian. Brian adjusted his cap, smiled at the coach, pounded his fist into his glove three times, and then set his feet for the next line drive. Coach Meyers looked at Kevin then at the Hens players standing silent in the dugout. Hoisting the bat on his shoulder, he turned back to Brian, looked past him and waved Lipinski in from the bullpen.

Coach Meyers tossed the bat to one of the players in the dugout. He walked over to Kevin.

"He play basketball?" asked Coach Meyers.

Kevin shook his head.

"I haven't seen hang time like that since I saw Jordan play the Pistons up at the Palace."

"I don't know how he does it myself," said Kevin. "But he's got that hanging throw move down pat."

Watching Lipinski take his warm-up throws, Kevin motioned to him. "What's he still doing here?"

Coach Meyers followed Kevin's gaze. "You were a pitcher?"

Kevin shrugged.

"You're right. He shouldn't be here. In fact I called Detroit this morning and said we're sending him back up. Coach Bruno will tell him after he finishes pitching to Brian." Meyers stared at Kevin. "But since he's here let's see how good your boy really is." Meyers shoved a wad of chewing tobacco in his mouth. "I know Coach Bruno said Brian's our second baseman." He chewed the tobacco. "I just want to know what I'm getting."

Brian used his bat to stretch while watching the Cannon work. He had never seen a pitcher throw a ball that fast. He couldn't pick up the rotations. The ball was just too fast. The Cannon stopped, pawed the mound with his foot and waited for Brian to step in the batter's box.

"Brian!" shouted Kevin.

Brian looked back at his Dad.

Kevin tapped his finger against the side of his head and shouted, "Get a helmet!"

Several of the players laughed. Brian jogged to the dugout and tried to ignore his dad. One of the players tossed him a helmet.

Brian swung way late as the first pitch blazed across the plate. He swung late missing the second and the third and the fourth and the fifth.

Kevin could feel Coach Meyers' eyes on him as Brian missed the tenth pitch and the eleventh and twelfth. "Come on, Brian," he whispered. "You can hit this guy. Concentrate."

Brian swung missing the twentieth pitch. He stepped out of the batter's box. He took a deep breath trying to slow his racing pulse. "I can't see it. The ball's just too fast." He glanced at his dad feeling his eyes boring into him. "Damn, I can't see it."

He tried to quell the panic creeping up from his stomach. "No one's ever thrown me a ball that fast."

Lipinski shouted, "Had enough, Kid!"

Kevin wanted to shout "NO!" as he saw Coach Meyers hold his hand up and walk towards Brian. "Just give him some more pitches."

Brian turned his back to Coach Meyers. He adjusted his helmet and stepped back into the batter's box. Coach Meyers stopped and waited.

Brian wondered what could he do as Lipinski went into his wind-up then hurled a fastball to the center of the plate. Brian pivoted, squared his body and bunted the ball down the first base line.

"What the hell?" shouted Coach Meyers.

Brian bunted the next pitch back to the Cannon. The players moved closer to edge of the dugout. Kevin heard one of them say, "What's he doing? Bunting?"

Brian fought off the third pitch, a high, inside fastball bunting it foul towards third base. He bunted the fourth pitch knocking it down right in front of the plate.

That's it, Brian, bide your time, thought Kevin. You've got to see it. You've got to see the ball leave his hand.

One after the other, the next three bunts all hugged the third base line. Lipinski stopped. He rearranged the dirt on the pitcher's mound with his foot. Brian stepped back and swept his foot shifting the gravel in the batter's box. Lipinski stood tall on the mound. Waiting. He juggled the ball in his hand inside his glove. Brian swiveled his back foot, digging, planting it in the batter's box. He brought the bat back, lowered his chin to his shoulder and stared at Lipinski.

Crack! Upper deck, foul, first base side. Brian didn't follow the ball, his eyes stayed glued on the pitcher. Crack! Upper deck, still foul but closer to the line. Crack! Lipinski, Brian, eyes locked. Neither one following the ball, as it sailed over

Lipinski's head into the center field bleachers. Crack! The ball rose and drifted foul by the third base line.

"Enough!" shouted Coach Meyers. "Lipinski, go ice your arm."

Lipinski looked intently at Brian then let the ball drop to his feet by the pitcher's mound. He walked to the dugout.

Brian stood in the batter's box, the bat still poised by his shoulder, staring at the empty spot where Lipinski stood. It seemed as if he were in a trance, his mind not ready to let go.

"Hey, Brian," Kevin said softly moving up behind him. "Brian," Kevin said louder.

Blinking his eyes, Brian lowered the bat from his shoulder. He turned and gradually focused on his dad. "Took me a long time, Dad. Took a long time to be able to see the rotations."

Kevin nodded.

"McBride! Come get your uniform," hollered Coach Meyers.

Brian extended the bat. Kevin grabbed the end and smiled at his son. Brian smiled back and slowly released the bat then jogged to the dugout.

Chapter 12

A *CONGRATULATIONS BRIAN* banner waved from the lower branch of the tulip tree in the McBride's front lawn. Gold and green streamers hanging from the gutters above the porch stirred in the slight early summer breeze. Kevin tried to think of what else he needed to get ready for Brian's high school graduation party. Throwing his hands up in frustration, he walked through the doorway to the front porch. He saw his father-in-law sitting alone on the porch swing resting his chin on top of his hands clutching his walking cane. "How's it going, Marty?"

Marty blinked. He looked like he was drifting back from someplace far away. As he recognized Kevin, he smiled. "I don't know. That chemo just leaves me tired all the time." Marty patted his stomach. "Hell of a way to lose weight, though."

"How much have you lost?" asked Kevin.

"Forty pounds." Marty chuckled. "I'm back to my fighting weight. What I weighed when I got out of the army back in '53." Marty reached over and squeezed Kevin's arm. "So my grandson's going to play for the Hens. When's his first game? I got to be there."

"Friday."

"I'll be there. Don't know if I'll be able to stay for the whole game, but I'll be there at the start. Where is he? I want to talk to him."

"He ran out to get some ice for the party. He'll be back soon."

Inside the house Karen stared out the front window and studied her father's profile. She couldn't help thinking he looked like a stuffed doll without the stuffing.

"Jesus, Mom, he's so gaunt."

"He won't eat," said Ellen. "He says the food looks good, smells good. He takes a bite and that's it. He just doesn't want anymore."

Karen asked, "Can't the doctors do anything?"

"They can't make him eat. They say a lot of that is the cancer. That's why he has no appetite."

Looking at her mother, Karen thought she had aged years in just the past few months. "How're you doing, Mom? You doing okay?"

Ellen shrugged her shoulders. "Doctor gave me some pills to help me sleep. Nighttime's always the worst. I lie awake thinking about what I'm going to do after Marty's . . . I can't picture my life without him."

Karen hugged her Mother. "I know it's hard, Mom, but I'm here and Mark and Matt and Patty."

"I know." Ellen returned the hug. "Enough." She stepped away from Karen and wiped the tears from her eyes. "Can't have me crying at Brian's graduation party. You said he decided to go to that university?"

Karen brightened and said "UW. It's a good school, Mom. It's where he wants to go."

"And he got a scholarship?"

"A partial scholarship."

"He's going to be so far away from home."

Looking out the window at her father, Karen suddenly realized that come the fall she would be missing both her father and her son. She leaned against the windowsill as a moment of panic overwhelmed her. She turned to see tears streaming down her mother's cheeks. She wrapped her arms around her mother and fought back her own tears.

Noticing the light was red, Brian abruptly slammed the brakes. The bags of ice in a box on the back seat slid forward tilted and crashed to the floor. The Jeep's tires squealed as the car lurched to a stop. Ali bounced forward. The seat belt flattened her breasts before she bounced back in the passenger seat.

"Sorry." Brian shifted the clutch to restart his Jeep. He glanced over his shoulder at the bags of ice on the floor then at Ali, his cheeks reddening in embarrassment. He decided it was much easier to talk to Ali online. Through the Internet he could fantasize how Ali looked as his fingers put his thoughts into words but when he was with her he had to look at her. It was a physical need to see her emerald eyes staring back at him. He couldn't stop his hand as he gently brushed through her wavy hair to lightly touch her soft ivory skin. Impulsively he quickly leaned forward and kissed her lips. A car horn honked behind them. Brian smiled and popped the clutch.

Brian pulled into the driveway and parked behind his grandfather's Bonneville. The car was ten years old yet gleamed as if it were brand new. He raced around his Jeep so he could have the sensation of holding Ali's hand as he helped her from the car. He kept a hold of her hand as he walked Ali to the porch.

Brian glanced away from Ali as they climbed the steps. He suddenly stopped as he looked at the swing on the porch. It took him a second to recognize his grandfather. He tried to quickly recover, knowing his face must reflect his feelings. He couldn't believe his grandfather's physical decline over just the last few weeks. He felt Ali squeeze his hand. He walked towards his grandfather.

"Grandpa, this is Ali," said Brian gently pushing Ali forward.

Looking up from his chair, Marty extended his hand. Ali clasped his hand in both of hers.

"Your grandma has been lying to me again. I'll have to talk to that woman. She said Brian has himself a cute girlfriend." Marty's mouth crinkled into a smile. "Cute, no." Marty paused, "You're beautiful."

Ali laughed and said, "Thank you."

"Here, sit down next to me," Marty pulled Ali down on the swing.

Brian grabbed one of the green plastic porch chairs and set it across from his grandfather.

"Brian, I hear tell you're playing for the Hens just like your dad." Marty smiled at Kevin. "Your dad probably doesn't even know I used to watch him pitch. Course, this was before he even started dating your mom." Marty chuckled. "With your dad pitching, if nothing else, you knew it wouldn't be boring." Marty looked at Brian and then turned to Ali by his side. "Looking at you two reminds me of the first time I met your dad. You remember that, Kevin?"

Kevin nodded.

"Your dad comes up the driveway on his motorcycle. Now, remember, I've never met him before and he's coming to take my daughter on a date. Walks up to the house with a helmet in each hand. I open the door and look down at the helmets . . ."

Kevin laughed. "And then you slammed the door in my face."

"Hell, yes, I did slam the door in your face. No daughter of mine was getting on the back of a motorcycle."

Ali laughed as she looked from Marty to Kevin.

"So what did you do, Dad?" asked Brian.

"I stood there." Kevin shrugged his shoulders. "What else was I going to do?"

"That's what your dad did." Marty turned towards Brian. "Any other kid would have taken off. But your dad just stood on the front stoop holding those two helmets."

"So what happened?" asked Ali.

Marty looked at Kevin and nodded.

Kevin continued the story, "About a half hour later."

"It wasn't that long," piped in Marty.

"Anyway, your mom comes walking out dangling the key to your grandpa's car and she says, "I guess I'll drive.""

Laughing, Marty said, "And she's been driving ever since." Marty held his stomach. "Oh, enough, that hurts," said Marty still laughing."

Leaning forward, Kevin put his hand on Marty's knee. "You okay?"

Marty held his hand up, nodded as he caught his breath. He sat back in the swing. "Ali, can you get me a glass of water, and ask Ellen for one of my pills."

As Ali quickly walked across the porch, Brian asked, "You okay, Grandpa?"

"I'm fine, Brian."

Brian swallowed. He knew, as he looked at his pale grandfather sitting across from him, that hidden from view the cancer cells were multiplying and that nothing science had in its arsenal right now could stop their multiplication. He felt helpless. He wanted to scream, Why now? Why couldn't they just wait? All we need is time. We can stop these cells. We can destroy the cells and heal the tissue. We just need time.

"Brian?" asked Kevin.

Brian turned. His dad had the same look on his face as he had after a fastball careened off Brian's baseball helmet.

"You said you had something for," Kevin nodded towards Brian's grandfather, "Marty."

Brian suddenly remembered. "I do." He sprang from the swing, jumped off the porch and ran to his Jeep Cherokee.

Marty watched him. "That's what I'm going to miss the most." Marty bit his lower lip. "Just seeing my grandchildren grow." He faced Kevin. "You got a lot to be proud of."

Kevin looked up as Karen walked onto the porch. "We both do."

Karen handed Marty his pill and a glass of water. "Ali's helping Mom with the fruit salad. You want a small bowl, Dad?"

"No, not now." Marty tapped his hand on the swing. "Here. Sit with me."

"Just for a minute. I've got all this stuff to finish inside before everyone gets here."

"That Brian's got himself quite a girlfriend."

Karen gently set her hand on her father's arm. "He does, Dad."

Marty glanced from Karen to Kevin. "Well, the way Brian looks at her reminds me of the way a certain young man would look at my daughter." Marty laughed. "And that would keep me up nights walking the floor when you two were dating."

"Dad," said Karen laughing as she sneaked a peek at Kevin.

"Don't "Dad" me. I might be old and sick but I'm not senile." Marty touched his daughter's hand. "If they do half as well as you two," Marty said looking from Karen to Kevin, and shaking his head, "they'll be fine."

Marty picked up his cane and rested his hands on top. Karen couldn't help staring at the white knuckles protruding through the tight skin.

"I need you to do me a favor." Marty looked at his daughter. "I want to go home."

"Dad, you just got here."

"Yeah and I saw who I wanted to see and now I want to go home." Trying to ease the disappointment he saw on Karen's face, Marty continued, "All these people are going to come up to me and ask me how I feel." Marty tightened his grip on the cane. "I don't want to tell them how I feel. Then they'll go into the house and whisper how bad I look. I look in the mirror every morning, Karen, I know how bad I look. Your sister Patty is going to sit with me and after a while she'll go into the house, find a chair in the corner and sit and cry. Then your mother will comfort her and she'll start crying too."

Marty pushed himself up from the swing. Karen took his arm to help steady him.

"I'm fighting, Karen, but we both know I can't beat this."

"Grandpa," shouted Brian as he leaped onto the porch. Skidding to a stop before Marty he held out a Hens baseball cap.

"I'll be," said Marty.

"It's not a souvenir. It's one of my official ones."

Marty ran his hand over his bald head. Laughing he took the cap and said, "Just what the doctor ordered." He put the cap on. "Brian, I need you to take me for a ride."

"Sure, Grandpa. Where we going?"

Marty faced Karen and said softly, "I want your mom to stay here. She needs this party. Don't let her come home. I'll be fine. I'm just going to sleep anyway."

"Okay, Dad," said Karen. She gave him a light hug and kissed his cheek.

Marty tugged the cap lower on his forehead. "Let's hit the road, Brian."

Karen watched her father shuffle along the porch. She felt Kevin come up behind her and wrap his arms around her waist. She leaned back against her husband.

As Brian waited for the light to change, he glanced to see if his grandfather was sleeping. His breathing was so rough yet steady; Brian thought he was snoring. His grandfather's eyes were open but staring vacantly at the road ahead. Brian wondered what was his grandpa thinking, wondered what you thought about when you were dying?

Marty blinked and looked at Brian. "Did you say something?"

Brian shook his head and accelerated as the light turned green.

"This damn medicine." Marty leaned forward and pulled his handkerchief from his back pocket then wiped his mouth.

"Half the time I don't know if I'm dreaming." Marty suddenly reached up and felt the cap on his head. He lifted the cap off and held it in his hands staring at the Hens logo. "This wasn't a dream. Damn. You are going to play for the Hens." Marty smiled and it seemed to Brian for that moment the constant pain left his grandfather's face. "You remember that grand slam you hit?"

Brian tried to think which grand slam his grandfather was talking about.

"Your first one. You gotta remember, 'cause I sure do. It was the first time you wore a baseball uniform instead of just those t-shirts."

"Third grade." Brian downshifted as they came to a red light. "That was the year the kids got to pitch instead of the coaches."

"But you didn't hit the home run off a pitch?"

Brian nodded as he remembered. "If you got four balls instead of getting a walk to first base, you got to throw the ball up and try to hit it. If you missed, it would count as a strike; so you could still strike out."

"The bases were loaded," Marty said. "You threw the ball up, man, did you wallop it! Your dad was coaching third base; he was over there yelling 'RUN! RUN!' But not to you," Marty laughed. "There was a chubby kid on first base; you caught up to him before he even reached second. Kevin's yelling 'RUN!' You got your hands on the kid's back pushing him ahead of you down the baseline." Marty laughed and smacked his knee. "Oh! Was that funny! I can still picture you pushing that kid and hear your dad yelling 'RUN!' The kid stumbled onto home plate and you fell on top of him. Then all the other kids on your team ran out and just piled on top of both of you."

Brian chucked as he remembered. "Wally Sankowich. He's not chubby anymore. He's fat."

Marty pressed his hand to his chest and took a couple of deep breaths.

Suddenly frightened, Brian swerved the Jeep to the side of the road. "You okay? Grandpa?"

Marty held his hand up and blew small puffs of air. The color returned to his cheeks. He let his hand fall into his lap. He stammered, "It's been so long since I had a good laugh."

Brian waited until both his grandfather's and his own breathing returned to normal then looked over his left shoulder. He steered the Jeep back into traffic.

Marty rubbed his thumb against the logo of the Hens. "My dad used to take me to Hens games when I was a kid. This was way back in the thirties. We were lucky. Dad had a job with the post office. At that time a lot of my friends' fathers were out of work. People just didn't have the money to spare on a ball game so we were always able to get pretty good seats. My dad would say, 'invite a couple of your friends.' He knew their parents didn't have the money to take their kids to the park so he always paid for their tickets and the hot dogs." Marty laughed. "As you can imagine, I had a lot of friends."

Brian pulled into the gravel driveway and parked in front of the wooden single car garage.

Marty didn't seem to know he was home. "All us kids had our heroes. We were all going to be professional ballplayers when we grew up and hit the grand slam to win the game. My dream was to play shortstop." Marty bent the bill of the cap then set the Hens cap on his head. He looked at his grandson as if he still couldn't believe it. "But you did it."

Marty rubbed his hands against the top of his knees. His voice grew serious, "You'll be carrying a lot of kids' dreams out there, Brian." Marty squeezed Brian's arm. "Don't let them down."

Not knowing how to respond, Brian just looked back at his grandfather.

Marty relaxed his hand. "You better get back to your party."

Brian walked around the Jeep and opened the passenger door. He offered his hand to Marty. As Marty took his hand,

Brian could feel his grandfather's grip weaken. Brian shifted his hand up Marty's forearm to help him from the car. He was shocked as he felt the sharp bone under loose skin. After years of maneuvering transmissions in the Jeep factory, Marty's forearms always felt like they were made of granite to Brian. As Marty stood wobbling slightly, Brian reached into the car and handed Marty his cane.

"I can get it from here, Brian."

"Nah, Grandpa. Come on." Brian took his grandfather's elbow to guide him up the walkway.

Marty tried to shake off Brian's hand. "Go on."

Brian held on to Marty's elbow. "I got to use the bathroom anyway."

Marty gave up and let Brian help him to the house.

Brian took the keys from Marty's hand and opened the back door. As the door opened, he couldn't help notice the smell. It reminded Brian of the hospital, when he sat in a wheelchair waiting to have his ankle x-rayed. It was so strange because his grandparents' house always smelled like a bakery. His grandmother constantly seemed to have something in the oven, cinnamon rolls, chocolate chip cookies, pound cakes. He still sensed a whiff of fresh bread, but the scent was overpowered by the medicinal odor.

Marty hung his cane on the coat rack then took off his Hens cap and set it on the hook above his cane. He seemed more self-assured in his own home. His hand skirted the tops of the kitchen chairs as he shuffled to the living room. He slowly made his way to his gray, lazyboy chair by the bay window overlooking his front yard. He collapsed into the chair and tried to raise the leg rest, but he didn't have the strength. Brian leaned over the chair and pulled the side handle. Marty settled himself then reached for the water pitcher set on the end table.

"Here," Brian snatched the pitcher, "let me get you some fresh water." Brian got some ice and filled the pitcher with cold water from the kitchen sink. Walking back into the living room, he found his grandfather's eyes closed, his chest slowly rising and falling. Brian quietly filled a water glass from the end table then set the pitcher and glass on the table. He looked around the familiar room, the color television in the corner that was almost as old as he was, the sofa, and the long wooden coffee table with the photo album resting on top. Trying not to make any noise he glided across the room and sat on the sofa. He looked down at himself. A page of photographs taken on the day he hit his first grand slam. In the top picture his grandfather was towering over him, his grandfather's large hand appeared to engulf Brian's slender ten-year-old shoulder.

Brian flipped through the pages. He stopped and turned back a page as he recognized his mother. She had to be nine or ten wearing her First Communion dress. She was standing on her parents' front porch her hands folded around a rosary. As Brian looked closer, he saw his mother was smiling in the picture but still trying to hide her missing front teeth. Her baby sister Patty was on the step below her, and her brothers Mark and Matt were sitting on chairs on the porch.

As he continued to flip through the album, the pictures were older. Some he had never seen before. There were army pictures of his grandfather. Brian was puzzled because he never heard his grandfather talk about the army. The old, grainy black and white photos seemed to have been taken at some army camp. One photo was a group picture of about ten young men. They weren't really wearing uniforms just identical t-shirts and pants. As he studied the picture he recognized his grandfather standing on the end. His grandfather's elbow was resting on the shoulder of the soldier next to him; his other arm was clutching something. It looked familiar. Brian peered closer trying to see what it was. Suddenly it came into focus. It was a baseball mitt. Brian wondered where they were when this picture was taken. Glancing at the other faces, it seemed like something was odd about these soldiers. Finally it dawned on Brian, it was like these guys had to force themselves to smile.

Brian traced his finger down the page of photos. He stopped at the photo in the bottom corner. Jesus. It was a soldier standing in front of what appeared to be a mountain of snow. A scarf or maybe a shirt was wrapped over the helmet and under the soldier's chin. It looked like water or ice was coated on his face, and the eyes staring from the photo seemed haunted. Brian felt a shiver pass through him. It felt as if the living room suddenly grew very cold. He couldn't take his eyes off the photo. He didn't know why but all of the sudden he said, "Grandpa."

The phone rang. Brian quickly glanced at his grandfather who mumbled something in his sleep then tried to turn on his side in the chair. As the phone rang again Brian hopped over the coffee table, ran into the kitchen and picked up the cordless phone.

"Grandma . . . no he's fine . . . he's sleeping." Brian looked at the clock on the microwave. Oh shit, he thought, as he suddenly realized he had left without telling Ali where he was going. She probably thought I forgot about her. Pressing the phone to his ear, he walked back to the living room. He saw his grandfather stirring trying to rouse himself from sleep. "Grandma, tell Ali I'm leaving now. I'll be home in ten minutes. What?" Brian relaxed and smiled. "You and Ali are making cookies . . . Kyle's helping? Don't let him eat them all . . . Grandma . . . Thanks."

Brian saw his grandfather's eyes slowly flutter then open. Marty reached for the glass of water. As he took a sip, he looked at Brian trying to figure out why Brian was standing there. Suddenly it came to him and he said, "Why are you still here?"

Brian set the phone on the end table next to Marty. "I had to use the bathroom, remember." Brian saw the photo album still open on the coffee table. He walked over and closed the book.

Marty pushed himself up in the chair. "Let me have that."

Brian carried the book over and gently set it on his grand-father's lap.

"Here." As if his fingers knew exactly where to go, Marty opened the album to the page of photos displaying Brian's first grand slam. He pointed at the photo of himself with his hand on Brian's shoulder. "That was the day." Marty smiled as he looked at the two grinning faces in the photograph. "You know, Brian, I was with you. I was helping you push that kid around the bases."

Noting the puzzled look on Brian's face, Marty continued, "You live through your kids," Marty nodded down at the photo, "and through your grandchildren."

Looking at his grandfather, Brian realized that Marty was trying in his own way to say goodbye. Brian quickly turned away. He didn't want his grandfather to see his face. He tried to stop the tears building in his eyes. He felt his grandfather squeeze his elbow.

"Hey! You got a party to go to. Tell your grandma to bring me some cake." Marty pushed Brian away.

Brian walked across the living room. He wanted to turn and say something, anything, but he couldn't. Not looking back, he just lifted his hand and walked to the back door.

Chapter 13

Kevin sat on the porch swing, reading the sports section of USA Today. He peeked up as he heard the bike fall on the driveway. The youth, wearing a St. John's baseball uniform, strolled to the porch.

"Kyle, what's new?" asked Kevin.

Taking off his cap and spinning it around his finger, Kyle plopped down on the porch chair. "James Dutch is moving to Atlanta. He doesn't want to go, but his dad's been transferred."

Kevin folded the paper and set it aside on the swing. "I don't think I'd want to move to Atlanta either."

"That's not the worst of it," replied Kyle. "His dad is our baseball coach."

"Well, you've got an assistant coach, don't you?"

"Keith's dad. But Mike and Bobby and Peter all said they'd quit if he becomes the coach."

"Well, that does sound like a problem. What's the matter with Keith's dad?"

Kyle sat up straight in the chair. "All he does is yell, yell, yell, and . . ." Kyle looked over his shoulder then back to Kevin and whispered, "and he cusses."

"No."

"He does." Nodding his head for emphasis, Kyle said, "He even uses the F word."

"What grade are you in now, Kyle?"

"Fifth, no sixth."

"Well, which one?"

"I was in fifth grade when this season started but now it's summer and we're still playing so I'll be in sixth grade when school starts."

"So, this coach has been cussing at kids in fifth, I mean, sixth grade."

"Screaming and cussing."

"Well, that's not good." Kevin stretched his legs in front of the swing and locked his hands behind his head. "That's not how you coach baseball, especially kids." Kevin looked at Kyle and said, "So . . ."

Kyle spun his cap faster around his finger. "So, Uncle Kevin, I told my mom and she said to come see you 'cause you're the best baseball coach St. John's ever had."

Kevin laughed. "Kyle, you know your mom kissed the Blarney stone."

Kyle's face showed he had no idea what his uncle was talking about.

"Never mind. So . . ." Kevin pointed his hand at Kyle and waited.

Kyle blurted out, "Will you be our coach?"

Kevin studied his nephew. He gazed at the curly hair above the anxious face.

"And how much does this job pay?"

Looking down Kyle shuffled his feet on the porch. "You know it doesn't pay anything." He glanced up at Kevin then to the front yard. His face brightened. "I'll cut your grass. Now that Brian's playing for the Hens, he's not going to have time."

"I'm not going to have time for what?" asked Brian as he opened the screen door and joined them on the porch.

"Brian!" Kyle said. "I didn't know you were home."

Brian slapped Kyle's outstretched hand and then made himself comfortable on the other porch chair. "Now what don't I have time for?"

"Kyle's going to cut the grass," said Kevin, "If I coach his baseball team."

Kyle quickly said, "You'll do it then."

"Whoa! What am I getting into here? What sort of team do you have? What's your record?"

"Well . . . Uncle Kevin, we're . . . really . . . not too good." Kyle crumpled his hat between his fingers. "We haven't won any games yet. We almost beat St. Charles but Bobby slipped and the ball went over his head. If he would have caught it." Kyle shrugged his shoulders.

"Sounds like there's a lot of room for improvement. How many games have you got left?"

"I don't know. Maybe twelve."

"You any good, Kyle?"

Kyle twisted his baseball cap. He mumbled as he glanced at his cousin sitting next to him, "I'm not as good as Brian."

Kevin laughed. "What do you play?"

"First base and pitcher."

Kevin pushed his foot and the swing started swaying. "Pitcher?"

Kyle nodded, "Jeff was our pitcher, but when we played Blessed Sacrament he walked ten batters in a row. They won't let him pitch anymore.

Kevin chuckled as he exchanged looks with Brian. "So you're the pitcher?"

"Me and Ben. Coach says he likes to start Ben 'cause he scares 'em away from the plate."

"Scares 'em away, huh."

"When we played Arlington he hit the first three batters."

Kevin rolled his eyes as Brian asked, "You're kidding right, Kyle?"

Kyle emphatically shook his head no.

Kevin asked, "Doast still the baseball commissioner for St. John's?"

"I think so. Jeremy Doast was in the other fifth grade."

Kevin pushed his feet to keep the swing rocking. "He must have had ten kids. I swear he has been the commissioner for twenty years."

Kevin's eyes darted to the driveway as he heard the squeal of brakes. Kyle ran down from the porch. He stopped in front of the car, rolled his bike from the driveway and laid it on the grass. He waved at his Aunt Karen.

Karen parked the car in the garage. She bent to smell the lilacs blooming on the bush before moving to the porch.

"I'm being propositioned," Kevin said loudly to Karen.

She paused and rubbed her fingers through Kyle's short tight curls. "Not by Kyle, I hope."

"He's trolling for a baseball coach. You're just in time. We're getting down to the serious negotiations." Kevin looked back to Kyle. "You know Aunt Karen's my agent." Kevin grinned at her. "I never sign a contract without her approval."

Karen gave one of her patented "Watch it buddy, looks."

"We've got about twelve games left," continued Kevin, "plus practices, two, nope." He glanced back at Kyle. "At least three times a week. Now, Kyle put on the table cutting the grass for the duration, but I'm thinking maybe he ought to throw in washing the cars."

"Of course," said Karen. "You don't expect me to attend your games in a dirty car, do you, Kyle?"

"Yeah. Right," said Kyle. "That's definitely do-able."

"Once a week," added Karen.

Kyle nodded.

Kevin turned his attention to his son. "What do you think? Brian? Your old man have any coaching left in him?"

Kyle's eyes darted from his uncle to Brian.

Brian laughed, "I think you might be able to scratch up another season."

Kevin asked, "You wouldn't be able to give me a hand?"

Kyle sprang forward to the edge of his chair, anticipating Brian's response.

Brian looked at Kyle then nodded to his Dad. "Well, since I learned from the master." He met his father's gaze. "As long as I don't have a game."

Standing up, Kevin said, "Let me see if I can get a hold of Doast. See if we can finalize this today."

A few minutes later Kevin walked out on the porch. Kyle shoved the rest of the cookie in his mouth and set the half-filled glass of milk on the small table.

"When's our next practice, Kyle?"

Kyle smiled broadly and wiped the milk mustache from his lips and said, "Tuesday."

Chapter 14

Brian jogged on the gravel path winding through the woods of Duck Creek. His chest heaving, he struggled to catch up with Ali. He felt a moment of panic as Ali rounded the bend far ahead of him and disappeared behind the dense trees and blossoming summer foliage. Ignoring the stitch in his side, he quickened his pace. As he rounded the bend, he saw Ali slowly walking with her hands locked behind her head. When she turned, Brian couldn't help staring at Ali's breasts moving in rhythm to her breathing. Ali dropped her hands to her waist and walked back to him.

"Brian."

He knew he was caught. With a guilty smile Brian looked into Ali's emerald eyes. "Pretty embarrassing."

Ali grinned and crossed her arms over her chest. "It's okay. Just don't ignore the rest of me."

Brian shook his head and laughed. "I was talking about getting beat by a girl."

"Oh, you were, were you?" Pretending to stretch, Ali locked her hands behind her back and arched her shoulders.

"That's cheating."

Ali sauntered forward and kissed Brian on the lips. She took his hand and led him down the path to the promontory.

"What? You know the way now?" asked Brian.

"I'm a fast learner."

Ali sat on the dry grass leaning back against the fallen tree stump. "I don't know how I feel. I know you're all excited and this is something you really want to do." She hugged her knees close to her chest. "But you just spring it on me and I really haven't had a lot of time to think about it." Ali took her wristband and wiped the beads of perspiration from her forehead. "This is going to change things, Brian. I thought we would be able to spend the whole summer together."

Brian took her hand and squeezed it. "This won't change anything. I won't let it." He took his finger and dabbed the moisture from her upper lip. Suddenly he shouted 'Ouch' and grabbed his calf.

"Cramp?" asked Ali.

Brian grimaced and nodded.

Ali scooted around and took his foot into her lap. Bending back the top of his running shoe, she massaged his calf. "You should have stretched out."

"Now you tell me," said Brian as the pain subsided.

Pressing back his toes, Ali squeezed the tight calf muscle. As her eyes drifted up his leg, she laughed. "Looks like you're getting another cramp."

Brian pulled his foot free from Ali's hands. Bringing his knees up to his chest, he sat in silence and looked off to the forest.

"Oh, you can look at me but I can't look at you."

"It's not the same . . . it's . . . ." Brian looked down at his lap "You know I can't help it."

Ali laughed again then suddenly stopped when she saw Brian recoil. She was surprised that Brian was embarrassed. She knelt by him and touched his chin with her fingers. "I'm not making fun of you. I would never do that." Her fingers skimmed along his cheek down to his neck as she kissed him. "I'm glad," she motioned to his lap and laughed, "you're like that."

"Yeah, right."

"If you weren't like that, I'd be worried." She took Brian's hand and sank back onto the short grass in the small clearing. The sunlight filtered through the overhead leaves as they both lay on their sides facing each other.

Ali whispered, "Have you ever done it?"

As Brian looked into Ali's eyes, he felt that all she wanted from him was the truth. Holding her gaze he shook his head no.

"Me, either." Ali stared at the leaves slowly swaying with the warm summer breeze. "Some of the other boys I dated . . ."

Brian shifted to his back and stared up at the trees unsure if he wanted Ali to continue.

"It seems that's all they wanted." Ali shuddered as if shaking off a bad memory.

When Ali stopped talking Brian turned to look at her.

Ali took a deep breath and told Brian what she had never told anyone else. "It's like I'm waiting for this voice to whisper to me. Now, now's the right time." Ali closed her eyes feeling she may have revealed too much about herself. "It does sound silly when you say it out loud."

Brian stroked her cheek gently with his fingertips. "I don't think it's silly."

Ali opened her eyes and held Brian's fingers against her cheek. "What about you? What do you think about doing it?"

Brian glanced down to his groin. When Ali followed his gaze he remarked, "It all depends on who you're talking to."

Ali laughed. She put her hand behind Brian's neck and pulled him so close their faces were almost touching. She stared into his blue eyes. "You, I'm talking to you."

Brian whispered, "I want you so much, sometimes I feel I can't breathe."

"Oh, Brian. Don't say that." Ali's fingers covered his lips as she closed her eyes.

Brian kissed her fingers then softly pulled away. "I want you so much, Ali." He kissed her fingers again and sighed. "I just wish you would want me as much as I want you."

"Brian, it's not a matter of want." She grabbed his fingers and tightly squeezed his hand. "I want you. You don't know how much I want you." Ali lay back on the grass and stared up at the twisting leaves trying to find the words to explain her feelings. "The first time will be mine for the rest of my life." She turned back to face Brian to see if he understood. "Once I do it," Brian felt her breath on his cheek, as she sharply exhaled, "I can't undo it."

Ali sat up, pulled her knees in and wrapped her arms around her knees. She rested her head on top of her knees and looked down at Brian. "I've always thought . . . I've always thought I would know when it was the right time." She held his gaze. Ali unlocked her hands and lowered her knees. Her fingers drifted to the top of her leotard. She asked plaintively, "You need me to prove how much I want you?" She slowly pulled the fabric down from her shoulders revealing the top of her breasts.

Brian turned and kneeled. He placed both of his hands on Ali's. He held her hands and looked into her glistening emerald eyes. He untwined his hands; the fingertips lightly danced up her smooth bare arms, and then flowed into her wavy hair. His palms gently caressed her slender neck as he brought her cheek next to his chest. "No. No, Ali." He felt her warm breath on his chest as she listened to the steady rhythm of his heart.

As she felt his heartbeat slow, Ali gently pushed away. She pulled her top back up then cupped her hands on the sides of Brian's face. Laughing, she looked at him. "You do this to me all the time. You know, you drive me crazy. We came here to talk about you and the Hens and the next thing I know," she stopped and kissed his lips then leaned back.

Running his fingers through her hair Brian said, "It's only for the summer."

"We were going to spend the summer together."

Brian's hands clasped Ali's shoulders, "We will."

"And what happens when you have out of town games. When you have to go to Buffalo or Columbus or wherever," said Ali sweeping her hand up towards the sky.

"You'll come with me."

"Wrong! One, my parents would go ballistic. Two, I have a job. You know I need to work this summer."

Brian straightened and walked to the edge of the promontory. He stared down at the slow waters flowing through Duck Creek.

Ali walked to him and pleaded, "Don't shut me out."

Brian faced her, "I don't know what to say, Ali." He turned away then suddenly spun around. "I want to play for the Hens."

"Okay, now I know. You're so quiet, sometimes. I don't know what you're thinking." Ali tapped her fingertips against his temples. "Brian, I don't know what's important to you unless you tell me. If this is what you want, we'll work it out."

"It's what I want to do this summer. I want to play for the Hens."

Ali studied Brian's serious face then slowly nodded her head.

Brian edged closer, "You'll come to my first game, Friday?" He took Ali's hands and pinned them against his chest. "It's a night game so you won't have to miss work."

Ali tried to pull her hands away. "I'll be there."

Brian tightened his grip on her hands. "You're not mad at me?"

Ali shook her head, "No."

Raising his eyebrows and biting his lower lip, Brian continued, "This wasn't like our first fight?"

In spite of herself Ali laughed and said, "No."

"Good." Brian released her hands and pulled Ali into his embrace.

Chapter 15

Brian sat on the grass of the new Hens stadium doing a hurdler's stretch, his right foot bent in next to his groin, his left leg extended straight out. He grabbed his left ankle and slowly lowered his upper body till his chest touched his left knee. He held the stretch for a few seconds feeling his calf and leg muscles relax. The pants of his Hens uniform felt stiff and coarse against his skin. As he straightened, he stared at the empty box seats he reserved for his family. Where were they? He gazed around the stadium to the fans trickling to their seats. He switched legs to stretch the other side. As he glanced up he saw his grandfather hobbling up the ramp using his cane like a walking stick. Brian laughed as his grandmother tried to help, but his grandpa just shooed her away. Brian jumped to his feet and raced across the field.

"I'm glad you're here, Grandpa," said Brian.

Marty smiled as his eyes caressed Brian and the baseball field. "Some day, huh?"

Leaning over the wall of the box seats between home and first base, Brian shook his grandfather's hand. He eased his grip as he felt the skeletal bones mesh together.

"Got my hat," said Marty as he pulled the visor of his Hens cap lower on his forehead.

"My, I've always had a soft spot for a boy in a uniform," said Ellen.

"Hi, Grandma," said Brian as he squeezed her hand.

As Karen and Ali and Kyle entered the box seats, Marty said, "You better watch it, Brian, looks like Kyle is trying to put the moves on Ali."

Brian laughed as he reached over and ruffled Kyle's curly hair. "Kyle wouldn't do that."

"Yeah, says who?" said Kyle grabbing Ali's hand.

"He did promise to buy me some popcorn," Ali joked.

Brian looked and nodded at his mother than turned back to Marty. "We're going to hit a home run, Grandpa."

Marty guffawed. "Babe Ruth lives! You going to point to where you're going to hit it?"

"Nah, I'm not that good."

Marty stopped laughing and said, "Just seeing you out there is enough." Marty raised his hand and pointed across the infield. "Is that your dad over there?"

Brian followed the direction of the shaking, pointed finger. "Over by the fence, next to our dugout, pacing back and forth?"

Marty nodded.

Without turning to look, Brian said, "That's him."

Shifting his eyes to Karen, Marty said, "This must be quite a day for him."

Karen wondered how Kevin felt as she gazed across the field at her husband.

"I got to get out there," said Brian backing away from the box seats. "Grandpa, look for that home run," he yelled over his shoulder.

"First time up," shouted Marty.

Brian pivoted then shouted, "I said *we* would hit a home run." He laughed. "I didn't say when."

Marty laughed and waved Brian away.

Kyle tugged on Karen's sleeve. When she looked at him, he asked, "Did Brian say we'd hit a home run?"

Karen, just as confused as Kyle, shook her head and said, "I don't know."

Brian stood in the dugout gazing from his grandfather to the spectators filling the terraced bleachers before the start of the game.

"Goosebumps. You can always tell the rookies."

Brian turned and looked at the catcher standing next to him then glanced down at his own arm. "Gees, you're right," said Brian as he rubbed his hand up and down his arm.

"Hey, enjoy them. They don't last too long," said the catcher.

Why am I so nervous, thought Brian as he listened to the starting lineup. Man, this is crazy. It's just a game.

"And starting at second base," the voice on the PA system announced, "Northwest Ohio's own, Brrrian McBride!"

Brian charged from the dimness of the dugout into the light. Surrounded by clapping and cheers he jogged across the infield. He stopped near second base. His eyes searched the rows of spectators until they found his grandpa. He doffed his Hens cap, then turning, he spotted the lone figure standing by the fence.

The bat resting on his shoulder, Brian waited in the on-deck circle. He tried but couldn't concentrate on the pitcher. He kept glancing around the stadium. He felt like he was in a petri dish under a microscope. A million eyes seemed to follow him to the batter's box.

"Strike one!" yelled the home plate umpire.

Brian stepped out of the box. He felt his heart jack-hammering in his chest. His hands oozed sweat inside his batting gloves. He searched for the figure by the fence. He found his father, and he remembered, *the game's not played in the stands. It's played on the field.* He exhaled as he stepped back into the box.

Silence. It was as if he dove and was swimming under water. He saw the pitcher as through a zoom lens but everything else was unfocused. He saw the rotations, the stitches revolving on the white sphere streaking towards the plate. The impact jarred his arms as the sphere cratered into the end of the bat. He tossed the bat to the ground. As he ran towards first, he followed the arc of the ball. He saw it start to drift. Rounding first base he heard the umpire call, "Foul ball."

He jogged back and picked up his bat. As he repositioned himself in the batter's box, he heard the voice, as if his father were standing right behind him. *The first swing's yours. After that you just try to put the ball in play.*

Brian rubbed his batting gloves along the bat's handle. He brought the bat high above his shoulder lowered his chin and eyed the pitcher. His wrists snapped driving the ball down. It streaked through the opening between the shortstop and the third baseman. As soon as he made contact, he sprang forward just as he would in the 100-yard dash. Rounding first base, he saw the left fielder race in and scoop up the ball. Not hesitating, he sprinted for second. Brian slid as he saw the second baseman lift his mitt to catch the throw. His toes touched the bag then the glove brushed against his calf. He called time, rolled then stood and smacked dust from his uniform with his Hens cap. He didn't hear the cheers as he looked to the box seats between home and first base. He felt as if someone had just punched him in the stomach as he stared at his grandfather's empty seat.

In the locker room after the game, Coach Bruno said, "You had a good game out there today, Brian."

"Thanks, Coach." The words came automatically. Brian's thoughts were with his grandfather. Why did he leave so soon? Was he okay? Brian pushed his mitt into his bat bag.

"Hey, Juan." Coach Bruno raised his hand and waved the catcher over. "Come here."

Loosening his chest protector, Juan ambled over. Brian looked at Coach Bruno then shifted his gaze up to the catcher. Juan was six inches taller and a good thirty pounds heavier than his black coach. Juan was stocky, carrying the weight in his thighs and in his Popeye-like forearms. With his Mexican ancestry, even though it was early summer, he was deeply tanned. His coal black eyes sharply contrasted his white teeth.

"What's up, Coach?"

"How long have you been here, Juan?"

"I don't know how many games," Juan lifted the chest protector over his head then held it at his side. "But I've been here three years."

"We're going to Buffalo for three games," said Coach Bruno as he put his hand on Juan's shoulder. "I want Brian to room with you. That way, you know, you can show him the ropes."

Juan glanced from Coach Bruno to Brian then back to the Coach.

"Okay."

Coach Bruno took his hand off Juan's shoulder then turned towards Brian. "See, Brian; that's what I like about Juan. Juan keeps things simple for me. If I'd ask some of these other guys, they'd tell me I got to talk to their agents and believe me that's worse than talking to their mothers. Thanks, Juan." With a satisfied smile, Coach Bruno strutted to his office.

Brian extended his hand, "Thanks."

Shaking Brian's hand, Juan said, "No problem."

"Hey, I gotta scoot." Brian picked up his bat bag and quickly left the locker room. As soon as he was outside he flipped open his cell phone and called his mom to see if she knew what happened to his grandfather.

Brian rolled over and looked at his alarm clock. The digital display clicked from 3:02 A.M. to 3:03 A.M. He untangled his feet from the sheets then rolled on top of his blankets. He kept reliving the day in his mind. It was a thrill; he had to admit: Hearing his name called over the public address system while thousand of fans shouted and clapped as he ran to second base in the Hens stadium. It definitely wasn't high school ball where the fans are usually just family, friends, and girlfriends. He could still envision Ali in the box seat. God was she beautiful. Brian rolled to his back and stared at the lines on the ceiling reflected from the streetlight through his window blinds. Grandpa was home. Grandma said he had just gotten dizzy and needed to go home and rest.

In the semi-darkness Brian crept across his bedroom carpet and powered up his computer. As the monitor glowed, the DNA helix of his screensaver cast a purplish hue over his face. He clicked on his favorites section and within seconds was connected with the computers for UW.

He clicked through an array of the latest computational models for molecular manufacturing systems. He studied the diagrams of proposed nano machines designed to assemble and store atoms, machines that one day could travel through the bloodstream and destroy the cancer cells that were destroying his grandfather.

He surfed his other sites for nanotechnology. Clicking from page to page he knew it could be done.

As sunlight crept though his blinds, he pushed his chair back from his computer. He stared at a picture of a submicroscopic robotic arm he had been designing to assemble atoms for a chemical reaction. Analyzing each component, he tried to determine how much was real and how much was still theoretical. After minutes of studying his submicroscopic robotic arm, the screensaver of his DNA helix popped up on his monitor.

Brian banged his fist against the keyboard and the DNA helix disappeared replaced by his design project. And this is just one small part. Totally frustrated, Brian glared at the screen. It was as if he knew the formula for a magic elixir to cure his grandfather but couldn't find the ingredients. There wasn't time. His grandfather would be dead long before the realm of nanotechnology opened the door to miracles.

Chapter 16

Karen sat at the kitchen table across from her mother. A warm, light July breeze stirred the lace, kitchen curtains of her father's home.

"They said the last chemo session didn't do any good," Ellen said. "They won't do any more." Even though the house was warm, Ellen wrapped both hands around her coffee mug, trying to bring warmth into her cold fingers. "They said there is nothing more for them to do, that we should call hospice."

Reaching across the table, Karen covered her mother's hands with her own. "Oh, Mom."

Ellen's lower lip quivered as tears ran down her cheeks.

"Does Dad know?" whispered Karen.

Ellen pulled her hands away from Karen. She took a Kleenex from her pocket and dabbed at the corners of her eyes. "He doesn't want hospice. He said he's going to rest and get stronger then have more chemo. He's convinced that the next chemo series will work." Ellen cocked her head towards the back bedroom. She shut her eyes and listened. "He's waking up." She put her hands on the table to push herself up.

"No, Mom." Karen quickly stood and gently pushed her mother back down. "I'll go."

Karen tiptoed down the hall to the back bedroom. She stopped and leaned against the wall, trying to gather herself. She steeled back the tears and forced a smile on her face. She pushed off from the wall and walked into the bedroom.

Glancing at the bed, she quickly looked away. She couldn't bear to see her father like this. He was always the strength, the foundation of her life and now to see him looking so helpless. Hesitantly, she approached the bed. She placed her hand on top of her dad's bony, blue veined wrist. His eyes fluttered open and slowly focused.

"Karen," said Marty in a hoarse whisper. His hand motioned to the glass of water on the night table. Karen brought the straw to his lips. "I get all dried out." He sucked some water, then waved the glass away. "Help me sit up."

Karen put one hand under his armpit and the other on his back. She eased her father forward then propped two pillows behind his back.

As his raspy breathing slowed, Marty said, "That's better." He stirred restlessly on the bed then pushed up with his hands to sit straighter. "What time is it?"

"It's about five o'clock."

Marty shook his head back and forth. "Slept another day away."

Karen took a Kleenex and gently rubbed some dried crust from the corner of Marty's mouth. "How are you feeling, Dad?"

"Not good. This pain in my stomach, it's like someone's twisting my guts."

"What about your pain pills? Do they help?"

"Some." He glanced at the prescriptions arrayed on the night table. "I don't like to take them. They make me feel like I'm half drunk." His eyes darted around the bedroom. "Where's your mother?"

"She's in the kitchen, Dad."

Marty sank back against the pillows then turned his pale face to his daughter. "I don't like the way she's looking. I think she worries too much. You've got to watch her, 'cause when she worries she doesn't eat enough. When Matt had his appendix out she lost more weight than he did."

"She's fine, Dad."

Marty rubbed his hand across his face and mumbled, "What day is it?"

"Friday."

"Friday!" Marty dropped his hand to his lap and stared sharply at Karen. "What are you doing here? Brian's got a game tonight. Go!"

"No, Dad. I'm going to stay with you."

"Like hell you are." Marty lifted his arm and tried to push Karen away. "Come back and see me tomorrow. Go! And tell Brian I'm listening on the radio."

Karen took hold of Marty's hand, "I'm not going, Dad." She held his hand down on the sheets her voice rising, "It's just a damn game!" Karen stopped as she saw anger fill her father's face. She felt her father try to lift his arm off the bed. Karen lowered her voice. "I want to spend time with you." She let go of her father's hand.

As quickly as it came the anger fled. Marty collapsed back on his pillow. "It's not just a game, Karen."

Marty swallowed and broke the lingering silence between them. "I don't talk about it, about my time in Korea." Marty looked away from Karen. He stared out the bedroom window. "We were rotated back for R & R. We had been through some pretty tough times." Marty sighed. "Those who could spent most of their time sleeping in their tents. Those who couldn't sleep, well, they seemed to hide in their tents. A Catholic chaplain, what was his name? Sweeney, Padre Sweeney pulled up in a Jeep. I watched him through the flap of the tent. He had a couple of duffle bags in the back. He opened 'em up and dumped these brand new bats, mitts and balls on the ground. I looked over at Henry in the next bunk and he looked at me. We both got up. We started tossing the ball back and forth. Then Sam came out, then Earl, and then Freddy. We set up a makeshift diamond on the field by the mess hall. Guys kept coming out of their tents. We played baseball." Marty paused then looked at his daughter. "Baseball brought us out of our tents, and when we were on that field, when we were on that field, we were home!" Marty gripped the sheets and pulled himself closer to his daughter. "It's not just a game, Karen."

Karen had never heard her father sound so serious.

"Help me up." Marty took his daughter's hands and she pulled him forward in bed.

"No." Marty shook his head. Karen released him, and he sank back onto the pillows. "Just too weak today," mumbled Marty. He closed his eyes for a few troubled seconds then shouted, "Ellen!"

As Ellen appeared at his bedside, Marty pointed to the closet and said, "Get me the shoebox."

"The shoebox?" questioned Ellen.

"It's on the top shelf, back in the corner. You know, with the stuff I brought back from Korea."

"I'll get it, Dad," said Karen walking to the closet.

Karen gently placed the shoebox on her father's lap. Marty fingered the strings tied around the old Tom McCann shoebox. His shaky fingers tried to undo the knots.

"Ellen." In frustration he pushed the box towards his wife.

Ellen deftly undid the knot then set the box back on Marty's lap. Marty slid the top off the shoebox. He stared at the mitt. He rubbed his finger on the heavily oiled, smooth leather. As he lifted the mitt, Karen took the box and placed it on the night table. Marty slid his bony, gnarled hand into the mitt. His hand quivered as he lifted the mitt up to his face, then let it drop against his chest. "We were going back up to the front. I wanted something . . . something that would bring me home. So I kept this."

Looking at Karen, he said. "I want Brian to have this." He gripped the mitt against his chest. "It brought me home." He sank back on his pillow. "It'll bring him home." As Karen met her mother's eyes she wondered, what does he mean? Marty drew a shallow breath and looked at his wife. "Mark and Matt, they'll understand." He turned to Karen. "This is for Brian."

"You give it to him, Dad."

"No," sighed Marty. His right fingers rubbed small circles on the leather. He closed his eyes and his head fell back against his pillow. With unbearable anguish he uttered, "Henry." He opened tear-rimmed eyes, "I can't." Tears slid down his cheeks as he shook his head, "I can't go back."

"Marty, don't." Ellen rubbed her hands on his cheek. "Don't." She kissed his forehead. Her hands rubbed his neck. "Don't." She pressed her damp cheek against his. "You're with me, Marty. You're with me."

They listened to the Hens game on the radio. Karen sat in a chair next to her father's bed. She watched the shallow rise and fall of his chest as he drifted off to sleep. One hand gently cradled his wrist while the other rested on the shoebox in her lap.

As she listened to the announcer, she could picture her son crouching by second base and her husband pacing the fence at the Hens stadium. Try as she might, she could not understand how the three men in her life all fell under the spell of such a simple game.

Chapter 17

Kevin watched the boys from St. John's fifth—sixth grade baseball team toss the ball back and forth as they warmed up before the game. The grass was still damp from the torrential downpour of the night before. One of the biggest players on the team, Will went running after a ball that scooted past his mitt, and slipped sending him feet first into a mud slick. Kevin tried not to laugh, but he burst out laughing with the rest of his team. Will struggled to his feet and tried to scrape mud from his pants with his mitt. Kevin mumbled, "Glad I'm not driving him home," then turned and looked back at the parking lot. He saw Keith with his dad towering over him coming from their car. Kevin adjusted the cap on his head as he thought, this is one conversation I'm definitely not looking forward to.

Keith's dad, Mitch, stopped about three feet away from Kevin and folded his arms across his chest. He motioned his son to go out to the field.

Not wasting any time, Kevin said, "I've found kids respond much better to a pat on the back than a kick in the butt."

Kevin gazed at Mitch trying to gauge his reaction. He had to peer up at him, as Mitch was a good four inches taller. Sherlock Holmes would take one look at Mitch's hands and forearms and easily peg him as a bricklayer. Although he was five years younger than Kevin, his weathered face made him seem five years older.

Kevin went on, "Kids make mistakes; our job is to make corrections. Not to yell, not to scream, but to help them learn the right way to play ball."

Mitch's ears reddened, but he met Kevin's stare.

"You won't swear around these kids, Mitch."

Kevin turned away from Mitch and looked over his St. John's baseball team. He watched his nephew Kyle throw the ball to Mitch's son.

Kevin swung back to Mitch. "You've got a good player in your son." He pointed his hand at Keith and Kyle. "He's got good fundamentals. I can tell you've done a lot of work with him." Kevin let his hand drift to the other St. John's players. He shook his head as he watched some errant throws and bobbled catches. "I could sure use your help, Mitch, but it's got to be on my terms." Kevin looked Mitch in the eye and waited.

"Where I work, swearing is just talking. Sometimes I forget and don't leave it at the job. I want to coach." Mitch glanced from the baseball field to the bleachers. "I'd go crazy just sitting in the stands. I'll watch my mouth."

"I give second chances to kids," said Kevin, "not adults."

Mitch looked at Kevin and nodded.

Kevin held out his hand. The hand that clasped his felt like a vise.

Mitch looked around the field. "Where's your son? Keith told me the Hens new star was going to help out."

Seeing the smile on Mitch's face, Kevin took it as a friendly barb. "I wouldn't count too much on him." Kevin snatched a ball from the bag and yelled, "Stanley" and tossed a high pop-up to the field. "Between his own practices and road trips he's going to have a pretty busy summer." Kevin looked at Mitch, "Besides for kids this age . . ." Kevin shook his head as he watched the ball land two feet in front of Stanley's outstretched mitt, "he might be more of a distraction."

Mitch nodded. "You're probably right. That's all Keith's been talking about."

Kevin called, "Time, Ump." He walked out to meet Kyle on the mound. He stood blocking his pitcher from the opposing team's view. "How's the arm feeling, Kyle?"

"It's okay, Uncle . . . I mean, Coach."

"You're sure? You're getting up in the strike zone. That tells me your arm's getting tired."

"It feels fine."

"Okay, Kyle. Remember what we talked about?"

Kyle wiped his forearm across his forehead and looked up at his coach.

"All I want is for you to get the ball across the plate." Kevin nodded his head towards the outfield. "Give those guys out there something to do." Kevin tapped the brim of Kyle's cap then headed back to the dugout.

The third baseman, the tallest kid on the opposing team strolled up to the plate. Mitch stood up and walked to the end of the bench. He shouted, "Back! Back!" He raised his arms and waved the outfield deeper.

Kyle threw the ball down the center of the plate. He jerked and pivoted to face the outfield as the ball took flight.

"You're good, Stanley," shouted Mitch. "Just stay there." Smiling, "It's coming right to you."

Dancing in place, Stanley brought his glove up. The ball hit right in the pocket of the glove and, before Stanley could squeeze his mitt shut, it popped right out.

As Stanley scrambled to pick up the loose ball, Kevin glanced at Mitch. He had never seen anything like it. Mitch's face looked like a water balloon just before it pops. Eyes bulging, Mitch stuck a finger in his mouth and bit down.

Stanley finally grabbed the ball, ran in a few yards towards the infield then threw the ball to the second baseman.

Mitch yanked the finger from his mouth, snapped a quick glance at Kevin then blasted, "That was a good throw, Stanley!"

Both teams met in the infield, single file, right hand extended, like two freight trains passing in opposite directions on bordering tracks.

"Good game, Coach," said Kevin shaking the other coach's hand.

"Yeah, good game."

"On the bench, boys," said Kevin.

They crowded on the single bench and looked everywhere but at Kevin. Stanley sat on the very end. His black face buried between his hands. He rested his elbows on his knees as he stared at his feet.

"Well, we almost won that one," stated Kevin.

Some of the boys looked at him, while others snuck a peek at Stanley.

Kevin moved down the line and stood across from Stanley. "That ball popped right out of your mitt, didn't it, Stanley?"

Stanley seemed fixated on his shoelaces.

"Well, I tell ya, Stanley, it's happened to me too and more than once. I got to ask you a couple of questions? When you dropped that ball, did the earth open up and swallow you?"

Still looking at the ground, Stanley shook his head no as a couple of the boys chuckled.

"Hmm. You didn't get hit by lightning, did ya?"

Stanley shook his head again as Keith and Kyle laughed.

"Well," Kevin walked alongside the bench past the other players. "I imagine your teammates are going kick you off the team."

"We are not," shouted Kyle. "I'm the one who let him hit it."

Stanley's head shot up and he looked at Kyle.

"I overthrew the first baseman in the third inning," added Keith.

"And I struck out three times," piped up Peter.

"Well, I guess you're still part of the team," said Kevin grinning at Stanley. "What we got to keep in mind and sometimes even I forget, this is just a game. Someone's going to win; someone's going to lose. One day you'll hit a home run, and the next you'll strike out. You'll make a diving shoestring catch, and the next inning you'll let the ball scoot right between your legs."

Kevin's eyes drifted over the faces of his team, "This is a game and a game is supposed to be fun." Kevin pointed at each one of his players, "If you're out there and you're not having fun, come talk to me. 'Cause if we're not having fun that means I'm doing something wrong."

Kevin bent and picked up the scorebook then looked at the boys. "Next practice we're working on fly balls and pop ups." Kevin continued, "I'll be hitting them. Coach Mitch will be out there with you. We're going back to the fundamentals." Kevin motioned to Mitch. "Coach Mitch is going to review how to approach the ball, position the mitt and use both hands for the catch. We'll keep doing it until we get it right." Kevin gave a nod of dismissal. "Wednesday, boys."

Kevin zipped the baseball equipment bag. "Kyle, you and Keith carry this over to my car. I want to talk with Coach Mitch for a moment."

Kyle grabbed one handle and Keith the other and between them they carried the green duffle bag off the field.

"Mitch, where was everyone today?" Kevin asked.

"What do you mean? All thirteen kids were here."

Kevin shook his head, as he looked to the other team's bleachers. He watched the families lingering, waiting for their kid's team meeting to finish. "I'm not talking about the kids." Swiveling to face Mitch, Kevin saw four of his players pile into one van in the parking lot. "I'm talking about the St. John's spectators, the friends and families."

Mitch shrugged his shoulders and gave a look of what do you expect. "We haven't won a game."

"Hey, Mitch," Kevin looked at him, "I'm not talking fans here. I'm talking about their mothers and fathers. I'm talking about these kids' brothers and sisters."

Kevin turned and Mitch followed Kevin's gaze. He watched the St. Charles team-meeting break up. He saw the players pairing up with their families and drifting off to the parking lot.

"Mitch, don't you see the way our kids look to those bleachers. How do you think it makes them feel?" Kevin jammed his hands into his back pockets. "Tonight, Mitch, I want you to call every parent. Tell them there is a MANDATORY parents-coaches meeting at the end of Wednesday's practice."

Chapter 18

As his fingers twirled through the waves of Ali's reddish blonde hair, Brian wondered how he had survived the last three days. He had been away from home before, summer camps, Boy Scout outings, where he had missed the familiar confines of his bedroom and the security of knowing his parents were down the hall. But he had never felt the momentary panic of returning home and finding they weren't there. That's how he felt with Ali. Dozens of times while on the road trip to Buffalo, an incomprehensible feeling that Ali wouldn't be there when he got home would seize him. The feeling was so intense, his heart raced rapidly and sweat beaded on his forehead. They were quick, fleeting moments, but he couldn't believe the intensity of the loss he experienced. Now as he brushed back Ali's hair and leaned across the center counsel of his Jeep to kiss her, he wondered how he would ever be able to go away again.

Brian slowly pulled away from Ali and reached into the back seat. "Here."

Ali looked at the brightly wrapped, palm-sized box Brian offered. She glanced up searching his face.

Brian smiled, shrugged his shoulders and extended the box further.

Ali slowly untied the red bow. She slit the tape with her nail reached into the box and lifted the cell phone. "It's so small."

Brian laughed, "I had the hardest time. I wanted to find one that would match your eyes. Wait." Brian reached into his pocket and extracted his cell phone. He flipped it open and said, "Call, Ali."

The green phone in Ali's hand chirped. Giggling she flipped it open and said, "Bond, James Bond."

Brian laughed and asked in surprise, "Bond?"

Studying the small cell phone Ali said, "I'm the son my dad never had. He took me to all the James Bond movies. About once a year we'd have a James Bond marathon. We'd pig out on popcorn and watch all the old movies." Ali examined the phone in her hands. "I just can't believe how small it is."

"I wanted it small," Brian said, "so you could always have it with you." Brian cupped Ali's hand. "When I was in Buffalo . . ." Brian searched for the words to describe his feelings, "there were so many times I just wanted." Without realizing it, he squeezed her hand. "I needed to talk with you. I just . . . I just needed to hear your voice." Brian turned and looked out the front window of his Jeep.

Sensing his uneasiness, Ali said, "Brian, I felt the same way. I can't believe how much I missed you."

"It's more than that, Ali." Not looking at her, Brian said quietly, "I just was so afraid that you wouldn't be here when I got back."

Ali lifted her hand and caressed the back of Brian's neck. "I'm not going anywhere, Brian."

"Ali." Brian looked at her and summoned the courage to ask the question that troubled him all the way back on the bus from Buffalo. "What are we going to do when I go away to college?" His face was so serious as he said, "I don't want to leave you, Ali."

Not having an answer, Ali just massaged the back on his neck.

"What are we going to do?"

Ali pulled Brian so his face rested against her shoulder. "We have the summer, Brian. We have the whole summer."

"Kyle, you do good work," said Karen as she walked by him on the driveway. "I'll get you a pop."

"Mountain Dew," shouted Kyle as he bent down, swept the cut grass and lifted it into the trashcan.

Karen sat in the swing watching Kyle gulp Mountain Dew. "Slow down, Kyle. You'll get gas."

Kyle's fist covered his mouth as he tried to muffle a burp. He looked at Aunt Karen and smiled, "'scuse me."

Karen shook her head then glanced to the driveway. Brian and Ali pulled up in Brian's Jeep. Brian took Ali's hand and escorted her to the front porch.

"So, my wandering son returns," joked Karen.

"Miss me?" asked Brian as he sat on the swing next to his mother while Ali took a chair near Kyle.

"Of course, I missed you. I forgot what it's like only talking to your father."

"Come on, it can't be that bad, Mom," kidded Brian.

Karen glanced to Ali, "Kevin is great at answering questions. But he's never learned the fine art of asking any."

Laughing, Ali turned to Brian. "So that's where you get it from."

Kyle looked from Ali to his Aunt and said, "I don't get it," which caused Ali and Karen to laugh harder.

"Kyle, it's a girl thing," Brian said.

Karen asked, "So, how was Buffalo?"

"Awesome. I mean the Falls were awesome." Brian looked at Ali and continued, "Juan rented a car and took me and a couple of the guys to Niagara Falls."

Karen watched as her son focused all of his attention on Ali.

Brian's eyes widened. "The water was just powering over the cliff and then you'd look down and notice these tour boats coming out of the mist."

"Juan?" asked Karen.

Brian turned back to his Mom. "Our catcher. He's my

roommate. I mean . . ." Flustered, Brian laughed and looked at Ali. "I mean he's my . . ."

Karen patted Brian's knee and said, "Roommate's fine. In fact you'll probably get a dorm mate when you go to UW."

Karen noticed the quick glance Brian shared with Ali. She said, "Can you two stay for dinner?"

"What ya having?" asked Kyle.

"I don't know," said Karen. "I can call Kevin and have him pick up some Chinese on the way home."

"Yuck," groaned Kyle.

Ali laughed. The look on Brian's face asked her if she wanted to stay. She turned to Karen. "I'd like that."

Karen faced Kyle. "Stay for dinner?"

"Chinese? No way."

"How 'bout if I scramble you some eggs?"

As Kyle mulled over the offer, Ali asked, "Do you like green eggs and ham?"

Kyle folded his arms across his chest and smugly replied as if the question was for a little kid, "No." He smiled, "But I like scrambled eggs with green ketchup."

Ali laughed and said, "Well, I like green eggs and ham. My mom," she glanced from Kyle to Brian, "used to read me all the Dr. Seuss books and *Green Eggs and Ham* is my all time favorite. I remember one time, I must have been like five years old and Mom took me to Dr. Zoll." Seeing both Brian and his mom's incredulous stares, Ali continued, "No kidding. Dr. Zoll was my dentist's name. I don't even remember how it started but Mom said one line and then Dr. Zoll recited the next line from Dr. Seuss' book." Ali laughed. "We're in this pediatric dentist office with all these kids and here's my mom and Dr. Zoll going back and forth, line by line, doing the whole book, *Green Eggs and Ham* from memory. The kids were laughing. The nurses were laughing. It was better than library story time.

I'll never forget that." Ali caught her breath. "What were your bedtime stories, Brian?"

Brian looked at his mother with a mischievous smile. "My mom wouldn't read me stories. No, not my mom."

"Brian," said Karen with a pretend, stern look.

"No, my mom would make up Prince Brian stories."

Kyle teased, "Prince Brian stories?"

"What are you laughing at pipsqueak?" said Brian. "You can learn an awful lot from Prince Brian stories."

"Yeah, sure," whined Kyle, "Prince Brian."

"Okay, here's one for you." Brian pointed in the direction of his second story bedroom. "Prince Brian wakes up and smells smoke. He went to open his bedroom door." Brian looked at Kyle and waited.

"Well, open the door," Kyle shouted.

Brian shook his head. "Did you put your hand on it first to feel if it was hot? What if there's a wall of flames outside the door?"

"Well, you break your window and jump out on the porch's roof."

"Now, why break the window, when all you have to do is open the lock and unsnap the screen."

"It doesn't matter," huffed Kyle. "At least you're out of your bedroom. Now you jump off the roof." Kyle turned to Ali, "When you hit the ground you make yourself into a ball and roll." Kyle blinked, "I saw that trick on one of the Ninja Turtle movies."

"Why are you going to jump off the roof? You could break your leg." Brian pointed to the gutter. "You sit on the edge of the roof then hang from the gutter. That would put even a shrimp like you four feet closer to the ground."

"Shrimp? Who are you calling a shrimp? I'm tall enough to ride Cedar Point's Magnum." Kyle grinned at Brian. "And I'm not afraid to go on it either."

Brian ignored Kyle's comment. "So, now you're on the ground, what's the next move?"

"That's simple." Kyle pointed across the street. "You run to the neighbors' and have them call the fire department."

"Did you stop and look both ways before you ran across the street?" Brian startled Kyle as he loudly smacked his hands together. "Prince Brian knows that even if your house is burning, you stop and look both ways before you run across the street."

Karen couldn't help laughing as she looked from Brian to Kyle.

"Mom," Brian looked at his mother, "that one Prince Brian story where the kids are throwing the football at the hornet's nest. There is no way . . ."

"Kyle," Karen interrupted. "What were your bedtime stories?"

Brian said, "What do you mean *were*."

"Ha . . . Ha . . . Ha . . ." Kyle ignored Brian's jest and spoke to Karen. "*I Spy* and *Where's Waldo* were my favorites."

"So Aunt Maureen would read you *I Spy* books?" asked Karen.

"Gees, Aunt Karen, everyone knows you don't read *I Spy*. You look for things in the pictures like thimbles and needles. Know how hard it is to find a needle?"

Brian laughed, "So that's why Aunt Maureen wears glasses."

"It is not," snapped Kyle. "My dad," Kyle stopped. They all looked at him and waited. He gave a little shrug then quietly said, "My dad and me would always go through the *I Spy* books." He gazed down at his hands in his lap as he swung his feet under his chair.

Wondering what she was missing, Ali looked to Brian.

Do you ever get over it, Brian thought watching Kyle stare at his lap. What would my life be like if I didn't have my dad. I probably wouldn't be playing for the Hens, that's for sure. Man. All these images of his father quickly sped through his mind. God, it's got to be tough. Brian tapped Kyle's shoulder. "Hey, Kyle, you want to see this new spell Merlwy can cast."

Kyle glanced up in interest and said, "You made another new one?"

"Come on, I'll show you."

Karen pensively rocked back and forth on the porch swing. Ali felt awkward. Not having followed Brian inside, she didn't know if she should stay on the porch. She looked up at the trees in the front yard, the myriad green leaves hanging listlessly in the summer heat. She heard the bumblebees buzzing around the azaleas. She started to rise and the movement shook Karen out of her reverie.

"I'm sorry, Ali. I just drifted off." Karen glanced at the front door then motioned Ali to sit next to her on the swing.

"Kyle's dad was killed in a car accident, must be two years now." Karen shook her head. "God, what a waste. He was driving home by himself after a football party for the OSU-Michigan game. He was drunk. He was a drinker, so Maureen always went along to drive him home. But Kyle's sister was sick with the flu that night and Maureen stayed home. He went by himself.

Karen sighed. "It's the stupid things people do that wreck other peoples' lives. Maureen can't forgive herself, for not being there to drive him home. She just cannot accept that the fault isn't hers but his. You have two kids who need a father." Karen paused, "If he could have seen the look on his childrens' faces at his funeral, if he could have known how he warped their lives." Karen unconsciously rubbed her fingers along her lower lip. "And all his so-called friends lined up to view the closed casket, the same ones that let a drunk stumble out to his car."

Karen's lips curled back against her teeth as she spat out, "I'm still so angry with him. I just cannot forgive him for what he's done to his family."

Ali sat still. She searched for some response as the swing like a pendulum rocked back and forth.

Chapter 19

Brian couldn't believe he was late. His fingers moved so fast they were just a blur as he laced up his baseball cleats. Why'd he ever boot up his computer? He tossed his bat bag into his locker, slammed the door, grabbed his mitt then raced out to the Hens field.

As he ran past the batter's warm-up circle, he was dazzled by sunlight reflecting off gold. Not a single chain but woven strands forming a rope entwined around a thick deeply tanned neck. Brian took in the unfamiliar, towering, six-six figure.

"What you looking at? Ain't you ever seen gold before? How the hell did I ever end up in this hick town?"

Brian quickly glanced from the chain to the piercing, jet-black eyes. He started to look away but stopped. It was the challenge. The look a pitcher gives you trying to force you back from the plate. The stare that says back up, or the next pitch will back you up. The man's bat didn't just rest on his shoulders but posed menacingly instead. Brian wondered: Who is this guy? Where did he come from? He's wearing the same uniform.

The player bulled forward to the batter's box as if Brian was not there. Brian pivoted to keep their shoulders from colliding.

"I see you've met the great Leroy Brown," said Juan.

Brian rubbed his eyebrows as he studied Leroy at the plate. "You got to be kidding me, that's him?"

As if he could feel their eyes on him, Leroy turned and stared at Brian and Juan. He spit on the ground next to the batter's box then turned back to the pitcher.

"What's his problem?" asked Brian.

"His problem. He started the season playing for the Yankees, they traded him to Detroit and then Detroit sent him back to the minors."

"Why?"

Juan looked around to see if anyone was in hearing distance. "The word going around is a lot more goes up his nose than comes out."

Brian stared at Leroy Brown as he took his batting practice. He sure isn't your typical baseball player. He remembered reading that Brown was the starting middle linebacker for three years at UCLA. Look at those shoulders. What was it Leroy said, when asked if he was going to play pro football or baseball? "I'm nobody's fool, people get hurt in football. Give me baseball and my money."

Brian fought it but he was mesmerized by Leroy's swings. He was fluid. It wasn't the bat he swung but his arms. It wasn't the bat that snapped but his wrists. The bat wasn't an extension of his hands it was his hands. Put that swing together with that power. Brian watched in awe as the balls sailed out of the stadium. He could see why Leroy was rookie of the year five years ago.

Flicking his wrist Brian hit the pitch as it dove to the outside corner of the plate. He lifted it over the outstretched mitt of the second baseman. He quickly rounded first then stopped as the centerfielder threw the ball to the second baseman.

Brian settled into his leadoff stance as Leroy Brown dug in behind the plate. Brian edged out further then quickly stepped back, as the first baseman caught the ball and swept the tag down to Brian's leg. Brian edged out again and the fans started chanting, "Go! Go! Go!" Brian crept a little further as he studied the pitcher. He knew the left-handed pitcher had the advantage and he wouldn't be able to get the lead he wanted. Brian dove headfirst back to the base narrowly missing the tag. He got up, brushed the dirt from his chest and spit dust from his mouth. The first baseman laughed and said, "Hey, do that again."

Brian saw Leroy check with the third base coach. Brian read the same sign for the hit and run. If Leroy makes contact, he'll keep going. If not, he'll steal second. Rising on the balls of his feet he shifted slightly forward, coiling, ready to go with the pitch.

Brian left with the pitch and exploded down the baseline. He felt the tag on his calf as his foot slid into second base.

"You're out!" screamed the ump.

Brian stood and dusted off his uniform. He jogged back to the dugout. He saw his teammates leaning forward, staring at Leroy as he positioned himself in the batters box. Brian sat next to Juan.

"He didn't swing," said Juan.

"What?"

"Everyone saw the sign. It was hit and run. Brown didn't swing," Juan said. "If he would have swung, you would have been safe."

Perplexed, Brian asked, "Why didn't he swing?"

"Who knows," Juan shrugged his shoulders. "Maybe he had a brain fart."

As Brian studied Leroy's back, he saw his arms snap forward. The Hens players stood and watched the ball as it sailed into the upper deck of centerfield. The fans cheered as Leroy jogged around the diamond. The on-deck batter high-fived Leroy as he headed to the dugout.

Coach Bruno met Brown as he walked down the stairs into the dugout. "You see the sign for the hit and run?" the coach asked while blocking Leroy's path to the bench.

"That wasn't my pitch." Leroy motioned over his shoulder to the fading cheers from the fans. "That was my pitch."

"I'm going to make this very simple for you, Brown," said Coach Bruno lifting his black index finger and holding it inches from Leroy's face. "The next time I give the hit and run, you swing." Coach Bruno moved closer and glared up at Leroy, "Whether it's your pitch or not." Coach Bruno shifted and pointed to an empty space on the bench. "If you don't, you ride the bench."

Leroy took off his batting helmet and flung it against the wall. He sidestepped Coach Bruno, shot a look at Brian as if it was his fault, then stomped his way to the water cooler.

Changed out of their uniforms and into shorts and T-shirts, Brian and Juan walked from the locker room to the parking lot. Juan alternated between humming and whistling a tune. He snapped his fingers and stopped. "That's it."

Brian looked at his friend. "What?"

"Leroy Brown."

Brian looked around the parking lot. "Where is he?"

"No. His name." Seeing Brian's perplexed expression Juan continued, "There was a song that went something like Big Bad Leroy Brown, baddest dude in the whole damn town."

Brian laughed listening to Juan's singing effort. "It's a good thing you can catch."

Juan insisted, "There was a song like that. My dad used to play it all the time. A guy named Croce . . . Jim Croce. Never heard it, huh?"

Brian shook his head and continued to the parking lot. He saw the red sports car parked in a handicapped spot at the front of the lot. "Look at that," said Brian. "God, it's awesome. Look at those lines." Brian moved closer, his hand hovered, not quite touching the car.

Juan said, "It's a 360 Spider Ferrari. Mid-mount V8 that tops off at over 180."

Not looking up Brian said, "You know cars?"

"Well, seeing that I can't sing. . . ."

Brian laughed as he kept walking around the Ferrari. His eyes glued to the sports car, Brian said, "The design, the aerodynamics, if you could take this molecular structure and miniaturize it . . . Work in reverse. Instead of designing from the atom up, take the structure and shrink it." Brian stepped back from the car and set his hands on his hips. "Nah, that wouldn't work." He laughed to himself. "Too much Jules Verne. You still have to build from the atom up, but if you can use the design for atomic molecular realignment. God, the lines. Aerodynamics, but the same principle of moving through air would apply to moving through water or . . ."

Juan said, "She can go from 0–62 miles per hour in 4.5 seconds."

Brian mumbled to himself, "blood."

"You have seen a Ferrari before?" said Leroy Brown as he walked up behind Brian.

Brian didn't hear the question. He was picturing atoms arranged like miniature Ferraris racing through the bloodstream after cancer cells.

Leroy shook his head, walked past Brian and opened the Ferrari's door. He slid into the bucket seat and turned the key.

Leroy spun the wheel and accelerated. Juan quickly jumped out of the way. One second the 360 Spider was there and the next it was gone.

"God, he's such an ass," griped Juan.

Brian didn't answer. As he watched the Ferrari weave into traffic, he pictured it weaving through the bloodstream.

Chapter 20

At practice Kevin lowered his cap to shield his eyes from the early evening sun. Resting the bat on his shoulder, he waited while Mitch set Stanley in the proper outfielder's position. He lofted the ball with one hand and smacked a high pop fly to Stanley. He could faintly hear Mitch help Stanley track the flight of the ball through the sun. Stanley skipped backwards, almost tripped, but kept his open mitt facing the downward trajectory of the ball. He snap the glove closed as his free hand covered the mitt.

"Good, Stanley," Mitch said. "From here your cut man is always the second baseman. Point your front foot towards Red, but throw off your back foot. If you don't think you can make the throw from here, then run towards Red before you throw."

Chris, the catcher, took the throw from Red. He tossed it to Kevin who caught it with his left hand. Kevin surveyed the field. He had his players positioned for their next game against St. Joan of Arc. "Keith!" Kevin motioned the lanky sixth grader over to have him pinch run when he hit the ball. "Keith's running!"

Keith sprinted as Kevin smacked a hard grounder down the third base line. Keith beat the throw to first by a step. Kevin walked towards the pitcher's mound. Raising his voice so all his players could hear, he pointed to Keith. "That's what I'm talking about. That's what's been missing, the hustle. You got to go all out! The difference between having a runner on first and an

OUT is a fraction of a second. Kevin swung his arm and leveled his hand at Red near second base. "When you're running to first, where are you going?"

"Past the bag," shouted Red.

"RIGHT! On a close play if you're just running to the bag, you're going to be out every time. You never let up! You go full speed past the bag!"

Kevin walked back to the batter's box. "Runner on first!" He bunted the ball to Kyle. Kyle charged off the pitcher's mound. He didn't use his mitt but grabbed the ball with his right hand. Spinning around, he eyed Keith running to second then pivoted and fired the ball to the first baseman.

"That's it, Kyle. Always take the out. Red! You got to get behind the bag. If you stand to the side of the bag that base runner will take your feet right out from underneath you!" Kevin took another ball from Chris. "Runner on second. Where's the play? Red?"

Red swung his head. His eyes darted from Keith on base next to him, to first then third. He cried out in his high-pitched, changing voice. "Play's at first. There's no force. I try to hold the runner on second but my play's at first."

Kevin paused. He let the bat drop onto his shoulder. He looked at Red and smiled. "You got it, Red." Kevin tossed the ball and lofted another pop fly to Stanley.

Kyle waved his cap over his head and yelled, "Hey, Brian!"

Brian strolled across the parking lot to the playing field. Kevin turned, watched his son and then shouted, "Bring it in." He motioned his players towards the batting box.

"I'm glad you could make it," said Kevin nodding at his son. As Mitch and the other boys gathered around, Kevin continued, "Mitch, keep working on those pop-ups. Brian, take Red and work with him at second base." Kevin shook his head. "I don't know what I'm doing wrong. I can't seem to get him in the right spot. Ben, Kyle, come with me." Kevin paused and looked over the sea of young faces. "And Chris, I need you to catch for my pitchers."

"Okay, Ben, remember what we worked on last time. All we need is one pitch. Just over the top." Kevin brought his right arm up, positioned it like the letter L, the ball level with his right ear. "Just let her go, right from the top."

Chris suited up in his catcher's gear and squatted about fifty feet from Kevin. He pounded his fist into the pocket of his catcher's mitt and waited.

Kevin wound up and thumped the ball into Chris' mitt. He caught the throwback from Chris and placed it in Ben's hand. He shook his finger back and forth near Ben's face. "No sidearm. I don't know where you got that, but that's why you keep hitting the batters. Besides if you keep throwing like that at your age, you're going to wreck your arm." Kevin tapped the brim of Ben's cap. "Let's get to work."

"I saw you last night, Brian," Red said.

"You did?" Brian asked while walking next to the second baseman with carrot hair and freckles.

My sister works in the souvenir shop. She took me with her so I could see the game while she's working. Red stopped near second base and looked up at Brian. "Is it . . ." Red hesitated; he wanted to ask but didn't know if he should.

"What?"

"Is it scary out there, Brian?"

Surprised, Brian repeated, "Scary?"

Red shivered just thinking about it. "I'd be scared to death having all those people watch me. What if you mess up?"

"So you mess up. Everyone messes up. You make a mistake; you forget about it." Brian tossed a ball to Red. "You go on to the next play. Red, when you're out in the field you don't have time to think about errors. Your head's just got to be in the game."

Red nodded across the infield to Kevin. "You sound just like Coach."

"But it's true." Brian smiled. "Take it from me, Red. I know."

Red kicked his cleats into the dirt and a cloud of dust covered his shoes. "What was it like having your dad be your coach?"

Brian said the first word that sprang into his mind. "Hard."

His face revealing that that was the last answer he expected, Red asked, "Hard? Why?"

Brian watched as his dad showed Ben the right way to grip for a fastball. "He was always harder on me than anyone else." Brian watched his father form Ben's right arm into an L, the ball up next to his ear. "I couldn't just be good. I had to be perfect and if that meant practicing an extra hour after everyone left or getting here an hour early." Brian heard Ben's fastball wallop into Chris' catchers mitt. "Then that's what we'd do."

"But, Brian," Red said as if none of that mattered. "You're playing for the Hens."

Brian lifted and opened his mitt. "Yeah." As he stepped back and Red tossed him the ball, he wondered why playing for the Hens meant more to a twelve year old than it did for him.

"Show me your change up, Kyle," Kevin said.

Kyle fiddled with the ball in his mitt." I hate throwing it, Uncle, I mean, Coach. It's so slow even Peter can hit it."

Kevin waved his catcher Chris towards him. "Ben, come on over here." Kevin took the ball from Kyle's mitt. He rubbed the league ball in both hands while waiting for Kyle, Chris and Ben to gather around. "Name the one thing I want from my pitchers," asked Kevin making eye contact with Ben and Kyle.

"Just get it across the plate," replied Kyle.

Ben nodded, "Just throw strikes."

"You got it," said Kevin. "Walks will kill us in this league." Kevin glanced at Ben. "So we just go over the top, right? Nothing fancy. No sidearm, no curves, no sinkers. Just over the top throwing strikes but." Kevin held the ball up. The boys watched as his fingers switched positions from being on the seams to across the seams. "To catch them off guard we've got the change-up. We throw it the exact same way as the fastball the only difference is where we put our fingers." Kevin gripped the ball and held it up in front of Ben. "What happens when I hold and throw the ball like this?"

"The seams slow the, the . . ."

"Spinning," butted in Kyle.

"Spinning or rotation," said Kevin.

"But even Peter can hit it," whined Kyle.

Kevin kept rotating the ball, flicking his fingers on and off the seams. "You got to set it up, Kyle. You get them looking for your fastball. If they're looking for your fastball and you throw the change-up, they'll swing early and miss it every time."

"But what if they know it's coming," cried Kyle.

"If they know your change-up's coming and they can hit," Kevin laughed and tossed the ball to Kyle, "they'll nail it every time."

Kevin looked over and watched the parents gathering by the visitors' bench. It was easy to match the parents with their kids. All he needed was to follow where they were looking. A few of his players stopped and waved to their parents. Other players completely ignored them.

"Brian!" Kevin shouted then waited as Brian jogged across the infield. "I need to talk with the parents. Can you take the kids and run the X pattern throw and run drill?"

"Sure, Dad."

"And, Brian, send Mitch over."

Kevin stood with his hands folded across his chest. He watched as Mitch ambled in from the outfield. He noticed Brian dividing the players into groups and sending them to the four bases.

Glancing at the cluster of parents, Mitch said, "Looks like they're all here."

"What did ya tell them?" asked Kevin.

"Just what you said, that this is a mandatory parents-coaches meeting."

Kevin studied the solemn expressions on the parents' faces. "Maybe it was the way you said it."

Mitch shrugged his broad shoulders and together they walked over to meet the parents.

"I'm Coach Kevin McBride." Kevin nodded towards his assistant coach, "I'm sure you know Mitch." Kevin took off his cap and wiped the sweat from his brow with his sleeve. He searched for the speech that slipped from his grasp as he faced the anxious adults.

Kevin caught a glimpse of Karen walking from the parking lot. He relaxed knowing he had at least one supporter. The parents seemed to follow his gaze. Kevin waited a few seconds then said, "This is our statistician, Karen."

Karen smiled and lifted her hand. "That's me." She looked at her husband and raised her eyebrows as if saying, *well*.

Kevin swept his eyes across the parents, stopping at Josh's father and mother. He nodded then said, "Some of you know me. I've coached your older kids." Kevin jammed his hands into his back pockets. "Through the years I've learned a lot about coaching kids and that's taught me a lot about parents. Here at St. John's, almost all the dads and most of the moms have at least one job. Most of you have more than one kid. You're involved with other activities going on at the parish. That there are not enough hours in the day and the one thing your heart secretly desires is to," Kevin glanced at Karen, "is to get a good night's sleep."

A few of the parents laughed.

Kevin continued, "We all have one thing in common, our children. As parents we've got a responsibility to raise them the best we can." Kevin shifted his weight from one foot to the other while searching for the elusive words. "I don't have to tell you what it's like when you're here watching your kids play a game." He looked at the boys running the drill, throwing the ball across the diamond, and then racing to that spot. He waited letting the parents search for their child. Kevin saw his son towering over the fifth-sixth graders.

He looked back to the parents and raised his voice. "But I can tell you what it's like when you're not here. During the game your kids' eyes are wandering, not to me, not to the other players." Kevin pointed. "But to the spectators bleachers. They're searching for you, for their brothers and sisters, for their grandparents." Kevin paced in front of the adults. He pointed at the St. Johns' baseball players. "They're still at that age where their life revolves around you. When they get a hit or make a good play, they crave recognition. They thrive on it but they don't want it from me, they want it from *you*."

"Through the years I've heard hundreds of excuses. There are hundreds of reasons why you can't make it to your kids' game. And the kids know all those reasons. They can recite your standard list of why you can't be here. Hey, they've got that down pat."

Kevin shook his head. "You know . . . that's what they're going to remember. You are handing them down your list of why you can't be here. That's what you are teaching them to pass down to their own kids." Kevin swept his hand back to his ball players. "I'll coach your kids. That's what I do. But I can't take your place."

Kevin turned his back on the parents. He folded his arms across his chest. "We've got four games left." He faced his players and shouted, "Brian! Bring 'em in!"

Kevin jammed the bats into the green duffle bag. Bending down to pick up the catcher's gear he spied the black high heels and black nylons. His eyes traveled up her body until they met his wife's face.

"Think I was too hard on'em?" Kevin asked.

Karen laughed, "I'm not going to miss a game."

Kevin struggled to zip the over-stuffed bag. "You know . . ."

Karen cut him off. "You said what you wanted and needed to say." She moved closer took his arm and pulled him to his feet. She looked into his blue eyes. "That's why you're the Coach."

Kevin placed his hand on top of Karen's. A slight smile crossed his face. They both turned when Brian and Kyle came towards them from the field.

Chapter 21

Brian stretched and held his right arm behind his head. He couldn't help smiling at Juan and his fellow teammates as they went through their pre-game warm-ups. He switched and stretched his left arm thinking there was no difference between this team and all the others teams he played on. He couldn't hear MacKay's joke but it must have been good because Juan burst out laughing. The Hens bodies were bigger, but he could just as easily be standing with Kyle's team. Ballplayers were kids. They didn't grow up, and like kids they loved to play games. Brian was surprised at how quickly his teammates accepted him and how quickly he felt he was part of the team.

Brian's eyes drifted over the sold-out stadium. Most of the fans were decked out in Hens red and white colors and a number of them had the Hens logo on their shirts and baseball caps. He remembered his first game on the team and how the stadium wasn't even half-filled. He told himself the crowd was due to the Hens being in contention. But in the back of his mind he felt they were coming to watch him play. It was a new sensation that had been creeping up on him. He always kept the game and the fans separate. The fans were always just the background noise and for the most part he just ignored them but now looking around the packed stadium he could feel their energy. It was as if they were behind him, pushing him forward.

After getting a solid single to start the Hens bottom of the first inning, Brian tightened then stretched the batting gloves on his wrists. He pulled open his helmet trying to ease the pressure on his ears. As the chant started his eyes swept the colorful undulating sea of fans.

"Brian! Brian! Brian!"

The chant sent tingles all the way up from his toes. Brian eased off first base. Sinking into his sprinter's crouch, he took the signal for the hit and run from the third base coach. He saw the slight nod from Leroy Brown as Leroy stepped into the batter's box.

"Brian! Brian! Brian!"

As Brian exploded down the baseline he heard the thwack of the bat against the ball. Seeing the ball out of the corner of his eye, he ducked and the ball whizzed over his head. Brian accelerated; his shoe barely touched second base. He flew along the base path watching the third base coach waving him on. His feet matched the rapid pacing of his heart. He felt as if he were flying. The catcher threw off his mask and moved into position to block the plate. Brian slid low and hard. He felt-heard the grunt as the cleats of his left foot dug into the catcher's ankle. He whooshed as the catcher collapsed on top of his chest. Brian instinctively rolled pushing the catcher away. Brian saw the ball lying near his feet and the umpire signaling safe. The catcher collapsed back kneeling on his feet. Brian sprang up and jogged to the dugout. The crowd exploded. His teammates lined the dugout rail, their arms extended to high-five Brian.

Smiling, Juan held his fists up. As Brian tapped his fists against Juan's, Ali's question came back to him. Do you love it? Do you love playing baseball?

Chapter 22

As Karen drove into the driveway of her home, Kyle held his hand up like a policeman stopping traffic. Opening Karen's car door he said, "You can leave your car right here, Ma'am." Karen saw Chris pull the hose from the side of the house as Ben walked out of the garage carrying a bucket in one hand and rags in the other.

Kyle extended his hand and helped Karen from the car. The heat hit her like the blast of an open furnace as she left the cool interior of the Cougar. "That's what I like, Kyle, service with a smile." Her black skirt and gray blouse wilted in the sun as her high heels clicked atop the driveway. As she glanced around, it seemed the entire St. John's baseball team was somewhere on her yard. She waved at Stanley who was pushing the vrooming lawnmower on the grass by the street. She saw Peter swinging the electric trimmer. Cupping her hands around her mouth, she shouted, "Watch out for my flowers!" She almost collided with Josh who was leaning over sweeping the grass clippings from the sidewalk. She bounced off his butt. Laughing Karen said, "Sorry Josh."

In the shade on the porch, Karen collapsed onto a chair. "Whew, damn, is it hot," Karen said as she fanned herself with her hand. Waiting for a response, she gazed at the tanned legs, sandals at the bottom, brown shorts at the top. Try as she might, she couldn't see through the USA Today newspaper covering the top of Kevin's body as he rocked back and forth on the porch swing.

"Working up a sweat over there?" Karen asked.

The newspaper ruffled as Kevin crumpled it onto his lap. He couldn't keep the grin from his face as he watched the boys working on the car and the grass. Karen glanced at his bare chest then followed his gaze out to the yard.

"Ya know, Kevin, it's just one win."

"First win."

"What are they going to do if they win another game? Paint the house?"

"Hold that thought."

"I'm going in. I've got to change into something cooler."

Kevin butted in, "Need any help?"

Karen ignored the question, "And then I'll make some lemonade."

Karen reappeared wearing white shorts and a matching halter-top. She set the tray with a pitcher of lemonade and a stack of plastic cups on the small, green end table. Pouring a glass of lemonade, she glanced at Kevin. "Don't give me that look!"

"What? I'm just looking at that mouth-watering lemonade."

"Don't start."

Kevin smiled at Karen. "I just realized how thirsty I am."

"I'm not kidding, Kevin. I'll throw this at you."

Kevin held his hand out. Karen hesitantly extended the glass of lemonade. Kevin's left hand snatched Karen's wrist as his right hand took the glass from her. He yanked her wrist forward pulling her down on the swing next to him. As Karen fell onto the swing, her elbow accidentally knocked the glass, splashing lemonade on Kevin's shorts. Kevin sprang up, his hands quickly knocking the ice cubes away.

Smirking Karen said, "That's one way to cool yourself off." She shrieked with laughter, "I imagine it shrinks those lemons right up."

Kevin peered down at her, tried to look angry but burst out laughing.

Brian parked his six-year-old Jeep behind his mother's car. He saw his mom and dad laughing and looking funny as they sat on the porch swing. He tried to picture himself sitting with Ali on that swing in twenty years. What will we look like? Will we have kids? As he watched his mom and dad joking and the way they looked at each other, he suddenly realized that his parents still loved one another. God, but they did fight at times. He remembered hiding his head under the pillows as a kid when they'd argued, but they always made up afterwards. He was sure he was the cause of more than one of their arguments, his dad and baseball, his mom and college.

As his dad stood and yelled something to Josh, Brian couldn't help thinking how much his dad influenced him. He was wearing a Hens uniform just as his dad did. He thought about the pictures in his dad's scrapbook from twenty years ago. Brian's picture could take his place. He looked so much like him. As his dad moved back to the swing Brian thought, still do.

Karen walked to the edge of the porch and straightened one of the flowers that were bent from the garden hose. Brian imagined her not on the porch but on a stage. How different would her life be if she had gone to Northwestern? If her father had pushed her, would he be going through a scrapbook of her pictures taken on Broadway?

His mother sat on the swing next to Kevin. It was just so weird when you saw them together. Brian was so used to dealing with them separately, his dad pushing and pushing baseball and his mom going on about nothing else but college. Seeing them sit together, Brian knew when they were young they both had their own dreams and now they had different dreams for his life. As his dad turned and Brian felt his eyes, he thought, I could play pro-ball. I'm only one step away. I'm good enough.

A sudden spurt of water from the hose splattered against the Jeep's windshield. His parents disappeared behind the surging spray. Brian shut off the engine and popped open his door. "Kyle, what are you doing?"

"Going to wash your car."

Brian walked around the Jeep. "Gees, Kyle, are you sweating?"

Kyle wiped his forearm across his forehead.

"Kyle, let me show you a secret to that nozzle." Kyle held the hose out as his teammates came over to see Brian.

"See this little latch here."

As Kyle bent closer, Brian squeezed the handle. The spray drenched Kyle's face and sent his baseball cap flying. Kyle shrieked, and Brian spun around and hosed the other boys. Soon it turned into a game of water tag.

Karen watched the laughing kids zoom in and out of the spray from the hose Brian held. She turned to Kevin. "You know he's still just a kid."

Kevin didn't answer. He just watched his son.

Chapter 23

Kevin walked through the front door of his house and onto the porch. He handed Karen the cordless phone. "It's your mom."

Karen took the phone and walked from the porch. She paced in the twilight under the trees in the front yard. Kevin watched as she pressed the phone tightly against her ear.

Seeing the concerned look on her face as she mounted the front steps, Kevin asked, "What's wrong?"

"I don't know," Karen shook her head. Her hand hung listlessly at her side still cradling the phone. "Mom said Dad's been asking for me all day. She said he's drifting in and out from his medication. I've got to get over there." Karen added guiltily, "I should've gone there Sunday."

"Want me to go with you?"

"No, I don't know how long I'm going to be there."

Kevin relaxed slightly, hearing the tone of the *no*. After being married for twenty years he felt he could finally understand the nuances of such a simple word between them. Here, it meant, *no* she didn't want him to go with her and not the *no, I'm just saying that, I do want you to go with me.*

"I'll be here," Kevin said. "If you need me, I can be there in ten minutes."

Karen closed the distance between them. She felt his strong arms circle the back of her waist. She let her head sink softly onto his shoulder. Her eyes drifted shut as she tightly clasped her hands behind his back and squeezed him against her. "I love you," she whispered.

Kevin tilted his head, bringing his lips against the hair resting on her ear. "I love you, too."

"How are you, Mom?" asked Karen as she walked into the kitchen. She set her purse on the table, bent over and kissed Ellen's cheek. As she pulled into her parents' driveway, she knew her mother would be sitting at the kitchen table, her hands wrapped around a cup of coffee. Karen poured a second cup from the under-cabinet coffee maker then sat across from her mom. As she studied her mother she tried to keep her concern from showing. Ellen's gray hair was uncombed. Without make-up, Karen could see every one of the sixty-nine years etched on her mother's face. She wore wrinkled baggy sweats that Karen knew doubled as pajamas.

"Why don't you take a shower, Mom?"

"In a bit."

"Has Patty been coming over?"

"Everyday. She used to bring Andy and Ashley with her. But I told her it was too much for the little kids. So now she comes over when Tim gets home from work." Seeing the look of guilt on her daughter's face, she added, "She doesn't have a job like you." Ellen took a sip of the lukewarm coffee. "Sometimes, I wish she wouldn't come over so much." Ellen shook her head. "I don't know . . . I feel like I'm taking care of both of them."

"What about hospice? I thought they were suppose to come every day."

"They would but I don't need them, Karen. I know how to give Marty his medicine." Ellen's eyes darted back to the bedroom. "He doesn't like them here." She laughed softly. "You should have been here the day one nurse tried to bathe him. I thought he was going to hit her. He pulled the blankets around him while screaming 'GET OUT!' She ran from the room. She hasn't been back since."

Laughing Karen said, "That's my dad."

The laughter faded and they both fell silent. Karen listened to her father's breathing coming from Patty's old baby monitor set up on the kitchen counter.

"There's really not that much to do. He doesn't eat. I don't even try to give him food anymore. He won't eat it." Ellen looked at her daughter. "He's lost so much weight. I give him liquids." She shrugged her shoulders.

Ellen pointed at the sheet of paper taped to the refrigerator. "They gave me that number. If something happens and I don't know what to do, I just call and they'll come right away." Ellen sighed then listened to the monitor. "He sleeps. That's what he does. When I get tired I just lay next to him."

Karen reached across the table and squeezed her mother's hand.

Ellen squeezed her daughter's hand back. "You're right. I need a shower." She ruffled her fingers through her hair. "And I need to do something with this hair."

Over the old pipes rattling and the cascade of water splashing against tile, Karen tried to listen to the monitor. She walked along the hall, gazing and lingering at the photo array on the wall. She vividly remembered as a child, standing on her tiptoes and touching her favorite picture. It was a photo of Marty and Ellen, taken on the day Marty returned from Korea. The photo captured the split second before they hugged. Only in that picture had she seen such a look of pure joy on her father's face.

She was shaken from her reverie by the rasping cough reverberating from the monitor. Karen entered the dimly lit bedroom, her senses assaulted by a mixture of flowers and medicine. She crossed the room, pulled back the curtains and slid open the window. She turned and froze. The sunlight fell on the pale, emaciated figure shrouded on the bed. As she gazed at her father, she was overpowered by the stark reality of death. All of her wishful thinking, her false hopes, deserted her. She tried to shuffle her feet forward but couldn't. She tried to lift her hands, but they were weighted at her sides. Like a child, she blinked her eyes to wake up from this nightmare.

As if in response, Marty blinked. His pale blue, cloudy eyes stared vacantly at the ceiling. He coughed. He slowly lifted his gnarled hand and wiped the spittle from his chin. Sensing movement, he turned his head. As her fingers touched his cheek, he said, "Karen." He closed his eyes and smiled. "I was having this most wonderful dream."

The coughing spasm started deep in his chest, racking his ribs. His hand feebly tried to reach the tissue box on the table beside the bed. Karen pulled the top few and shoved them into his hand. Marty hacked into the tissues then collapsed back.

Karen guided the straw into his mouth. She held the cup steady as he sipped greedily. When he stopped, she placed the cup back on the table.

"I got to sit up. You got to help me, Karen."

"Just tell me what to do."

Marty swallowed. "Take my feet, push them off the side of the bed." Marty waited while Karen untangled his feet from the sheets then pulled them over the side. "Now take my hands." Karen took his hands and pulled him towards her. Marty sat up on the side of the bed with his feet resting on the floor.

Her hands steadying him, Marty fought the waves of nausea and dizziness. As the spinning diminished, Marty placed his hands on his knees and tapped his feet on the rug. He shook his head. "Gets harder every time."

Karen slowly removed her hands but quickly snapped them back as Marty started falling to the side. Marty chuckled, "Whoa, don't have my sea legs yet."

"That's okay, Dad. Here." Karen sat on the bed next to him using her shoulder to prop up Marty.

Marty's hand patted Karen's knee. "You're here. Your mom tell you to come?"

Karen nodded, "I was going to come . . ."

Marty lifted his hand and signaled Karen to stop. "We need to talk." Marty peered at the clock on the bedside table. "Four-thirty, right?"

"Yeah, Dad."

"Good, we have time."

Karen quizzically looked at her father.

"I've been timing it. The medicine's pretty much worn off but the pain hasn't got too bad yet. This is 'bout the only time I can think clearly." Marty absently ran his hand along the top of the sheets trying to smooth the wrinkles. "I've had so many conversations with you in my head. So many things I want to say . . . need to say." Marty glanced to the hallway. "I want you to make sure your mom's okay. It's going to be hard on her." Marty looked around the bedroom. "You live with someone forty-five years. Spend forty-five years in the same bed. She's going to hate me for leaving her."

"She'd never hate you, Dad. She'll miss you. We're all going . . ." Karen stopped she couldn't finish. She looked away. Marty leaned against his daughter.

"Being the first born . . . I made all my mistakes on you. God, I was too hard. I was way too hard on you. It's like those damn eggs. Your mom still talks about it." Marty shook his head. "I'd make you eat those eggs even though you hated 'em. By the time Patty came along, I didn't care what she'd eat as long as she ate something." Marty lifted his head and looked at Karen. "I didn't know better. Karen, I had to learn how to be a father." Marty sighed. "The mistakes I made."

"Dad, don't."

"You're the most like me. Stubborn and bull-headed, but you're strong, Karen. You have more strength than Mark, Matt and Patty put together." Marty bunched the sheet into his fist. "When the time comes you got to make the tough decisions, 'cause they won't. But you got to let them know that it's your decision!"

Marty reached for the water cup. Karen watched as his fingers curled around the paper cup. As he slowly brought it to his mouth, his hand quivered splashing water against the cup's lid. Marty took a few short sips. The tremors increased as he tried to set the cup back on the table.

"Want to lay down, Dad?"

Marty shook his head no. He closed his eyes. His body sagged. Karen listened to the water gurgling through his system.

"Ow!" Marty leaned forward and clenched his hands against his stomach.

"Want a pill?"

Shaking his head back and forth, Marty sucked his lower lip between his teeth willing the spasm to pass. His shuttered eyes slowly opened. He started tapping his feet against the carpet. "I've had a lot of time to think. Too much time. Things I would've, should've done differently. You and that college." Marty paused trying to remember the name. "Northwestern. I was wrong." Marty shook his head.

"Dad, you don't have to say anything."

"Hear me out, Karen!" Marty said more harshly than he meant.

Karen stared out the window at the rope swing hanging from the branch of the elm tree.

"Decisions. It was *my decision*. Not yours, Karen. I didn't have the money to send you to that school. I had to do what I though was best for all my kids. You're my firstborn. I would have given you the world if I could." His voice faltered. "I would've driven you myself to that school."

Through tear filled eyes Karen watched as a slight breeze stirred the rope swing. She could remember her father's hands on her back as he pushed her higher and higher. Like a summer downpour the tears cascaded down her cheeks. She turned and buried her face into her dad's shoulder. In a choked voice she cried, "It doesn't matter, Dad."

Marty rested his face against his daughter's hair. "It matters to me."

Karen felt her father jolt as he gasped.

"You're taking a pill, Dad." Karen reached for the medicine on the table. After slipping a pill into his mouth, she held the cup while he sipped from the straw.

Marty nodded his head when he was finished and Karen eased him back on the pillows. He groaned as she swung his feet onto the bed.

"Cold," mumbled Marty.

Karen wrapped the sheet around him then took one of the blankets Ellen had folded and placed on her side of the bed. She covered her father with the blanket.

"Karen." Marty lifted his hand and held it out to her.

Karen sat on the chair by the bed. She took his cold hand and warmed it between her hands.

"How's my ballplayer? I wish I could see him play." Marty smiled and closed his eyes. "He tell you about the home run?"

Karen rested his palm against her face. She felt his cool fingertips press against her cheek. As he drifted off to sleep she felt his weak pulse. She couldn't help feeling that with each breath he drew he was slowly leaving.

Karen stumbled into the kitchen. Ellen was standing by the stove stirring noodles into a pot of boiling water. She had changed into clean sweats. Her hair was still damp from her shower. Karen poured another cup of coffee. She listlessly walked over and sat at the table.

"Did you give Marty his pill?" asked Ellen.

Karen absently bobbed her head as she took a sip of coffee.

"Oh! I almost forgot." Ellen walked to the counter and turned on the baby monitor. "I turned it off while you were with your dad."

Karen nodded not really hearing what her mother had said. She felt like a schoolgirl again, sitting at the table doing her homework as her mother cooked noodles. She curled her arms on the table then rested her head on top of them.

Chapter 24

"Time, Ump!" said Kevin. He walked to the mound and wiped the sweat from his forehead onto his sleeve. "Kyle, it's got to be at least 90 degrees."

Kyle looked at the ground while kicking clumps of dirt with his cleats.

"How's the arm? asked Kevin.

"It's good, Coach."

The catcher, Chris, came up from home plate and stood across from Kyle. As he took his mask off, Kevin could see his damp hair pasted to his forehead, his rosy cheeks and the sweat dripping down his neck.

"You need a break, Chris?" Kevin asked.

Chris didn't reply, just shook his head no.

Kevin glanced at the runners on first and second base. He looked intently at his other pitcher, Ben, playing third base.

Kyle glanced up and followed Kevin's gaze to Ben. "Coach." Kyle waited until Kevin looked at him. "We only need one out."

"You walked the last two."

Kyle tossed the ball firmly into his mitt. He stared at the batter waiting by the plate. "I won't walk this batter."

Kevin wondered if Kyle's statement was for his Coach or to himself. Seeing the determination on his young nephew's face, he thought, we're getting there, Kyle. Pitching is a mind game.

You'll never make it on the mound if you don't have confidence in yourself. Kevin nodded and said, "I'll give you one batter."

Kevin walked past his assistant coach. Mitch didn't say anything. The look on his face said it all. Kevin knew Mitch wanted him to pull Kyle and put Ben on the mound. Kevin stopped in front of Karen. She sat on the edge of the players' bench wearing one of the St. John's baseball caps.

"We're up by one?" Kevin asked.

Karen nodded.

"Who do they have coming up?"

Karen scanned the scorebook on her lap. "Number 18. He tripled last time and got a double before that."

Kevin smiled at his wife. "You're melting." He rubbed his finger under her eye.

Karen snapped the scorebook shut. She grabbed some tissues from her purse, which she kept under the bench and wiped below her eyes. She grimaced as she held the tissue up and saw it covered with mascara.

As Kevin stood by Mitch and surveyed the baseball field he couldn't help think, how many times have I stood in this dugout in this same situation? He watched Kyle kicking dirt around the pitcher's rubber trying to resettle the mound for his small feet and Red pounding his fist into his glove at second base. As he glanced at Stanley bent over with his hands on his knees in the short grass of right field, he pictured the dozen other boys that he coached in that same position. He breathed in and the hot July air filled his lungs. Feeling the eyes on his back, he pivoted and let his vision roam the full bleachers. Josh's mom and dad were sitting close together under a golf umbrella. Chris' mom was bouncing his baby brother on her knee and Ben's dad was fanning his face with a newspaper. All of his players had someone in the bleachers. He watched his substitutes on the bench sitting quietly and staring intently at the diamond. Glancing across to the other team's dugout, he could hear the boys offering words of encouragement to their number eighteen as he stepped up to the batter's box. Kevin knew that one pitch could win or lose the game. This is why I coach, he thought. To be right here. Right now. When Kyle glanced his way, Kevin smiled and shouted, "Throw strikes, Kyle." Kyle nodded. As the young pitcher went into his wind-up Kevin whispered, "God . . . I love this game."

Mitch glanced at Kevin then looked to the outfield. "Stanley, . . . Josh," he shouted, "back . . . back." He waved his arms, motioning his outfielders deeper towards the fence.

"BALL ONE!" screamed the ump as Kyle's fastball just missed the outside corner.

Kevin looked at Mitch and said, "Change-up."

Mitch took off his sunglasses and lifted them up in his left hand. He shouted, "Kyle!"

Kyle glanced at the coach and took the signal for the change-up. He fingered the stitches on the ball inside his mitt.

Number 18 swung fast and hard. He spun well before the ball crossed the plate.

"You've got him, Kyle," Red shouted. "Come on now, two more strikes, two more strikes."

Kyle glanced at the coaches. A slight smile played across his lips, and a look of "I did it" flashed on his face then vanished as he stared back at the batter.

"STRIKE TWO!" screamed the ump as number 18 just stood and watched the ball catch the inside corner.

"Hey, batter, batter, batter," chanted Red. The rest of the infielders and outfielders joined in, "Hey, batter, batter, batter." The players on the bench took off their caps and shook them in their hands adding to the crescendo. "Hey batter, batter, batter. . . ."

The chant died with the crack of the bat.

"OH SH . . . ," Mitch swallowed the ending. "Come on, Stanley, it's coming right to you." He watched spellbound as Stanley's feet danced a few steps forward then a few to the side.

Kevin followed the arc of the ball while out of the corner of his eye he saw the parents rise up in the bleachers. He saw the batter rounding first base as the runner from second base headed home. He watched Stanley squinting, lifting his glove to block the sun.

As the ball hit the webbing, Stanley snapped his mitt shut and covered it with his other hand. He turned the mitt over and stared at the ball like a nugget of gold in his palm.

"WAY TO GO, STANLEY! WAY TO GO!" screamed Mitch as he marched down the baseline pumping his fist in the air.

Red tackled Stanley. Josh piled on top followed by his teammates. Kevin stood with his hands jammed deep in his back pockets, watching his team laughing and rolling on the burnt out outfield. He felt Karen slip her hand through his arm.

"It's the little things, right?" she said as her lips brushed his cheek.

"This," Kevin pointed to his team romping in the outfield, "It's just a game."

Karen tugged on his arm pulling his eyes back to her. "It's always been more than a game for you." She nodded at the eleven and twelve year olds jostling each other as they came in from the field. "And that's what you give them."

Kevin stared into his wife's eyes. Surrounded by the bois-terous young voices, he shouted, "LINE UP, ST JOHN'S." As the boys formed a single line to slap hands with the opposing team, Karen watched her husband fall in line behind them. She saw the parents and families milling around the bleachers and Brian standing in the parking lot, his arms across his chest, leaning back against his Jeep with a look of such wistful long-ing on his face.

"BRIAN!" Kyle shouted. He sprang from the bench where he sat with his teammates for the after game team meeting. Catching the look from Coach Kevin, he plopped back down. Brian stopped at the edge of the baseline and gave Kyle a quick wave.

Kevin glanced at his son then turned back to his team. "Stanley, I have to ask you one question. When you caught that fly ball the earth didn't open up and swallow you, did it?" As some of the boys laughed Stanley looked from Kevin to assistant coach Mitch and said, "Nope."

"That was a good catch, Stanley," said Mitch.

Kyle smacked his fist against Stanley's arm, "You sure saved my ass." Soon as he said the word, Kyle's hand flew and covered his mouth.

Kevin shook his head and said, "That just cost you two laps around the field." Kevin felt like there was a two-ton elephant in the ballpark. The boys tried to look at him but their eyes kept drifting to Brian. He turned to his son, "You see the catch, Brian?"

"You mean the one that saved Kyle's rear end." Brian nodded at Stanley. "That was a catch."

Reaching into his back pocket, Brian walked up to his dad. He pulled out an envelope and handed it to the coach. "Maybe you can help me out. I've got all these tickets to tomorrow's game against Indianapolis."

"Tickets?" marveled Kevin. "I thought the game was sold out?" As Kevin fanned the tickets the boys left the bench and gathered around.

Brian said, "Well, if you can use them."

"Wow, you mean it, Brian!" exclaimed Red.

"Yeah, you guys come to the game. I just hope the Hens can give you a game as good as the one you just won."

"So my wandering son returns," Karen said as Brian walked up to her.

"Hey, Mom."

"What? Are you too big and important now to give me a hug?"

Brian smiled and hugged her. As he pulled back, Karen said, "Look at you." She reached up and stroked his cheek. "You're all grown up." She looked at the boys leaving the field.

"It's not fair. All boys should stay twelve forever. That way their mothers could stay young forever, too." She waved her hand as if blowing away a cloud of smoke. "So, what brings you here? Courting your fan club?"

"I had some extra tickets . . ." Brian stopped and laughed as he realized that's what it seemed like he was doing.

"Courting your fan club," Karen chuckled.

Brian saw Red stop at his parent's car and wave. He waved back to the young player. He was courting his fan club. He liked the feeling he had when the kids looked at him. He couldn't put it in words. It was just a feeling, something new to him.

"Brian." Karen arched her eyebrows and waited until Brian looked at her. "At night, you've been getting home pretty late, young man."

Brian blushed. "Gees, Mom. It hasn't been that late. Besides, I'm eighteen. You just said I'm all grown up."

Karen walked over to her son. "Body wise, but I'm not sure about what's up here." She poked her finger against his temple and then against his chest, " Or what's in here." She looked at her son. "I'm always here if you want to talk."

"I know, Mom."

"Not to judge."

"I know, . . . Mom"

"Just to talk . . . or listen."

"I . . . know, . . . Mom!"

Brian turned away and watched Kyle jog around the field. "How's Grandpa? With the road games in Columbus I haven't seen him since Monday." As he glanced back at his mother she seemed to deflate in front of him.

"Not good. He's pretty comatose right now. I'm heading home to see him." She went to get her purse from under the bench.

"I'll go with you."

Karen paused to look at her son. "Aren't you going out with Ali?"

"We were going to get a pizza." Brian shrugged. He remembered how gaunt and pale his grandfather appeared when he saw him on Monday. "That doesn't matter, I'll go with you. I'll just call Ali and let her know."

Karen nodded surprised how her son could be so happy one moment and somber the next. "I came with your dad."

"We can take my Jeep."

"I'll tell Kevin."

Brian crossed his arms and leaned against his Jeep. He knew that he should see his grandfather. He knew he should spend more time with him. He knew how much it hurt to do so. In his eyes, his grandfather could do anything. There was nothing he couldn't fix, no problem he couldn't solve, no question he couldn't answer. Brian thought of all the times he heard the familiar knock on the front door and the booming "Is anyone home?" Brian would run down the steps, and then he and his grandpa would be off mushroom hunting in Duck Creek Park or fishing out of his canoe. In the winter they'd track deer through the snow or venture out on the frozen creek to cut a hole for ice fishing. Somehow his grandpa always knew the times when he got in trouble with his parents and got grounded. He'd mysteriously appear and get Brian out of the house to help him with some chore. With his grandpa it never seemed like work, definitely not a punishment, and somehow he'd always manage to steer the conversation around to the grounding. He'd never judge but just make Brian backtrack. Like he would do in the woods when Brian had the lead and took the wrong path. He'd make Brian backtrack to the spot he wandered off course then let him try again.

Brian clenched his fists. If only he could backtrack for his grandfather, backtrack to stop the cancer before it started to spread. He glanced across the parking lot to the field where his mother was talking with his father. He was suddenly struck by a new fear. What if his mother was genetically predisposed to the same cancer? He watched his mom lean forward and kiss his dad's cheek. How would he feel looking at his mother on her deathbed?

Karen touched Kevin's shoulder. "I'm going to run home and see Dad."

Kevin shouted, "Kyle, just one lap today, it's too dang hot." He peered at Karen. "Want me to go with you?"

Karen shook her head. "Brian's going to drive me over. We'll just stay for a little bit."

"You sure?"

"You take Kyle home." She nodded at her son leaning against his car. "This is hard on him."

"It's hard on all of us, Karen."

Karen shook her head, trying to shake off the sudden wave of depression. She looked at Kyle as he slowed from a jog to a walk. "I would have pulled him."

"So would've Mitch. And you probably both would have been right." Kevin continued, "If Stanley had muffed that ball we would have lost the game."

Karen glanced from her young nephew to Kevin. "Stanley made the catch. He made it because you and Mitch spent all that time teaching him how to catch." She saw Kevin's face respond to her words. "I've got to run." She leaned closer and kissed his cheek, "Coach."

Kevin waved as Brian and Karen pulled away in Brian's Jeep. He popped the lid on his car's trunk. Kyle said as he struggled to lift the heavy equipment bag, "Sorry, Coach, it just slipped out."

Kevin lifted one end of the green canvas bag. The aluminum bats clanged together as they dropped the bag into the trunk. "You know I can't let that slide, Kyle."

"I know, Coach, I'll try . . . I won't say it again."

Kevin looked at the beads of sweat on Kyle's upper lip and forehead. His short, tight brown curls were matted under his baseball cap. Kevin pulled his damp shirt from his pants. He fanned the shirt to dry it and keep it from sticking to his back.

"Forget the AC, let's just roll the windows down." Kevin climbed into the car and started the engine.

As Kyle slid into the car seat and shut the door, he said, "But Stanley did save my butt."

"Did you throw a strike?"

"Right down the center."

"That's all I ask for. You throw strikes. We'll win games."

Kyle put his arm out the window and let his hand hydroplane in the breeze. "You know, Coa . . . , Uncle Kevin, I don't understand Coach Mitch. Since you took over the team he doesn't swear, doesn't yell at anyone. I mean . . . he's really . . . okay. And gosh, he knows a lot about baseball."

"Sometimes it's just the way you're brought up, Kyle. If parents swear all the time, then kids are going to do the same thing."

"But it's not just the swearing, Uncle Kevin. You don't get mad. You don't yell at any of the kids."

Kevin laughed. "I get mad, Kyle. Believe me, I get mad."

"But you don't yell."

"Kyle. You know anything about philosophy?"

Kyle thought for a second then shook his head.

"There are different philosophies," Kevin saw Kyle looking at him, trying to understand. He continued, "different ways to coach baseball. The one that I always follow is positive reinforcement. You reinforce the good things that your players do. It's like today, Kyle, you threw a strike. I don't care if the kid hit it. That's why we've got eight other guys on the field. You did exactly what a pitcher in this league needs to do and that is throw strikes. If Stanley had dropped that ball, we would have lost the game. I'm not going to yell at you and I'm not going to yell at Stanley. As long as you're out there doing your best, that's all a coach can ask. You did your best. You got it over the plate." Kevin stopped the car at the red light and looked at

Kyle. "That was a big time play. You got the strike when we needed it."

Kyle looked at Kevin and nodded.

"We're going to build on that right, Kyle?"

Kyle nodded again.

"You got me going now, Kyle." Kevin accelerated as the light turned green. Lifting his right hand he pointed his finger like he was lecturing a class. "When a coach is continuously badgering a kid, one, the kid will not have any fun and won't want to play the game and two, he's going to be so worried about making mistakes that he will make a mistake. When you're on the mound, Kyle, if you're worried about me yelling at you for walking a batter, then, you're not concentrating on the game. If you're not concentrating on the batter you probably will walk him." Kevin took a breath. "We're always going to make mistakes. That's part of the game. So we just acknowledge the mistake and go on. I don't want you worried about someone yelling if you make a mistake. I want you to concentrate on throwing strikes." Kevin glanced at Kyle. "Does this make any sense to you, Kyle?"

Kyle took his cap off and twirled it around his index finger. "Well, I know when Coach Mitch would yell at me, my stomach would get all twisted up." Kyle put his cap back on and looked out his window. They drove in silence for awhile as the hot breeze dried their damp skin.

"Is that why Brian is so good?" asked Kyle.

"What?"

"Cause you never yelled at him."

"No." Kevin laughed. "Brian's good . . ." He thought of the countless hours he spent pitching to his son. "Because he practices."

"But you taught him, right?"

Kevin mulled the question. "Brian has a lot of coaches, Kyle."

"But you coached Brian when St. John's won the city championship. I saw the trophy at school. It's down in the glass case by the cafeteria. In the team picture Brian's standing right next to you."

It seems like so long ago, thought Kevin and it seems like only yesterday.

When Kevin didn't answer Kyle said, "and now Brian's playing for the Hens." His voice jumped two octaves. "You can see him on TV."

"You want to play for the Hens, Kyle?"

Kyle laughed. "No way! I'm not that good."

"You just need to practice, Kyle. You practice hard enough and you want it bad enough, it'll happen."

"Did Brian always want to play for the Hens?"

Caught off guard by the question, Kevin scanned the traffic and said slowly, "I thought so."

When his uncle didn't continue Kyle leaned against the car door and hydroplaned his hand again in the breeze.

Kevin drove a few blocks in the quiet car then swallowed. "You ever go to Steak and Shake?"

Kyle pulled his hand back inside the window. "What?"

"Steak and Shake. Brian and I would go there after practice sometimes to get burgers. I haven't had a chocolate shake in a long time. Not hungry are you?"

Kyle shrugged, "I could eat a burger . . . maybe a double burger and fries. I don't like milk shakes, but they have lime freezes."

Kevin shook his head, "Don't eat dessert, do you?"

"They've got fudge brownie cake and you can get it with a scoop of vanilla ice cream."

"I'll call your mom when we get there."

Chapter 25

The wipers streaked the misted windshield as the Jeep meandered down the side streets of the old north side neighborhood. Karen stared out the window at the small, single-family homes, some like her parents', enlarged and remodeled through the years. She turned and studied her son's silent profile as it passed back and forth from light to darkness under the streetlights. His blue eyes glinted from the headlights of an on coming car. She carefully searched his face but what she wanted to see wasn't there. In repose Brian had a natural smile, but not today. Today he looked more like his father with his blond eyebrows arched, the same worry lines, like tiny crow's feet next to his eyes. There was none of his usual fidgeting or the tap of his blunted fingernails on the steering wheel. The silence hung between them, broken only by the steady, rhythmic sweep of the wipers.

"I don't want to remember him like this," whispered Brian.

Karen felt like she was in a confessional. "Grandpa doesn't want you to remember him the way he is now."

Brian shook his head back and forth. "It's not living."

"No, it's not," murmured Karen. She folded her hands and let them rest in her lap. "It's dying. It's the process of the body shutting down."

"I don't want to die like that. No way!" In the closed space of the Jeep, his voice sounded like a scream. Brian smacked his hand on the steering wheel. "I want to go fast! I just want to be gone!"

"There's a reason for everything, Brian."

"What?" Brian abruptly pivoted his head towards his mother. "A reason to suffer like that?"

"He's not suffering, Brian."

"Come on, Mom! Gasping for breath is not suffering?"

"The medication blocks the pain."

"Yeah! Right! Did you look at Grandpa's face?"

Karen squeezed her hands together and leaned forward in her seat.

"Why? Why go through it?" Brian lifted his right hand from the steering wheel and downshifted as the Jeep approached the red light. "Grandma says he's not going to wake up?" His foot pressed too hard and the brakes squealed as they slid to a stop on the damp pavement.

Karen slowly turned and looked at her son. She asked plaintively, "What would you have us do, Brian?"

"I'd . . . I'd," Brian looked away from his mother.

Karen watched him retreat into his seat.

As the light turned green, Brian slowly accelerated onto Douglas Road. "I just don't want him to suffer." Brian rubbed the back of his hand against his cheeks.

Karen unfolded her hands and gently rested her left palm on Brian's shoulder. The rhythmical sweep of the wipers brushed the silence like a ticking metronome. "What's your best memory . . . your best memory of Grandpa?"

Karen waited as she watched the oncoming car lights illuminate Brian's face.

"Mushroom hunting," said Brian. Unknowingly a slight smile returned to his face. "Grandpa would drive over to our house then we'd walk to Duck Creek. Remember?" He looked at his mother. "He'd always come early. So early in the morning there would still be dew all over the grass and leaves and my gym shoes would get damp." Brian chuckled. "I wouldn't wear socks and I could feel the cold wetness against my toes. Grandpa would say, . . . 'Even though I'm retired, I'm still on that damn factory schedule, up at five every day.' That spring I was . . . ten? Grandpa had to be . . ."

"If you were ten," Karen injected, "Grandpa had to be sixty-two. It must have been the spring he retired."

"He knew everything."

Karen felt the touch of awe in her son's voice.

"Every tree, every bush, all their names. How to spot poison ivy, poison oak, sumac. He'd take out his Swiss army knife and break apart decaying tree stumps to show me all the worms and bugs crawling inside. He'd point out where the snakes would lay on warm rocks down by the creek, where the hornets had their paper nests hanging from branches. We'd go deep into the woods and he'd show me where the deer would sleep."

"He'd always bring a paper sack with our lunch inside and it was my job to carry it." Brian laughed. "I don't know how many times . . ." He shook his head. "I'd be looking at something and just set it down. Later Grandpa would say, 'I guess it's time for lunch.' I'd look around in a panic for the bag only to see it hanging from Grandpa's hand. We'd take our shoes off and sit on a flat boulder down by the creek. Our feet would dangle in the cool water while we ate bologna sandwiches and drank from the canteen that Grandpa would unclip from his belt. I'd break off little pieces of bread, toss them in the water, and watch the blue gills bob to the surface."

"On the way back we'd fill the sack with mushrooms. I don't know how he did it." Brian glanced at his mother. He shook his head laughing. "I still don't know how he did it. He could always find them. He'd say, 'It's time to be heading back.' We'd walk along the path and all of the sudden I'd feel him yank my shoulder. He'd dart off the path and I would hurry to keep up with him. It was like . . . he could smell them or something. He always knew where to look. We were surrounded by all these trees and he would zero in on one tree." Brian continued, his voice conveying his incredulity, "And they'd be there. We'd walk around this tree and there, right at the bottom, would be a whole bunch of mushrooms. But we'd never take them all. Grandpa would say, 'Save some for the next time.' Then he'd stand up, look around the forest and dart off again. The sack was always full when we came home."

Brian downshifted and the Jeep slowed. Karen felt as if her son was still back in the forest with her father. As the light turned green, Brian accelerated and glanced from the street to his mother. "Remember when we thought I broke my ankle?"

Karen looked at Brian and asked, "Was it that summer?"

"Yeah," Brian nodded, "It had to be." Brian shook his head back and forth. "It was my own fault. We were on the ridge. You know," Brian glanced at his mother, "the one above Duck Creek by the swinging bridge."

Karen nodded and waited for Brian to continue.

"There was this butterfly resting on a leaf. It was big . . . yellow with black spots. Man, it was really cool. It just kept slowly opening and closing its wings like a fan. I'm looking at it, trying to sneak closer before it flies away. I'm almost there. I take another step but my foot doesn't touch the ground. I remember falling and rolling, rolling until my foot got trapped. Oh God! Did that hurt!"

Karen watched Brian wince.

"I don't know," Brian went on. "My foot got caught on some sort of root. Gees, it felt like it was yanked right out of my leg. I must have blacked out 'cause the next thing I remember, Grandpa was standing over me. His face was all red and he was breathing so hard. Somehow he got my foot untangled. I remember he said, 'It's going to be okay, Brian. I'll get you home.' He picked me up and swung me over his shoulder in a fireman's carry. Then he . . . wait . . . he couldn't have gone back up the ridge."

Karen felt the Jeep sway as Brian slowed through the curves on Douglas road by the university. She watched Brian chew on the inside of his lower lip, his mind sorting through the memories.

"He must have taken one of the deer paths through the floodplains. Yeah," Brian nodded his head. "That's what he must have done. He kept stopping because his hands were so wet they would slip on my bare legs, and I kept sliding down him. Every time he stopped, I'd hear his heavy breathing and feel his legs shaking beneath me." Brian laughed. "And I could smell his Old Spice." Brian peaked at his mother, "Remember, we'd always ask him what he wanted for Christmas and he always said, 'Well, I could probably use another bottle of Old Spice.'"

"Somehow we got home. I remember him setting me on the front porch swing. Then he went in the house and came out with your pasta pan. He had filled it with cold water and threw ice cubes into it. He didn't even take my shoe off. He just lifted my leg and put my foot in the pan." Brian looked at his mother. "He must have called you at work . . ."

Karen continued, "Said you twisted your ankle and it might be broken. He said I should come home so that we could get some x-rays. Your father was at a conference in Cleveland." Karen smiled. "I set the speed record getting home that day. Soon as I got out of the car and walked up the sidewalk I saw," she put her hand on Brian's shoulder. "You sitting on the porch swing covered with dirt. Your face and arms are scraped and bleeding, your lip is swollen, you've got twigs in your hair and your foot . . . your foot's in my pasta pan. You're holding onto Grandpa's arm. You looked from me to Grandpa and I swear my heart stopped."

Karen drew a breath and slowly exhaled. "He was sitting on the swing next to you. His head was tilted back, his face red, his eyes closed and his mouth hanging open." Karen swallowed and shook her head. "I ran across our porch so fast. I screamed, DAD! At the same second he let out this hoarse snore and the next thing, I was hugging both of you."

Brian flicked the turn signal as they pulled into the driveway of their home. The wipers streaked the mist on the windshield. Brian leaned forward, resting his arms on the steering wheel. He slowly turned his head and looked at his mother. "You know, Mom, I can still see his face." Brian shook his head as if his mother didn't understand. "No, not today, Mom, but that day at Duck Creek. I can still see Grandpa's face as he stood over me and said, 'Everything's going to be okay, I'll get you home.' And I knew he would. I knew he would get me home."

Chapter 26

Karen sat in a chair by her father's bed. She cradled his cold, thin bony hand with her palm. She could feel his faint heartbeat, the pulse coursing through purple veins near the surface of his skin. She looked up as her mother entered the room filled only with the sound of Marty's jagged breathing. Ellen squeezed Marty's toes covered by a blanket. She glanced at her husband then walked over to the dresser and turned on the old RCA radio. Karen watched her father's face as they traveled to the ballpark.

There were two places where Brian did not have to confront the reality of his grandfather's impending death. One was sitting before his computer and becoming Merlwy, the other was standing in the batter's box. He escaped into the game. Whether his fingers danced across the keyboard or the bat swung in his hands, his only thought was the reality of the game for that moment. Nothing else entered his mind.

Brian stood in the batter's circle oblivious to everything except the pitcher taking his final warm-ups. He stretched his fingers in his batting gloves and tapped his helmet with the heel of the bat as he strolled to home plate. He took a couple of swings in the box while facing the Sox's ace lefty Hoyt Miller. He didn't wait. He jumped on the first pitch. Hearing the way the bat made contact with the ball and feeling the jolt race up his forearms, Brian knew he got all of it. Running to first base, he watched the ball sail to the right field bleachers.

Kyle almost knocked Stanley over as he jumped on top of his seat to watch Brian's home run land in the upper decks behind him. He shouted down to Ben on his other side, "Did you see that! One swing!" Kyle mimicked swinging an imaginary bat.

"He nailed it!" shouted Ben.

A sea of St. John's baseball uniforms surrounded Kyle. Brian stopped by the dugout and lifted his cap to the cheering stadium. Kyle waved his hands above his head hoping his cousin would see him.

Standing by the fence, Kevin didn't follow the flight of the ball. As soon as it left Brian's bat, he knew it was a home run. Instead he watched the pitcher. He wondered would Hoyt Miller shake off his last pitch and concentrate on the next batter. Seeing the way Miller glared at his son as he circled the bases Kevin mumbled, "Shit. Watch him Brian, next time up he's going to be coming for you."

Brian pounded his fist into his open glove. He darted glances at the three base runners. As the Hens pitcher went into his windup Brian sank lower in his crouch at the same time coming up on the balls of his feet. The tip of his glove almost touched the dirt of the infield.

Thwack! A hot grounder to the shortstop. Soon as the bat hit the ball, Brian started moving towards second. The shortstop, Kern fielded the ball, scooped it from his mitt and tossed it underhand to Brian. Brian caught the ball with his open right hand. As his left toes scraped the plate, he pushed off and up with his right leg. He was airborne. He saw the runner sliding beneath him. He pivoted in mid-air and hurled the ball like a javelin to the first baseman's mitt. He didn't see the catch because he was watching, then spreading his feet, so he wouldn't land on the runner beneath him. The roar of the crowd told him he got the double play.

Brian lifted his bat from the rack and grabbed a helmet. He started up the steps out of the dugout.

"Brian!" shouted Juan.

Brian turned back at the sound of his name.

Juan looked from Brian to the pitcher, Miller, on the mound. He debated if he should say anything. Finally he just said, "Be careful out there." He started taking off his catcher's gear.

The look on Brian's face seemed to ask "what are you talking about?" Feeling a hand on his shoulder, Brian turned and peered into the eyes of Coach Bruno.

The coach said, "Miller KO'ed a kid in Buffalo last month. Shattered his helmet with his fastball. They suspended him five games, but I don't think that changed him. Juan's right, just be careful out there. Look for that fastball up and in."

"I will, Coach." Brian skipped up the steps into the sunlight.

The crowd fell silent as Brian stepped into the batter's box. Hoyt Miller's brown eyes glared at Brian. His Fu Manchu mustache and long, wavy dark hair bristled as he shook off the sign from his catcher. Brian lazily swung the bat across the plate to stretch his muscles. He brought the bat back above his shoulder lowered his chin and waited.

Brian could hear his father's words drilled into countless little leaguers. Never turn into the ball. Never open yourself up. Always turn away. Always turn your back to the ball if it's going to hit you. Turn your back and fall away.

The ball seemed to come right out of the sun. Brian started to turn his back, to fall away, but the ball was too fast. Instinctively Brian's head turned away from the pitch. The stitches of the ball, like a scalpel, sliced the top layers of skin from Brian's left cheekbone. He fell to the ground.

The fence rattled as Kevin jumped against it to get a better view of his son.

Kyle and the St. John's baseball team stared dumbstruck, as Brian lay motionless on the ground.

Ten thousand spectators held their breath as Coach Bruno and the trainers ran onto the field.

Brian pushed himself up on one elbow. He could still see the ball streaking towards his eyes. He was dazed. He might as well have been hit because mentally he was shocked. He couldn't believe the ball was that fast. It seemed to gain speed rather than lose momentum. His cheek stung where the ball had scraped the skin and with the pain came the realization that this pitcher's ball could have killed him. He could hear voices and movement around him He stared at the pitcher standing on the mound, his glove hanging at his side. The pitcher meant to hurt him. He tried to hit him in the head with his fastball.

"You okay?"

Brian tried to focus on the face of the umpire who was squatting next to him. He didn't answer as he watched Coach Bruno and the trainers running from the dugout. He twisted his face away from the umpire and stared at Miller who stood motionless on the mound, waiting, studying Brian. Brian instinctively snatched the bat from where he dropped it as he fell. He stood. The bat in his right hand hung down by his leg. He squared off and faced Hoyt Miller.

Kevin running down the ramp slowed to a jog as he saw Brian push himself up from the ground. The collective release of the spectators' breath seemed to blow like a gust of wind across the infield. As the fans inhaled all eyes swept back and forth between Brian and Miller.

Juan, followed by the Hens players, charged from the dugout to the pitcher's mound. Coach Bruno turned and held up his hands while yelling, "STOP!" The Sox players erupted from their dugout and raced across the diamond. They surrounded Miller and waited. Coach Bruno grabbed Juan by his shirt. The shirt buttons popped as Juan fought to break free.

"Don't, Juan!" shouted Brian taking a few steps forward.

Juan stopped struggling against Coach Bruno as the Hens players huddled behind him. Brian's eyes were riveted on the pitcher.

"Come on, back to the bench, before you all get thrown out and we lose this game," Coach Bruno said as he pushed Juan backwards.

The Sox players peeled away from Miller and slowly returned to their dugout.

As Brian turned back to home plate, the umpire said, "Don't worry, Brian, he's out of this game and if I can do it, he's out of this league."

"NO!" Brian swung around and faced the umpire. "He didn't hit me!"

"Are you crazy? He tried to take your head off."

"It was a wild pitch, that's all . . . Just a wild pitch." Brian narrowed his eyes as he stared back at Hoyt Miller. "Come on, let's play ball."

Brian stood at the edge of the batter's box. He yanked his batting gloves up his wrists, tightening them against his fingers. He took his bare forearm and pressed it against his left cheek. The sweat on his arm seared the scrape that looked like a crescent moon on his cheekbone. There was no blood, but if anyone looked closely they could see the veins throbbing beneath the missing top layer of skin. Pushing his helmet down on his head he tapped it with the bottom rim of his bat. He swung the bat upright, held it out in front of him and as he stared at the bat, took a deep cleansing breath. He stepped into the batter's box and planted his right foot. He pivoted his right foot back and forth digging his ball and heel into the dirt then shifted his weight back to his right foot and lifted his left, front heel slightly off the ground. He swung the bat a couple of times across the plate and finally brought it back above his right shoulder. And then . . . he looked at Hoyt Miller.

The only sound in the vast stadium was the slight breeze flapping the flags. The fans all stood like silent sentinels.

Brian's concentration was so intense his eyes hurt. The ball thumped the catcher's mitt. The bat never moved from above Brian's shoulder.

"Strike one!" yelled the umpire.

Brian watched the ball leave Miller's twisting hand. He watched the rotations. It wasn't enough just to hit this ball. He calculated the impact and trajectory. "Strike two!" screamed the umpire as Brian continued to stare at Miller, the bat frozen in his hands.

"Ball three!" Brian seemed as immobile as a statue. The only sign of life, the intensity of his blue-eyed stare. Brian locked eyes with Hoyt Miller. Blinking, the pitcher broke the stare down as sweat from his forehead dripped into his eyes. Miller wiped his arm across his forehead. He shook his head and sweat flew from the thick mustache. He stared back at Brian then went into his windup.

Brian exhaled as he watched Miller's arm arch back and then up. He saw the rotations. Brian flicked his wrists downward. The bat snapped like a whip in his fists.

Miller was on the ground.

Brian let the bat drop from his hands by home plate. He slowly walked to first base as the infielders gathered around the pitcher. Miller held his right shoulder, his face contorted in pain. Brian's ball was on the ground by his feet.

Looking at Hoyt Miller, Brian realized he got the pitch he needed. He wanted to strike back. He didn't think it was possible. You can throw a ball to a spot with pinpoint accuracy, not hit it. No one could do that, but he did. He waited for some emotion to sweep over him but nothing came. As he watched the trainers help Miller to his feet, he felt empty.

The buzz started as the relief pitcher Suthoff began his warm-up throws. It rose in crescendo until Brian felt as if he were inside a beehive. The seats with the talking, buzzing, standing fans spun like a kaleidoscope. He felt dizzy and drained. Brian knew the fans were all talking about him. He had a sharp headache centered behind his eyes. He just wanted to lie down and close his eyes. Standing by first base Brian hunched over, lowered his head and put his hands on his knees.

"You okay, Brian?" asked the Hens first base coach.

Brian didn't look up. He just nodded his head. He could hear the steady rhythmical thump of the pitcher's warm up throws into the catcher's mitt.

"Here."

Feeling the hand on his shoulder, Brian stood up and took the water bottle. As he drank, he looked across the diamond. His eyes searched and stopped at the familiar figure by the fence. As he focused on his father, he pressed the cold water bottle against his burning cheekbone. The dizziness passed. He handed the water bottle back to the coach. As the umpire yelled, "Play Ball!" Brian nodded once to his Dad and eased into his lead off crouch.

The fans began their chant. "Brian! Brian! Brian!"

Chapter 27

"A lot of people have taught me about living," said Kevin. "Your grandfather has taught me about dying. I don't know if I have his courage. I don't know if I could keep fighting like that when you know you're not going to win." Kevin shook his head as he drove down the North End Streets. The sun had been up for an hour. The air was filled with the hum of lawn mowers as people raced to get their lawns cut before the heat built up during the dog days of August.

Brian kept reliving the scene over and over again in his mind. The words just came as he tried to catch up to his feelings. "Grandma told him to go, that he can't stay here anymore." He swallowed and looked away from his father. He rubbed his hands together in his lap. "She took his hand and told him that she loves him and he'll always be with her. She said, 'Go Marty, it's time, go. You can't stay here anymore.'" Brian couldn't keep the tears from rolling down his cheeks. "And then he died." Brian wiped the tears from his cheeks with his finger. "How does that happen?" His eyes searched his father's face looking for an answer. "It was almost like Grandpa was waiting for her to tell him to go."

"I don't know, Brian. Maybe it wasn't so much Ellen telling Marty to go but letting him know it was okay to go."

Brian stared out the front window as he pondered his father's answer. When Kevin stopped for a red light, Brian watched a young mother scoop her toddler up in her arms and carry him across the street. "Do you think Mom's going to be all right? I've never seen her cry like that."

Kevin eased the car forward as the light turned green. "Something happened between your mom and your grandpa when she was about your age."

Brian looked at his dad and waited.

"She . . . they . . . no one ever talks about it, but it's always been there. You'd see it in glances between them or hear it in the words they didn't say. I don't know what it was, but I always thought it had something to do with college. A couple of days ago your mom came back from visiting your grandpa. She was crying." Kevin shook his head remembering his wife's face before him. "She wasn't really making any sense. She said something about how it wasn't fair that they both lost their dreams." Kevin glanced away from the street and looked at his son.

Brian met his father's stare and said, "Mom wanted to be an actress. She wanted to go to Northwestern and study acting." He stopped and considered what he could say next, but he couldn't cast any blame on his grandfather. He shrugged and said, "They just didn't have the money."

They drove in silence. Brian couldn't escape the image of his grandfather on his deathbed. Cancer killed the man whose footsteps he followed in the snow. A man who didn't know how to stop fighting. His strong body ravaged until he looked like a child's skeleton. His sunken cheeks pulled back against his teeth as he struggled to breathe. Brian wanted to talk with his dad, wanted to tell him why he wanted to go to UW, to tell him about his dreams to be part of the research to help find a way to stop cancer. As they pulled into the driveway he looked at his dad, but before he could say anything, Kevin said, "You're going to miss the three game series in Columbus."

Brian couldn't believe it. He hadn't even thought about the Hens.

Kevin said, "It can't be helped. If you want, I'll call Coach Bruno."

Brian couldn't say anything. He nodded. He sat in the car as his dad walked up to the house.

Brian didn't want to go back to his grandmother's house after the funeral. He and Ali drove to the park. Brian took off his dark blue pinstripe suit coat and tossed it into the back seat of his Jeep. He shucked off his tie, spun it into a loose ball and tossed it on top of his coat. As he walked to the passenger door he rolled up the long sleeves of his light blue shirt to his elbows.

Ali said, "Give me a minute, Brian." Brian walked to the entrance path through Duck Creek Metro Park and waited. Ali kicked off her low black pumps. She pushed up on the passenger seat, slid her hands under her sleeveless black dress and yanked down her panty hose. She folded the panty hose and placed them in her purse.

Ali slid her hand down Brian's forearm. She could feel the light gleam of perspiration on his skin from the late afternoon sun. Her fingers entwined his. She squeezed his hand and they both started down the path. The air cooled as they entered beneath the canopy of listless leaves. Their steps found a matching rhythm, and they turned as one onto the deer trail leading to their promontory above the winding Duck Creek.

Brian lay with his head on Ali's lap. Ali leaned back on the overturned tree stump gazing at the ducks paddling in lazy circles in the low murky water. The short grass felt damp and cool against her bare legs. She looked down at Brian. Her finger hovered above the white, crescent moon scab on his left cheekbone. She didn't touch the scab but instead let her hand rest gently on his cheek. Brian opened his eyes and stared up at Ali. Ali gently slid her fingertips over Brian's mouth. Brian kissed her fingertips then closed his eyes.

She could stay like this forever, gazing at his short sun bleached blonde hair bristling against her black dress, her hand lightly cupping his cheek and hearing his breath softly whistle through the gaps of her fingers.

Brian stirred and lines furrowed his forehead. As Ali gently massaged the deep wrinkles, Brian slowly came awake. He looked up into Ali's sparkling emerald eyes. She inclined her head as her lips brushed his and lingered.

"How long was I sleeping?" whispered Brian.

"Not long."

Looking at Ali, Brian lifted his hand and absently entwined his fingers in her reddish blonde hair resting on her shoulder. "Part of me just feels empty. Like a part of my life is gone that I'll never get back." He took Ali's hand and rested it on his chest. "I just wasn't . . . ready. When they closed the casket . . . I never said goodbye."

Ali stroked his cheek with her fingertips.

"I couldn't say goodbye to him." Brian squeezed her hand realizing he couldn't bear another loss. "I can't say goodbye to you. Come with me, Ali."

"Brian." Ali looked away from his beseeching eyes. "I can't go to UW. My parents . . . we don't have that type of money. Do you know how much out of state tuition is? Brian, there is no way I can go there."

Brian's fingers covered Ali's lips. "Just think about it. We'll find a way." Brian's coarse fingertips gently touched her cheek. "Just think about it."

Ali leaned back against the tree stump and gazed up at the thousands of leaves hanging silently above and around them. She felt his head stir in her lap. She stroked his short hair then followed the sun filtering through the leaves to his intense blue eyes. "Can't we stay here forever?"

Brian slowly shook his head and whispered, "No."

Ali's finger gently traced a circle around the scab on Brian's cheekbone. "What about baseball?"

Brian flinched. Ali quickly pulled her hand away. "I'm sorry, does it hurt?"

Brian shook his head.

"Can you walk away from baseball?"

Brian sighed and looked away from her eyes to the leaves stirring in a slight warm breeze rising from the creek. "I don't know." His eyes darkened as he pondered the question. "I've never not played baseball." He sat up and leaned against the tree stump next to Ali. "For me swinging a bat is like walking. I've always done it. It's always been my life." He stared down at Duck Creek.

Ali asked, "Is it your life or is it your dad's life."

Brian said harshly, "He's not on the field, I am." Seeing the hurt look on her face Brian gently stroked her arm. "I don't know, Ali. I've always played baseball. It's what I do."

"You never talk about baseball."

"It's hard . . ." Brian peeled a piece of bark from the tree stump. "It's what I am. I'm a ballplayer." He tried to think through the question. "Ali, I wouldn't still be playing ball if I didn't want to. Not for my dad. Not for anyone. When I put on that uniform I become a different person. Baseball will always be part of my life."

Brian stood up. He walked to the edge of the promontory. He stared at a family of ducks paddling across the creek. Ali stood and followed him. Standing close behind she wrapped her arms around him and leaned her chin on his shoulder.

"I've always had this feeling, Ali. That I was meant to be part of something important."

Ali squeezed Brian closer to her body.

"When I was a kid I thought I'd be part of the team that won the World Series."

Ali watched Brian as he tried to see into the future.

"My mom says there is a reason for everything. Watching Grandpa suffer . . ." Brian swallowed and tried to chase away the image of his grandfather on his deathbed. "Knowing how cancer kills. There's got to be a way to stop cancer." Brian spun around. "Something important. What's more important than trying to save someone's life? Baseball's a game, Ali. It's just a game."

Chapter 28

"Okay, guys, five minutes. That's all," said Kevin looking down at his peewee team decked out in their St. John's uniforms. He gathered his team outside the door to the Hens locker room. "I still don't know how Brian was able to swing this." He pointed his thumb over his shoulder at the door. "They're in there getting ready for the game. So when I say five minutes, I mean five minutes. Got it!"

He saw his wide-eyed kids nod their heads. They quietly walked through the door as if they were entering St. John's church.

"Mitch," said Kevin, "You got 'em? I need to see Coach Bruno."

"Sure," replied Mitch. "Five minutes, right?"

Kevin lowered his voice, "Fifteen max."

As they walked through the doorway Kyle brushed against Red and saw the long, cylindrical paper tube. "What do you got there?"

"No . . . nothing," stammered Red.

"Come on. What do you got?" asked Kyle.

Standing on the other side of Kyle, Stanley poked him in the ribs. "Look, there's Brian."

"Brian!" shouted Kyle as he ran across the locker room with Stanley by his side.

"Hey, you guys made it," Brian said.

Looking at Brian, then around the locker room Kyle said, "This is pretty cool. You even got whirlpools in here."

"They're mainly for the pitchers." Brian tugged Kyle's St. John's baseball cap down over his eyes. "You know how those pitchers are, nothing but a bunch of big sissies."

Kyle laughed and said as he pushed his cap back up, "Are not."

Brian noticed Red hanging in the background with some of his teammates. "Hey, Red, that was some double play you turned against St. Joan of Arc."

Red's ears blended with his red hair. He held the paper tube out and pushed his way between his teammates. "Brian, could you . . . sign this?"

Kyle and Stanley stepped to the side as Red held the tube out to Brian. "My sister, Kim, works in the souvenir shop." Red swallowed. "She was able to save me one of the first ones."

"What is it?" asked Brian taking the tube.

"It's a . . . a poster."

"Well, let's have a look."

Brian pulled the plastic top from the tube. He slid the poster from the container. He handed the tube back to Red then turned and started to unwind the poster against his locker. The St. John's team pushed and shoved trying to see over Brian's shoulder. As the poster opened, Brian saw himself hanging high in the air over second base, a base runner sliding beneath his feet, the ball just leaving his fist.

All the kids all stared dumbstruck as Kyle managed to utter, "Wow!" Brian was as hypnotized by the poster as the boys. He could feel the ball leaving his hand hurtling to first base.

"It's like Michael Jordan," Chris said with awe. "How do you jump so high?"

Red reached into his pocket. "I have a pen, Brian."

Brian couldn't take his eyes from the poster. When he was younger, the same age as the kids surrounding him, he filled his bedroom with posters of his favorite players. Ken Griffey Jr.

used to loom over his bed. He couldn't believe he was now on a poster that would hang on some kid's bedroom wall. As he pivoted to take the pen, he saw the upturned faces. He wondered if he had the same look of awe on his face when he got the autograph from Ken Griffey Jr. These young faces staring at him as if he was larger than life. All of the sudden his grandfather's words came back to him, "You'll be carrying a lot of kids' dreams out there. Don't let them down."

Kyle said, "Brian?"

Brian motioned for Kyle to hold one end of the poster while Stanley held the other end up against the lockers. He grinned at Red and asked, "Do you want Red or your real name?"

"Red, Brian."

"Your number's eleven."

Red's face beamed in a smile of surprise as he nodded yes. Brian took the pen from Red and wrote on the top edge of the poster. *Red, St. John's (11) From one second baseman to another, Brian (21) McBride.*

Brian tapped the pen against Red's hand. Red reluctantly looked away from the poster and took back his pen.

As if it were a sacred manuscript, Kyle and Stanley rolled the poster and slid it back into the tube. St John's teammates all started talking at once. A few of the team players broke away searching for their other favorite Hens players. Chris, St. John's catcher, saw Juan coming from the back near the showers. He took his Hens team photo from his pocket and went to intercept him.

Juan shouted to one of the team trainers. "You need more paper towels back there." He wiped his hands on the front of his pants and slowed as he saw the stocky, crew cut, twelve-year-old blocking his path. "Whoa." Juan glanced around at the other St. John's teammates and with a flash of recognition said, "Oh, Brian's team, right?"

Chris nodded and extended both pen and team picture.

Juan took the pen in one hand and the picture in the other. "Turn around."

As Chris spun around Juan placed the picture on this back. "What do you play?"

"Catcher."

"Catcher, huh? What's your name?"

"Chris."

"Well, Chris, let me give you a word of advice. Never, never eat hot Mexican food the night before a big game. Just don't do it."

"Why?"

Juan spun Chris back. "Why? You ever hear the term . . ." Juan looked down at the young, expectant face. He reconsidered. "Just because I said so, that's why." He saw Chris' bewildered expression. As he handed the picture back, he winked and tapped Chris on the shoulder. "It's a catcher thing."

"Oh, yeah, right." Chris winked back and nodded as if he understood their private joke.

Juan walked away from Chris. He suddenly stopped and swung back. He leaned down and studied Chris' teeth.

"Good teeth." Juan tapped his own two front teeth. "Fake." He pointed his finger at Chris and waved it back and forth. "Never, ever, warm up a pitcher without your facemask. Got it!"

"Got it!" Chris said.

Juan gently slapped Chris on the shoulder then turned and walked away.

"Juan," Chris said.

Juan looked back over his shoulder as Chris held up the picture and said, "Thanks."

Juan shrugged. "No problem."

Stanley's black hand tightly clutched the white ball. He stared at Leroy Brown's back as Leroy bent over to tie his cleats. When Leroy sat up, Stanley hesitantly edged forward.

Feeling his space being invaded, Leroy swung around on the bench.

"What you want?" snapped Leroy.

Stanley averted his eyes from Leroy and looked down at the ball. He softly mumbled, "Could you autograph this." He lifted the ball higher. "It's yours."

"It's mine?" asked Leroy.

"It's the home run you hit against Indianapolis."

Leroy quickly snatched the ball from Stanley. "Then I'll just be keeping it." He laughed seeing the startled look on Stanley's face. He studied and rotated the ball. "Yep, there it is. That's my tattoo." He pointed to the indentation in the hardball's cover. "How'd you end up with it?"

Stanley looked away and shuffled his feet. "I ran faster than anyone else."

Leroy looked at Stanley appraisingly. "There ain't much to you, ya better be able to run fast. Where's your pen?"

As Stanley tapped his pockets an "aw gees" look appeared on his face.

Standing up Leroy towered over Stanley. "You got to come prepared. You can't be wasting a man's time." He reached into his locker and picked up a pen from the top shelf. He took his time boldly signing his name on the leather-covered sphere. As he handed the ball back to Stanley, he looked at the white faces of the St. John's team still gathered around Brian. He nodded his head at them. "They treating you okay?"

Stanley looked puzzled as he glanced at Brian and a half dozen of the St. John's team. "What?"

Raising his voice Leroy asked, "Your teammates, they treat you okay?"

Stanley looked up at Leroy, "They're my friends."

Leroy looked away from Stanley and shook his head, "Whatever." He looked down at the autographed league ball. "Hold on to that till I get back to the majors."

Noticing the confused look on Stanley's face, Leroy said, "It'll be worth more when you sell it."

Stanley shoved the ball in his pocket. He gave Leroy his twelve-year-old stare. "I'm keeping it."

Leroy laughed and turned back to his locker.

"St. John's!" Mitch shouted in the Hens locker room. "It's time to go!" He pushed Kyle and Chris towards the exit. He held out his hand to Brian. "Good luck out there today." After Brian shook his hand, Mitch turned towards Juan and offered his hand. "Thanks for having the kids here.

"No problem," replied Juan. He waved at the St. John's players heading through the locker room door. "You got to take care of your fans."

As the St. John's team left the locker room, Red held the poster like a baton in his hand. "Whatever you do, Red," said Kyle in a low voice, "don't set it down. Someone might steal it."

"Or," added Stanley as they walked through the corridor up to the bleachers, "someone might sit on it and it'll get all crushed."

"We can take turns holding it," said Kyle. Red turned and looked at Kyle suspiciously.

"Good idea," Stanley said. "That way we'll be sure nothing happens to it. One person's job is just to hold it while the other two watch the game."

"We'll go by innings," Kyle exclaimed. "That way each of us gets to hold it for three innings."

"Unless there's extra innings," Stanley added.

"Then we'll rotate back to the first person." Kyle put his hand on Red's shoulder as they climbed up the steps into the bleachers. "You can hold it for the first inning." He looked across Red's shoulder at Stanley. "Then me 'cause Brian's my cousin." Stanley rolled his eyes and gave a, "well-I-can't-top-that," look. "Then Stanley."

Stanley glanced up the steps to the bleachers. "Wait, Red. There are some people up there. Let me go first so they don't accidentally hit Brian's poster."

As Brian left the locker room he thought, no one talks about it. All the players knew if they won today's game they'd tie the Clippers for first place in the Western Division. It was like if they talked about the pennant they'd jinx it. In his entire life the Hens had never even come close to winning the pennant. Brian jogged onto the field, another sellout. The first game Brian had played, the stadium wasn't even half full, but now his dad said, there were scalpers in the parking lot. Brian laughed, scalpers for a Hens game.

Kyle and Stanley stood and leaned against the support rail as they looked down in the twilight as the Bison's players took their positions on the field. Kyle looked back at Red sitting between two empty seats, the poster held like a scepter in his right hand. The stadium lights were coming up. Kyle glanced at the scoreboard. The Hens were leading five to one going into the bottom of the third inning. A smile spread across Kyle's face as he raised his fist and pumped it in the air while looking at Red.

Kyle rocked forward against the rail and screamed, "Yes!" As Brian tossed his bat to the batboy and jogged to first, Red lifted the poster tube and pointed the top of it at Brian.

Jogging to first base, Brian could feel the resonance of the chant prickling over his skin.

"BRIAN! BRIAN! BRIAN!"

Wow, he thought, this feeling is overpowering. He could still see the poster, still see the young faces staring up at him. He looked around the artificially lit stadium. He saw the aisles packed elbow-to-elbow with a sea of fans, and every one of them seemed to be chanting his name. The chant swept over him like a warm wave. He wanted to sink into its embrace.

Brian yanked his batting gloves higher on his wrists. He walked off first base, crouched down and placed his hands on his knees.

He stared at the back of the pitcher. He knew the pick-off move wouldn't start with the pitcher's feet or the hands but with the quick upward jerk of the shoulders. The secret of stealing was to know the minute difference between the pitcher's pick-off move and his throw to home plate. Once Brian understood the difference, once he knew that the pitcher was going to pitch to the batter instead of first base, he would start the steal before the ball would leave the pitcher's hand. As he watched the shoulders, he shifted the balls and heels of his feet across the baseline. His body appeared not to move yet he edged further and further from first base. As the pitcher's shoulders jerked, he crossed his right foot behind his left and lightly sprang back to first base. He was so quick the first baseman didn't even attempt the tag.

Slow, so slow, thought Brian. He walked off and this time crouched down six inches further. He skipped back to the base as the first baseman caught the ball. Brian looked at the pitcher and smiled. He got what he hoped for as the pitcher glared back. He wondered, why do so many pitchers have such massive egos?

He edged out further. As he crouched, he came up on the balls of his feet. The shoulders jerked, and he hesitated a nanosecond then dove head first for the base. The first baseman swept his mitt down on Brian's glove clinging to the base.

Brian dusted himself off then looked at the first baseman and shrugged. Yanking his gloves up on his wrists, he edged away from the bag. He glanced back at the first baseman. He whistled softly between his lips while watching the pitcher's shoulders. He left before the ball. Brian tried to ignore the cheers as he slid into second.

Brian stepped off second base as Leroy walked from the on-deck circle. As Brian went into his crouch, he rested his elbows on his thighs and let his hands dangle between his knees. He flicked his gloved fingers as if he were tapping them on a piano's keyboard. He glanced at the third baseman who was playing Leroy deep in the pocket, then at the second baseman who was hovering near the bag. He took the sign from the coach for the hit and run. He watched Leroy's eyes register the sign. Leroy bent his head left and right, rolled his shoulders, then stepped into the batter's box.

Brian was running to third as he heard the crack of the bat. He slowed and watched Leroy's ball sail over the centerfield fence.

Stanley was the only person sitting in the stadium. He held the rolled up poster between his legs. Kyle looked back from his spot at the rail and said, "Three to go. Just three to go, Stanley." Kyle leaned over, grabbed Red's shoulders and shook him. "Just three to go!"

The batter popped the ball up behind the plate. Juan threw his mask off, ran to, then leaned over the rail, reached into the stands and just got the glove on it.

Kyle pounded his fists on the rail like he was beating on a drum. Stanley couldn't take it any more. He got up from his seat, cradled the poster against his chest and sandwiched himself between Kyle and Red at the rail. As the next Bisons player stepped to the plate, it felt like the air was sucked out of the stadium as all the fans drew a breath and held it. With a diving catch, Brian snagged the line drive for the third out.

Kyle and Red jumped in the air and high-fived each other, Stanley lifted the poster like a sword and pointed it at the stadium lights.

"Brian!"

Brian slowed to a walk across the infield, turned and searched the bleachers. He heard Kyle's young voice shouting his name while Stanley waved the poster in the air He veered to the bleachers as the boys ran down to the rail.

Kyle leaned against the rail and stretched his hand to Brian. As Brian slapped his hand and saw the look of pure joy on

Kyle's face, he was overwhelmed. Fans that were leaving stopped and as if drawn by a magnet made their way down to the rail. Beaming at Brian, Stanley shook the poster in his hand. A young boy wearing a Hens cap ducked under the rail and held out a program and pen. Brian grabbed the program and quickly signed his name. When he went to give it back, he saw a dozen hands waving programs.

His fingers cramped. He didn't think he could sign his name one more time. Finally he backed away from the rail. "Got to go, guys. Next game okay." Brian stopped at the top step of the dugout. He looked across the field to the fence where his dad usually stood. Maybe his dad was right. Maybe he should play ball. Looking to the spot where Ali usually sat in the bleachers, he realized he could stay here with Ali. He glanced at first base. He could hear the fans chanting his name urging him to steal and feel the thrill as his foot slid into second base.

Chapter 29

Brian lingered in the locker room after the game. He laughed listening to Juan singing in the showers. He sat on the bench, his arms draped over his knees nodding as his teammates walked by. He felt at home.

Coach Bruno said, "You're in the record books now, Brian." The coach took off his cap and smoothed back his sparse salt and pepper hair on his high forehead.

"How's that, Coach?"

Coach Bruno looked at Brian to see if he was kidding. "You don't know, do you? One hundred and thirteen stolen bases, that's the league record." He put on the cap then ran his fingers down his thick, bushy mustache. "You need anything?"

Brian smiled up at his short, stocky coach. "No, I'm good, Coach."

"How 'bout shoes? You burning out those cleats. Need new ones."

"No, these are fine. I've got 'em broken in, just how I like 'em."

Juan still singing, a towel wrapped around his waist, walked out of the showers. He stopped when he saw his coach. "What. You don't like my singing?"

"You keep shagging those pop-ups behind the plate like you did today," said Coach Bruno, "you can sing as much as you want. I'll even get my harmonica."

The shortstop Kern shouted, "Hey, Coach. You got company."

A smile of recognition spread beneath Coach Bruno's mustache as he saw Tim O'Connell from the *Make-A-Wish* foundation. The slightly overweight middle age misplaced Texan wearing his trademark cowboy hat extended his hand.

"Coach, we were listening to the game during Bobby's therapy session. I told Bobby we'd swing by and take a chance, see if a couple of the boys were still hanging around."

Brian noticed the thin boy standing close to O'Connell.

Seeing the camera hanging around O'Connor's neck, Coach Bruno said, "Looks like you caught our catcher out of uniform."

"Hey." Juan tightened the white towel around his waist.

"But our second baseman's still suited up. If you want to take couple of pictures."

The young boy stepped forward. "With Brian McBride?"

Looking at the boy's pale face, the bald head beneath the Hens baseball cap, Brian saw his grandfather.

Juan said, "Brian?"

Brian heard Juan's voice but couldn't look away from his grandfather's image.

Juan shook his shoulder. "Brian."

Feeling his face flush, Brian stood up and ran back to the toilets. He held onto the sides of the sink trying to stop the room from spinning. After the dizziness passed he splashed cold water on his face then looked up into the mirror. His mind cleared. It wasn't Grandpa. He thought, Jesus, what has he done? What's the kid thinking? He snatched some paper towels from the dispenser.

Wiping his face, Brian walked back to the locker room. Juan was autographing a ball for Bobby. Juan studied Brian then tossed him the ball. Brian caught the ball while ignoring the stares from O'Connell and Coach Bruno. He took the pen from Juan. "Bobby." The pale face looked at him then quickly turned away. "Bobby." A small hand reached out for the ball. "Come on. Let's go outside and take some pictures."

Brian sat on the edge of the promontory, dangling his feet from the ridge. He chewed on the end of a long stem of grass. His blue eyes stared vacantly at the low, slow moving creek. He could faintly hear the water rippling over the rocks. He kept replaying the scene in the locker room. He rationalized that it was just the similarity, the bald head beneath the Hens cap that made Bobby seem like his grandfather, but he knew it was more than that, he knew he saw his grandfather for a reason. But why? Backtrack. Wasn't that what his grandfather always had him do.

The buck moved quietly, his brown coat blending with the tree trunks. Brian only noticed him when he froze at the edge of the creek, lifted his antlered head and sniffed the air. Brian sat motionless, the stem of grass hanging from his lips. The doe and then a yearling emerged from the woods. The yearling quickly scampered down the bank, ducked her head to the creek and drank. Brian wondered if it was the same buck. They were coming home after beating Start High School 5-4 in extra innings. It was dusk quickly turning to night. They were on Glendale, the winding road that split Duck Creek Metro Park. As they rounded the curve and entered the darkness of the forest, the buck was standing in the road, frozen in the glare of the headlights. He remembered his dad hit the breaks and the car skidded. The deer's large brown eyes were fixed on the headlights. The deer couldn't look away. Brian tensed his body waiting for the impact as the deer loomed before the car. His dad instantly switched off the headlights. Everything went black. He heard the buck's hoofs scraping the pavement. As his eyes adjusted he saw the buck leap. He heard the high screech as the toes of the back hoofs scraped the hood of the car.

Sensing motion the buck shifted his head towards Brian.
He snorted and pawed the earth. The doe and yearling fled
back to the forest. The buck wasn't staring at Brian, but beyond
him. The buck shook his head then bounded into the trees.

Brian chewed on the end of the grass stem. He thought, is
it to remind me, Grandpa? How could I forget how you died?
Is it to let me know what's in Bobby's future? Brian tossed the
grass stem to the ground. I know what's in Bobby's future.

He heard her coming up the path. As she sat next to him he
couldn't look at her. Ali rested her head against his shoulder.

In a voice so weak that he could barely hear himself Brian
said, "I have to go, Ali."

"I know."

Brian tried to stop the tears but couldn't. "I have to leave
you, Ali."

Ali put her arm over his shoulder and just whispered,
"Brian."

Lying in bed, Brian groped in the dark hearing the chirping of his cell phone. He untangled his arm from the sheets.
His hand fumbling across the night table knocked the alarm
clock over. He grabbed the phone and flipped the lid open as
he brought it to his ear.

"Brian?"

"Ali?" Brian sounded like he was talking through his pillow.

"You awake?"

Brian glanced at his turned over clock. "What time is it?"

"It's five. I couldn't sleep."

Brian stretched out his legs while rubbing his face with his
free hand. He yawned into the phone.

"You're tired. I should let you go back to sleep."

As he fell into the rhythm of her voice Brian rolled over
and lay on his back. "No, I'm awake now."

"I want to go to the park. I want to go jogging."

"It's dark out."

"No, I'm looking out my window. There's a lot of light from the moon. Besides the sun will be up in a little while."

"Jogging?"

"We haven't gone jogging for awhile. I miss it."

"The gates for the park won't be open."

"I can park my car on that side street. You know the one by the two-mile marker where the path curves out by Glendale. We'll just go through there. If you walk down, we'd both be there about the same time."

Brian asked, "Can I at least brush my teeth?"

"Hmm, good idea."

Brian slipped on a sweatshirt and black shorts. He grabbed a pair of socks from his drawer and his running shoes from the bottom of his closet. He quietly opened his bedroom door then used the bathroom. He stopped in the kitchen and bent over the table to scribble a note to his parents.

Near the park Brian glanced at the dew melted on the warm hood of Ali's empty car parked under the streetlight. He looked across the street at the small opening in the bushes then jogged through the bushes and onto the path. He slowed as he saw her silhouetted in the moonlight. Ali stood on the edge of the clearing, looking up at the fading stars. She turned as she felt his presence. Brian slowed, watching her. Ali's loose spirally hair seemed to catch the moonlight. She wore shorts over her leotards. A small fanny pack was strapped to her waist. She turned and started jogging down the path. He watched her, and then followed.

He came abreast of her, matching her rhythm. Their breaths seemed as one. The sheen of the sweat on their skin reflected the moonlight. As they jogged down the path the overhead branches hid the stars. Ali slowed, searching. She veered onto the deer path. Brian slowly jogged behind her on the narrow trail.

Breathing deeply, Ali slowed to a walk and rested her hands on her hips as they came to the promontory. Brian stopped and watched as Ali walked to the edge and looked down at the creek. The wind stirred and the mist from the creek flowed up the hillside and enveloped her.

Brian could see the faint light of dawn creeping across the top branches of the forest behind her. She turned and stepped out of the mist towards him. "I can't let you go without me." Ali took another step forward. "I've been up all night trying to figure out what we can do. I'll work while you're going to school, at least until we establish residency, then I'll go to school with you." She stood before him. He heard the snap and then saw the fanny pack fall to the ground. Her hands crisscrossed her shoulders and in one fluid motion she slid the leotard from her breasts. Her hands uncrossed and slid underneath her leotard and shorts. She pushed them to the ground.

Brian searched her face hidden in the shadows of the rising light behind her and asked softly, tentatively, "Are you sure, Ali?"

She glided forward and pressed her index and middle fingers across his lips as she looked into his deep blue eyes filled with the first rays of dawn. She replaced her fingers with her lips. She gently broke off the kiss. Her hands slid under his sweatshirt. Intense heat radiated from his skin through her hands as she glided her warming hands across his naked damp skin. She lifted the sweatshirt above his head. She set the sweatshirt, like a blanket, on the grass.

Ali pressed her palm against his chest feeling his pounding heart. She looked and swam into the blue sea of his eyes. Her hand rose, caressed his skin and rested on his cheek. "I want . . . no . . . I need to spend my life with you." She kissed his lips. Then lay on top of the sweatshirt.

Not taking his eyes from her, Brian tugged down his shorts and stepped out of them. The first light fought and filtered its way through the tangled leaves rustling in the breeze. The branches swayed and a beam of sunlight burst through and flashed a streak of crimson across Ali's hair. As he sank to his knees, she handed him her pack. He looked into her laughing emerald eyes. The wind stirred and the leaves cascaded down upon them.

Chapter 30

Coach Bruno jerked his head around and spotted his assistant coach, Toby. Seeing the look on Toby's face Coach Bruno growled, "Now, what!" He stomped across the locker room. When he stopped, Toby whispered in his ear.

"God damn son of a bitch!" Coach Bruno screamed. He picked up a batting helmet and threw it against the lockers. The Hens players fell silent and stared at their coach. Coach Bruno kicked the helmet back against the lockers. "Toby." He grabbed his assistant by the arm and spun him around. "Find Kevin McBride get him down here, now!" As Toby raced off, Coach Bruno watched Laplante and Moran walk through the door of the locker room.

The players looked on as Coach Bruno glared at Laplante and Moran. The silence was broken when the shortstop Kern said, "Well, I know they're not here for me."

Moran walked forward and said, "Hi, Coach, where's McBride?"

Coach Bruno sat stiffly behind his desk. He took one of the toothpicks from the holder on his desk, slipped it between his teeth and chomped down like he was biting the end of a cigar. Brian glanced back and forth between Coach Bruno behind his desk and Laplante and Moran sitting on two chairs before the desk. No one spoke. They turned as one when the office door opened and Kevin and assistant coach Toby entered the room.

Kevin surveyed the room. He saw Coach Bruno flip the mashed toothpick into the garbage can and snatch a fresh one from his holder. Brian stood with his back to them, staring out the wide glass window at the Hens diamond. Kevin took in the dark blue suits as both men got up and walked towards him.

"You must be Brian's dad," said the first. He was as tall as Kevin but fifty pounds heavier with a bull neck that threatened to snap his shirt collar open. "I'm Clyde Moran. I'm glad they caught you. This will save us a trip to see you."

The second man was about the same height. He was thin and so pale his skin seemed translucent. He stepped forward and extended his hand. His Adam's apple bobbed up and down as he spoke. "Jeff Laplante. You got yourself quite a player there, Mr. McBride."

Kevin shook his hand and looked past him at Coach Bruno who tossed another toothpick in the trash. "Can I ask what this is all about?" asked Kevin.

Laplante darted a glance at Clyde Moran who appeared momentarily insulted but quickly recovered and burst out, "We're with the Tigers. We want Brian to come up to Detroit."

Brian spun around from the window. He didn't see the men. He only saw his father. He would never forget the transformation that crossed his dad's face, from shock and disbelief to a look that his dad had just thrown the last strike for a no hitter. Kevin couldn't keep the grin from his face as he looked at Moran and Laplante. When he noticed his son, the grin vanished.

Brian leaned back against the window to keep from falling. He never saw it coming. You don't play high school ball in June then play for the Tigers in August. This couldn't be happening. He made his choice. Soon as the season was finished he and Ali were going to UW, and that would be the end of his baseball career.

Laplante walked back to his chair and picked up his briefcase from the floor. He set the briefcase on top of Coach Bruno's desk and started ruffling the papers inside. Moran walked over and stood across from Brian. "Wow, kid. Take a breath." He playfully slapped his hand on Brian's shoulder. "You look like we're walking you to the gallows." He glanced over his shoulder at Kevin. "He's got a funny way of showing how happy he is." His head swiveled to face Brian. "You know, Brian, I was going to say, when you were a kid did you ever dream about growing up and playing for the Tigers?" He laughed, "But I got to tell ya, Brian, looking at you, you're still a kid." He laughed again and looked at Kevin.

Seeing his son look like he was going to get sick, Kevin thought, what's the matter with him?

Jeff Laplante pulled the contract from his briefcase. "You have an agent, Brian?" When Brian didn't reply, he looked at Kevin. "You can get one but I'm telling you, you don't need one."

"Brian," Moran added, "you can keep number 21. We want you in uniform by Friday's game."

Brian couldn't meet his father's eyes. He turned back to the window. He put his open palms on the glass to steady himself and looked out at the stadium. He watched the groundskeepers working on second base, his base. He looked to the box seats, to the spot where his grandfather saw him play his first game as a Hens.

"Brian."

He heard his father's voice but he wouldn't turn around to face him. His eyes focused on the flagpoles, all he could think to say was, "Why, now?"

"What?" Moran practically shouted.

Staring out the window Brian asked again, "Why now? The Tigers are what ... twenty games out of first. They're not going anywhere. Their season's done."

Moran turned to Laplante and gave him a look that said is this kid loony or what?

"It's about filling seats, Brian," said Laplante. "You put excitement in the game. The fans will come to see you play. We need to give them a taste. A taste of what you'll be able to do for the Tigers next year." He glanced at Coach Bruno. "Just like you've done for the Hens this year."

Brian exhaled. He knew if he signed a contract and played for the Tigers that college was out. Major league ball was a full time commitment. He felt trapped. He wanted to smash his hand through the glass and jump down to the bleachers.

"Brian." Kevin's tone was insistent.

He couldn't turn and face his dad. He knew if he looked into his dad's eyes, he'd crumple. He'd give in and live his dad's dream. He had to find a way out. His palms pressed against the window, pushing so hard his fingers turned white. He looked to the bleachers where his grandfather had sat and then again to the flagpoles. Thinking out loud he said, "In my whole life the Hens have never won a pennant. This is the first time in over twenty years where we have a shot to put a pennant up there on the flagpole." He spun around and stared at Coach Bruno. The Coach bit down on his toothpick and held it motionless between his teeth. "You gave me my chance, Coach. We have a contract, right? Says I play for the Hens for the season. That's what I'm doing, Coach."

"Now, wait a minute," shouted Moran. "The Hens are the Tigers farm team. We have first rights on that contract." His face red, Moran stopped, drew a breath and held his hands up. He tried to speak calmly, "The Hens play Triple A ball. Brian, we're talking about playing for *the Detroit Tigers*." Seeing the look on Brian's face he smacked his hands together and shouted "Jesus, kid. I could walk down into the Hens locker room right now and any one of those guys would give me their right nut to play major league ball!"

"Clyde," said Laplante.

Clyde Moran dropped his hands and backed up a couple of steps from Brian.

"Brian." Laplante motioned Brian to the desk. "Why don't you come over here and look at the figures I put together."

Brian shook his head and stayed by the window.

Moran whirled and faced Kevin. "McBride! Talk some sense into your kid!"

"Brian." His father's voice had the same tone that would stop him in his tracks when he was a kid.

Brian kept his eyes on Coach Bruno. "I'm finishing the season, Coach." He couldn't meet his father's eyes. He focused on the door. His father, Moran and Laplante were just a blur off to the side. He put one foot in front of the other. He saw Moran move forward to block his path.

"Let him go."

Brian followed the voice to his father's face. It wasn't a look of anger -he could handle that-but one of immense disappointment. He sagged and said, "Dad . . ."

"Go. Just go."

I can't undo this, thought Brian as he saw his father look past him to the baseball field. Brian walked across the room opened the door and left.

Chapter 31

Kevin sat on the green porch swing. Beads of moisture from the cold Miller Light trickled down and left a ring on the arm of the swing. After wiping his damp hand on his shorts, he took a swig of beer. The hot August air seemed to suck the moisture from his lips. He felt the beads of sweat roll from his armpits down the sides of his bare chest. With one foot on top of his knee, his other foot pushed the swing, unconsciously falling into the rhythm of the oscillating lawn sprinkler. He stared at the empty driveway and waited.

Her car seemed to hold until the last second before making the tight arc into the driveway. It stopped, and as the car shut down Kevin listened to the pinging from the heat of the engine. He saw Karen sitting behind the wheel talking on her cell phone. He looked up and watched two squirrels scrambling from branch to branch on the tall, fully leaved tree in his front yard. He listened to the click of Karen's high heels on the driveway then felt her hand touch his as she took the beer from his hand. He stared up at her long slender neck as she took a deep sip. As she returned the beer to in his hand she said, "Quite a day, huh?"

When Kevin didn't respond Karen ran her hands down the back of her skirt then sat next to her husband. After being married for twenty years she thought she knew all of his moods. Looking at his face, when he is angry, really angry as he is now, he wouldn't talk. It's like he goes into a cave and expects her to wait outside until he's ready to come back out. She watched the two squirrels scampering from branch to branch. One squirrel stopped near the top branches. It turned on the other squirrel. Its tail flared and swished back and forth like a rapid metronome, as it made angry clicking noises. The second squirrel stopped then leaped to a lower branch. They reversed the chase as they darted through the leaves, down the tree and across the front yard. "I'll be back."

Karen pushed the screen door open with her hip. She carried a beer in one hand and a cup of coffee in the other. Kevin turned as he heard the screen door slam. He looked up at his wife. The heat had loosened the soft curls, her raven hair brushed against the top of her shoulders. As she walked forward and extended the beer her breasts swayed freely under her black tee shirt. Kevin took the beer. Karen sat and tucked her bare feet under her black shorts. Kevin pushed with his foot and the swing again fell into rhythm with the sprinkler.

Karen blew across the top of her coffee mug then took a sip. When they first got married she would let him sulk for days, letting him have time to work out his feelings before he felt ready to talk. But as she grew older she realized she didn't want to waste all those days, time they would never have back. Maybe he didn't want to talk, but she did. "Brian told me. He called me on his cell phone soon as he got out of . . . what would you call it, a meeting?"

When Kevin didn't respond, she went on. "Do you know how hard it was for Brian to do what he did today? Do you have any idea, Kevin? Since he was a toddler he's done whatever he could to win your approval. Don't you see the way he looks at you?" Karen sighed and set her coffee cup on the armrest of the swing. She felt her frustration build as Kevin just sat there. "It wasn't that he said no to baseball, he said no to you. To your dream."

Kevin's angry eyes flashed on her. He slammed his foot down and stopped the swing.

Karen held onto her cup as the lukewarm coffee spilled and ran across her fingers. "That's what really hurts, doesn't it?"

Kevin snapped, "How would you know?"

Karen raised her hand and licked the coffee from her fingers. She leaned back against the swing looking out at their driveway. "I can still see the two of you out there." Karen motioned to the driveway. "You with your bucket of plastic whiffle balls and Brian with his oversized Hens cap that kept falling in his eyes as he swung that jumbo orange plastic bat. I've watched you both through the years, watched Brian grow into one hell of a ballplayer. There's only one reason he would give that up." She waited until Kevin looked at her. "There's something more important to him."

His face full of anguish Kevin asked, "What?"

"You have to ask him."

Kevin stood up from the swing and walked across the porch. He stopped, his hand on the door handle. He slowly walked back. He leaned against one of the white wooden pillars supporting the roof. "He's a ballplayer, Karen. He can be one of the best. It's not only a dream, Karen, it's the money. Do you have any idea what sort of money he's walking away from?"

Her face reflected disappointment that Kevin didn't understand. Karen shook her head. "Money's never been a driving force for Brian. Maybe part of that is our fault. We've always met his wants. But what are they? A computer? A used Jeep? The kid's never gone hungry, Kevin. It's not that." Karen curled her hands around the coffee mug in her lap. "As a ballplayer you're always talking about Brian's vision. How he sees the play before it begins. How it's something you can't teach, a player either has it or he doesn't. Brian's got vision." She looked at Kevin. "But it's not just for baseball. There's a whole different side to our son. He hides it from you and I

don't know why. Maybe he feels you'll think it's not masculine."
Karen leaned forward on the swing, trying to get closer to her
husband. "Where would the world be if Thomas Edison played
baseball and never pursued his other dreams?"

Kevin turned away from his wife and leaned against the
pillar.

"He's made his choice, Kevin. He's our son. I will do whatever I can to support him. This summer is the turning point in
his life, and he'll look back and always remember what we do."

Kevin stared as the water from the sprinkler rained on the
burnt, dry grass withering under his tree. He heard the swing
stop rocking and felt his wife come up behind him. Her arms
encircled his waist. She leaned her cheek against the gleam of
sweat on his naked shoulders and whispered, "I know it was
your dream for him." She sighed as she squeezed him to her.
"But he has his own dreams."

Chapter 32

They met over the breakfast table. Kevin was drinking coffee and munching on buttered toast. Brian walked into the kitchen, wearing shorts and a tee shirt, his hair still tousled from sleep. He dropped two Pop Tarts into the toaster, then grabbed a gallon of milk from the refrigerator and swung it down on the table.

Kevin smoothed the newspaper folded on the table. "Stebli's pitching today. He'll lead with his curve ball. If he can't get it over he'll go to his fastball. That's all he got."

Kevin's pitching background allowed him to analyze the technique of each pitcher much as a surgeon would critique an intern performing an operation. There were no notes to be filed away. The pitcher's tendencies, strengths and weaknesses, favorite pitches, even the velocity of his fastball, Kevin committed to memory. Much like a meteorologist could predict the direction of a moving cold front, Kevin could accurately predict what kind of ball a pitcher would throw in a given situation. When Brian was in high school, if Kevin knew the pitcher, he would always prep Brian during the ride to the game.

As Brian plucked the Pop Tarts from the toaster and sat at the table, Kevin continued talking on their common ground, the one thing they could always talk about, baseball. Kevin had watched Stebli pitch two times before against the Hens. "When Stebli gets behind in the count, he goes almost exclusively with his fastball." He took a sip of coffee. "He likes to lead with his curve, but if you wait, three out of four times it curves out of the strike zone. Sit on the first ball. Let him fall behind in the count, forget the curve and just look for the fastball."

Brian, chewing on his Pop Tart, nodded at his father.

"Brian! Are you up?" Brian saw his dad smile as they heard the pounding on the front screen door.

Kevin shouted, "Come on in, Kyle."

They heard the front screen slam and quick footsteps along the hallway. Kyle rounded the corner glanced at Kevin then stared in awe at Brian.

Brian shifted uncomfortably in his seat as Kyle kept staring at him. "Are you okay? Kyle?"

Keeping his eyes fixed on Brian, he nodded.

"Have you had breakfast, Kyle?" asked Kevin.

"Cheerios." Kyle watched as Brian took another bite of his Pop Tart.

His mouth full, Brian asked, "Want one?"

"Okay."

Brian pointed to the toaster and the box of pop tarts on the counter.

As Kyle reached the counter he said, "Strawberry, huh? I'll have to get my mom to buy some."

When Kyle joined them at the table, Kevin noticed the bruise on Kyle's cheek. He pointed to the purple bruise and asked, "What happened?"

Kyle broke the Pop Tarts into little pieces, picked up the ones with crust and ate those first. "Justin hit me." He quickly added, "But I got him back."

Kevin asked, "Why are you two fighting?"

Kyle looked across the table at Brian. "He called you a stupid idiot for not going to the Tigers. I called him a stupid idiot back and said everyone knows Brian can play for the Tigers whenever he wants but," a look of hero worship crossed Kyle's face, "Brian wants to stay and help the Hens win the pennant first." Kyle tossed another Pop Tart chunk in his mouth. "I didn't think he'd hit me, but he did."

"What'd your mom say?" asked Kevin.

Kyle put his curly head down and hunched lower in his chair. He played with the broken pieces of Pop Tarts on the plate. "Well, I kinda told her . . . I fell off my bike."

"Oh." Kevin tried to keep the smile from his face.

Kyle looked up at Brian. "That's why you stayed, right, Brian? To help the Hens win the pennant."

Brian thought yes, but . . . was that what everyone was thinking? They thought that was the reason he didn't go to Detroit. He saw Kyle waiting for his answer. What could he say? It was part of the answer but not the complete answer. He'd be lying if he said that was the reason he didn't go to Detroit.

His fingers wrapped around his coffee mug, Kevin waited for his son's response. He saw Brian look more and more confused as he sat there staring at Kyle. Kevin finally said, "Hey, Kyle, let Brian just worry about today's game."

As he heard the crowd erupt, Coach Bruno glanced up at the scoreboard; Norfolk just beat Columbus six to four. He smiled and flicked his toothpick to the corner of the dugout. He knew what all of his players did, win today's game they'd tie Columbus with eighty-eight wins and force a playoff game Monday night in the Hens stadium with the winner taking the Western Division pennant. Word quickly passed from one player to the next. Coach Bruno looked at his players and said, "Get it done, boys."

Brian ran onto the field wearing his home game uniform, white with blue pin stripes and blue sleeves and the Hens red logo on his chest, red number 21 on his back. The bleachers were a sea of pulsating red, white and blue; the Hens home game colors. He glanced to "The Roost" the second story section of the stadium built around the right field foul line three hundred and twenty feet from home plate. If a ball landed in the right section of "The Roost" it was a foul ball, in the left section it was a home run. Kyle and his St. John's baseball teammates were jumping up and down and waving their caps. As he met their eyes, Brian felt a strange sensation. He felt the boys trying to live through him. Suddenly they switched. He was in the stands cheering with them. And then it hit him. In his entire life he never had the chance to cheer the Hens on for a pennant. He remembered the look of awe on Kyle's face from this morning. He turned slowly. Ten thousand cheering faces stared back at him. A moment of sheer panic gripped him as he thought, God, what if we lose, to come this close then lose our last game. He saw his dad leaning against the fence. As their eyes met, his dad tugged the brim of his Hens cap. Brian nodded and automatically tugged the brim of his cap then settled into his crouch by second base. He rubbed his palm on the edge of his mitt. As the batter walked from the on deck circle to the plate, he tuned out the fans just as he would turn off the volume on his computer. He went into the game.

Brian watched the pitcher Stebli rub the ball in his mitt. As the ball left the pitcher's hand, Brian was taking the whole way, he wasn't going to swing. The bat never left his shoulder.

"Ball one!"

There goes his curve, thought Brian. Let's see what he's got next.

"Ball two!"

Close Stebli but you missed. Now you've got to bring the heat. Brian held up his hand to call time then stepped out of the batter's box. The bat rested between his legs as he tightened his batting gloves. He glanced around the stadium. He looked to "The Roost." He took off his cap then wiped his forearm across his brow. He could see Kyle and the St. John's baseball team standing by the rail watching him. He smiled as he replaced his

Hens cap and looked at the pitcher, knowing he was going to throw his fastball.

Brian stepped back into the batter's box. As the ball left the pitcher's hand, he knew exactly where it was going. His swing wasn't to make contact, to get on base but to knock the ball out of the stadium. He drove his hips forward, powering his weight behind his swing. He kept his head down to see the point of impact. His fists jarred, tingles raced up his arms. His feet moved without thought. As he raced to first base he saw the ball land on the roof of the building across the street from the stadium. He slowed to a jog. The roar of the crowd was deafening. The strangest feeling crept over him as he rounded the bases, he felt he wasn't alone. He darted a glance to "The Roost". Kyle and his friends were jumping up on their seats and cheering. As he rounded third base, his teammates were standing by the rail in the dugout pumping their fists in the air. He crossed home plate, headed to the dugout and high-fived open palms as he jogged by.

As the umpire yelled ball four, Brian jogged to first base. Before he even touched the bag the chant began, "Brian! Brian! Brian!" The chant was a surge of electricity coursing through his muscles. The volume increased as the fans clapped their hands in rhythm to the chanted beats of his name. Flexing his gloved hands, he stood on base. As he peered around the standing room only crowd, he smiled. He shook his head, trying to shake off the sense that he was their center of attention. He stepped off the base then edged out into his no man's land staying up on the balls of his feet. He went into the game. There was no thought of winning or losing, of pleasing or disappointing his fans. His only thought was of the moment, the moment when he would turn and steal second.

Kevin shook his head. "You can't give Brian that big of a lead." He ignored the stares from the fans around him, realiz-

ing he was talking out loud instead of to himself, but he was so
wrapped up in the game he didn't care. He watched the catcher
hold the ball in his hand as his son slid then popped up on second base. "Brian's on second with the go ahead run. We got
Brown coming to the plate. Shit, a single will score Brian from
there." Kevin came up on his toes as Leroy hit the ball deep
towards centerfield. "The wind's got it." The centerfielder
backed onto the warning track then timed his jump. He
snagged the ball right off the wall. Kevin saw Brian tag up then
slowly jog to third base. "What the hell you doing, Brian?
Move it." As the centerfielder made a soft throw to the shortstop, Brian kicked in the afterburners; he quickly rounded third
and streaked for home. The catcher waved his arms while
screaming for the ball. Brian dove headfirst and slid under the
tag. Kevin laughed and smacked the fence. "Damn, Brian, you
even faked me out."

Brian could feel the pebbles digging into the skin of his
forearms. He pushed himself up on his hands then jumped to
his feet. The umpire was still signaling safe. Blood was trickling from the scratches on his forearms. He felt light-headed.
It took a second for his breathing to catch up to his heart. He
heard thundering applause and somewhere fireworks were
going off. As he stumbled to the dugout, he was surrounded
by his teammates. He felt Juan's hand grab his arm and steer
him down the steps. He collapsed on the bench as Jamal,
the trainer, used an antiseptic wipe to clean the blood from
his forearms. Brian heard his name chanted through the
stadium.

"Brian! Brian! Brian!"

Juan urged, "Go on!" He grabbed Brian's arm and hoisted
him up. He shoved Brian towards the steps. "Go!"

Brian turned around. "What?"

Juan pointed to the field, "Go."

Brian walked up the steps and out onto the field. Ten thousand clamorous fans were on their feet. He lifted his cap and listened to the cheers. As he stood there, he knew he would still hear the cheers when he woke the next morning.

Kevin watched his son lift his cap. The cheers were deafening. "How can you walk away from this, Brian?"

As Brian walked out of the Hens locker room, he saw Ali leaning against the wall, waiting. Her face broke into a smile. She ran and hugged him then, looking into his eyes, she laughed and said, "You're beaming. I don't believe it, you're actually beaming."

Brian blushed and said, "What are you talking about?"

"I've never seen you look so happy." She leaned forward and kissed his lips. "Well, maybe a couple of times."

"When'd you get here? I kept looking for you?"

"I missed the first couple innings. I just couldn't get away from work. Finally, I gave them my two weeks' notice and just walked out." She rubbed her palm along his cheek. "Maybe, I won't have a job tomorrow."

As the locker room door opened Ali heard shouts and boisterous laughter. She saw Juan and the shortstop Kern walking towards them. Juan threw his arm around Brian's neck and pressed Brian's head against his chest. Grinning at Ali he said, "You see him out there, Ali?" Juan rubbed his knuckles on Brian's cap. "Faster than a speeding bullet."

"Let go." Brian struggled out of Juan's grasp then reset his cap on his head.

Pointing his finger at Brian, Juan said, "You're coming, right?

"Yeah. I'll be there."

"You better or I'll come get you." His finger swiveled. "You too, Ali."

"Yeah, yeah, yeah." Brian waved Juan and Kern away.

As they left, Ali asked, "What was that all about?"

"They're all going to the Dugout, it's a bar by the old stadium. Want to come?" Brian took Ali's hand and they started walking to the parking lot.

"No." Ali glanced back over her shoulder as a group of Hens players came out of the locker room laughing and jostling each other. "I think it's going to be a guy thing."

"Come on. We'll just stop for a little bit."

They walked across the near empty, lighted parking lot to Ali's car. Ali took her keys from her purse and unlocked her door. "No, you go and have fun. They got you for the season." She kissed his lips, "And then you're all mine."

"You sure?"

Ali opened the car door and sat on the seat. Looking back over her shoulder she said, "Besides, I've got a lot of packing to do." She watched Brian's face in the rear view mirror as she drove away.

Chapter 33

Hearing the horn blast, Brian popped the clutch as the semi-truck's lights filled his rearview mirror. His Jeep's tires squealed as he accelerated from the stoplight and raced down Anthony Wayne trail. He couldn't concentrate on his driving. He kept seeing the look on Ali's face as she said she was going home to start packing. He couldn't believe she was actually going with him to UW. His mind was bombarded with a hundred different questions. "They couldn't live in the dorms. Where were they going to live? How were they going to live? He had the money he saved from his Hens salary. Ali said she'd get a job, but how much money could she make?"

He saw the Dugout in a strip mall off a side street. When the new stadium opened downtown many bars sprang up within walking distance. Each vied to become the new home for the Hens. But none could match the allure of sitting on wooden picnic benches, leaning your elbows on tables scarred with the carved initials of long departed Hens players while lifting quart size, frosted glass beer mugs. Hens team photos, going back over fifty years plastered the walls. Behind the bar Hens memorabilia, hats, mitts, bats and balls laid in state on glass shelves.

The parking lot was full. Brian finally found a spot near the back of the lot. Leaning forward he rested his arms on the steering wheel and stared at the old wooden double doors. He remembered the times his dad would bring him here. They'd sit on one of the benches eating burgers and fries, his dad's upper lip covered by beer foam. Kevin seemed to know everyone in the place and either his dad or his friends had a story for every picture hanging on the walls. Brian smiled as he remembered and thought those were good days. Brian got out, locked his Jeep and slowly walked up to the door wondering if he would feel any differently as he entered the Dugout for the first time as a Hen.

Brian shook his head and mumbled, "gees" as he spotted Leroy Brown's red Spider Ferrari parked in the only handicapped spot by the front door. As he pulled open the heavy wooden doors, he was engulfed by the smell of stale beer which had seeped into the cracks on top of the wooden tables. Looking up at the slow spinning paddle fans, his foot accidentally kicked one of the two golden spittoons aligned like matching lions on each side of the doorway. He walked through the entranceway and glided past the team photos while looking at his teammates gathered around the tables.

The third baseman, Parker, jumped up from one of the picnic benches and shouted, "Brian, go back!" Two other Hens took up the shout, "Go back!"

Brian froze. He couldn't understand what was wrong. Why was everyone staring at him? Juan stood up and swung his leg over the bench. He held his hands up in a signal for Brian to stay put. When Juan reached him he put his massive hands on Brian's shoulders. "It's okay," said Juan. "Just walk backwards."

Brian let Juan guide him back to the threshold flanked by the spittoons. Juan dropped his hands and said, "No problem, Brian. Okay?" Brian nodded his head while looking at Juan quizzically.

Juan laughed seeing Brian's expression. "Just do what I do." Juan turned and walked along the photo-arrayed wall. He slowed as he neared an empty spot about two feet by two feet on the wall. He tapped his open palm against the empty spot as he walked by. Brian followed in his footsteps and tapped his hand on the same spot. The room suddenly filled with the babble of voices and laughter.

Juan walked back and stared at the empty spot. "That's where it's going," he pronounced. "Our team photo." He leaned one hand on Brian's shoulder while his other pointed at the spot. "Hopefully, our pennant team photo." Juan tapped the spot again with his open palm. "For luck." His hand on Brian's shoulder, Juan pushed him towards the benches. "Come on, go squeeze your skinny butt in that bench over there. I'll get you a Mountain Dew." As Juan pushed him along, Brian couldn't stop his hand from reaching up and tapping the spot again.

Juan did a double take as he saw a young college kid with a shaved head standing at the tap trying to get at least as much beer as foam into the pitcher. "Where's O'Malley? He's always here."

The young bartender slid the pitcher on top of the counter. "He got a call. His wife took a tumble down the stairs at home. She thinks she may have broken her ankle. O'Malley was going to run her over to St. Luke's to get some x-rays."

"That's a tough break." Juan bit his tongue as the words left his mouth to keep from laughing at his own joke. He took Brian's Mountain Dew turned and almost collided with Leroy Brown.

Leroy pointed to a bottle on the shelf behind the bartender. "You're sure that's Chivas and not some of your stock shit in there?"

Juan shook his head and walked back to the tables as the bartender pulled the bottle of Chivas from the shelf and filled a shot glass. Leroy studied the amber color then held the glass under his nose and inhaled. The young, part-time bartender stepped back away from the bar. Leroy took a sip then smacked his lips. "Yep. That's my Chivas." Leroy set the glass back on the bar. "What's your name?"

"Bob."

"Listen up, Bob. This is my party, tonight." Leroy pointed to the three picnic tables jammed with Hens players. "Hey!" he shouted. As the players looked at Leroy, he made a show of pulling a gold money clip from his front hip pocket. He slid a platinum Visa card from the middle of the folded wad of bills. He held the card up in the air then flipped it between his thumb and index finger. Looking at the Hens, he handed the card to the bartender. Raising his voice he said, "Tonight, everything goes on this card."

"Leroy!" barked Bellman, the backup catcher. Another chorus came from some of the other Hens. "Leroyyy!" They pounded their hands on the table then lifted their beer mugs in a toast.

Brian sat on the bench jammed between Juan and Parker. The caffeine from the Mountain Dew kicked in as he glanced around the table. He was the only one who didn't have a mug of beer in front of him. He couldn't follow half the conversations at the long picnic table. All he could hear were loud disjointed words. The guys kept laughing as they refilled their mugs from the beer pitchers. After Leroy finished basking in the toast from the Hens, Brian felt Leroy staring at him.

Leroy turned his attention back to the young bartender. He sipped his Chivas as he watched Bob run his credit card. Taking the card back he studied Bob's eyes as he slid the card back between the hundred dollar bills. Leroy peeled the top two bills from the pile. He laid them face up on the bar. He drained his shot glass. "Ahhhh." He slid the empty shot glass to Bob and watched him refill the glass. "Bob, this is just between us." Leroy laughed. "Kinda off the record. You know, Bob, so that your boss doesn't know." Leroy flicked one of the hundred dollar bills towards him. "You're going to take good care of my friends, right, Bob?" As Bob nodded Leroy drained his shot glass and slid it back to Bob. Leroy turned and watched the Hens laughing and jostling each other. Beer splashed on the tables as they filled their mugs too quickly from the pitchers.

Brian was laughing at one of Juan's stupid jokes. Leroy curled his big palm around the full shot glass and then poised the long middle finger of his other hand above the remaining one hundred dollar bill. As Leroy peered into the bartender's eyes he said, "They get whatever they want, right?" The bartender glanced from Leroy's face down to the bill. He nodded. Leroy laughed and flicked his middle finger. Before the bartender could catch it, the hundred-dollar bill slid and fell over the edge of the bar. As the bartender bent to pick it up, Leroy snatched his shot glass and headed to the tables.

Juan pounded his open hand on the table. Laughing he shouted, "Then Brian said, I hear ya . . . Get it?" He laughed again as Brian shook his head and chuckled. Seeing that his teammates at the table were not falling over in spasms, Juan conceded, "Ah, you had to be there."

Brian watched as the pitcher MacKay got up from the other table and stumbled back towards the restrooms. MacKay's hand instinctively came up and smacked the empty spot on the wall as he walked by. Brian elbowed Juan and pointed at MacKay and asked, "How'd that start?"

Juan shook his head. He focused on MacKay as he went through the men's doorway. "What?"

Brian replied, "You missed it. Slapping the wall like that."

"Oh," Juan looked around at the other tables. "Where's Kern?" He saw Kern sitting on the end of the next table. He nodded at him. "Kern started it. O'Malley showed us the spot where he was going to hang our team picture. As he got ready to pound the nail in the wall, Kern smacked the empty spot and said, 'you mean our pennant winning picture.' O'Malley pulled the hammer back and said, Juan tried to mimic O'Malley's Irish accent, 'I'll not be spoiling your luck. We best be waiting till you win the pennant then before I hang your picture."

Brian laughed. Looking at Juan's Spanish features and hearing him mangle an Irish accent was just too much.

"It's not that funny," said Juan.

Brian caught his breath. He watched as another Hens player walked by and tapped his palm on the wall. "So, that's how it started . . ."

"Yep. Ever since then, any Hens player who walks by smacks the wall and whispers, "Pennant.""

The large figure moved in and blocked Brian's view of the empty spot on the wall. Brian peered up at Leroy. The paddle ceiling fan spun lazy circles behind Leroy's gold rope chains draped around his neck. Leroy set his shot glass on the table and watched as the bartender slid two more pitchers and a frosted mug across the wooden top. "I thought that was you, Brian," Leroy said. "'Bout time you showed up in the Hens coop." Leroy lifted his left leg and set his foot on the picnic bench. He leaned forward and rested his forearm on his knee. "Some of your teammates think you're too good to hang with us."

"You're blowing smoke, Leroy," said Juan as he picked up the pitcher and made a show of topping off his beer mug. "Guys never said that."

"Well, Juan," Leroy stretched the name out with a Spanish inflection in his voice. He motioned with his head to some of the other players sitting at the next table. "Maybe, you don't hang with the same guys." Leroy turned his attention back to Brian, lifted one of the pitchers and slowly poured the beer into the frosted mug. He watched as the ice coating the outside of the mug slid down the glass and pooled on the table.

"Brian, a toast to the Hens." His eyes darted to Juan then back to Brian. "To all the Hens." Leroy glided the wet mug across the table until it bumped against Brian's hand. "Shit, man." He laughed, "Look at your face." He twisted the mug around so the handle rested next to Brian's fingers. "I'm not offering you drugs. God Damn, this is nothing but watered down draft beer. You have had a beer before?"

Bob grabbed one of the empty pitchers and deliberately looked away then walked back to the bar. Brian jerked his damp fingers back to the edge of the table. He rubbed his thumb over his fingers trying to dry them.

Leroy picked up his shot glass and held it between his thumb and index finger. He grinned at Brian as he dangled the glass over his knee. "Hens!" Leroy stood up straight. He seemed like a giant towering over the sitting players. He lifted his shot glass. The room fell silent. Leroy let his gaze sweep over every player until it finally rested on Brian. "A toast." He waited as the Hens lifted their beer mugs. "To the team that's going to win the Pennant!" He held the shot glass steady as he stared at Brian.

Juan nudged Brian "Don't let him get to you. Just drink your Mountain Dew."

"Yeah, Brian." Leroy laughed. "Drink your pop."

Brian felt every eye in the room on him. His fingers unconsciously curled around the glass handle. He thought, what's the big deal. A sip. I'll just have a sip. His hand quivered and foam splashed on the table as he lifted the heavy mug. His voice broke as he shouted, "TO THE HENS!"

"HENS!" His teammates shouted in unison.

Leroy drained his glass. He laughed looking at Brian. "You could be in that commercial." He reached out with his finger. Brian jerked back as Leroy's finger wiped the white foam from Brian's upper lip. "Only, it's not milk." Leroy carried his empty shot glass to the bar.

His teammates refilled their mugs and returned to their loud stories. God, they all seem so happy thought Brian. He stared at the almost full mug still in his hand. He was surprised when he lifted the mug and took another sip.

Bob set two more pitchers of beer on the table. He tried to pretend that Brian wasn't there.

In the back of his mind Brian knew MacKay's joke was so dumb, so incredibly stupid but he still couldn't stop laughing. He sat transfixed as MacKay refilled his mug. Gees, he wondered how many beers have I had? He tried to focus on his wristwatch. It can't be that late. The foam overflowed and oozed down the sides of the glass. Brian's hand tightened on the handle but as he lifted, the full mug slid down his wet palm. The bottom of the mug knocked against the table causing the beer to splash over the top. Forgetting he was on a bench, Brian tried to push away from the encroaching puddle of beer. Beer seeped over the table's edge and drenched his pants.

"Brian! Jesus! Watch what you're doing," said Juan as he slid off the bench and backed away from the table.

Brian laughed as he awkwardly wobbled and at the same time wiped beer from his pants. He lost his balance and crashed down on the bench. "Whoa!" He stuck his hands out to catch himself, but they slid across the wet table soaking his arms.

MacKay shouted, "Brian, you're supposed to drink the beer not wash in it." Brian curled both hands around the mug and brought it to his lips.

Juan took the bar towels and soaked up the beer from the table. He watched Brian stagger along the wall of team photos on his way to the john. Brian halted, staggered back a few steps and smacked his wet hand on the empty spot. Juan looked around the bar. He saw Leroy sitting two tables over, watching Brian and laughing.

"Juan."

Juan glanced up and found the shortstop Kern standing next to Brian's empty seat. "This ain't no good," said Kern. "The kid's drunk."

Juan pulled the wet rags into a pile. "Shit. I know. I'll get him home." Juan turned away from Kern and carried the rags to the bar. After tossing them into a bucket behind the bar, he watched the restroom's door waiting for Brian to appear. He saw the door open and Brian lean against the doorframe as he wiped his face with paper towels. Brian crumbled the towels and attempted to throw them into the wastebasket. He pushed off unsteadily from the doorway. He concentrated on walking in a straight line along the wall. He glanced at the team photos as he lurched past them. He stopped and leaned against the wall caught by the year in the top right hand corner. He rested his palms on either side of the photo. The room stopped spinning as the team picture slowly came into focus. He lifted his index finger and placed it on the jersey of a figure standing in the back row of the photo. He felt the hand on his shoulder.

"You okay, Brian?" asked Juan.

Brian kept staring at the photo. "That's my dad." Brian shook his head back and forth. "This is strange." He slurred the words. "It's like he's looking at me standing there in his Hens uniform." Brian traced his finger from the figure to the year on top. "I wasn't even born yet. I don't even think he had met my mom . . . yet." As he said "mom" his face changed. Brian leaned his head against the wall above the photo. "Oh, Shit! God, Juan. How'd I get so messed up? My mom's . . ."

"Come on," Juan said. He grabbed Brian's left arm. "Let's go sit down."

Brian sat on the bench. He slowly pushed the mug full of beer away. He mumbled, "My mom's going to kill me."

MacKay slapped the table with his hand. "What? Is your mom like the one on the TV show? You know, Malcolm's mom, Malcolm in the Middle." He lifted his beer, "Did you see the one where she's got Reese . . ."

Juan snapped out, "MacKay, shut up!"

Brian stared at the beer in front of him. "She'll never forgive me. I promised. I promised her . . ."

Juan shook Brian's shoulder. "It's going to be okay."

Brian shoved off Juan's hand. "NO, IT'S NOT! You don't understand. I promised."

MacKay and the other teammates at the table stared at Brian.

"My uncle, Kyle's dad was killed when he was driving drunk. I promised my Mom I wouldn't drink." With a look of utter anguish Brian said, "I promised her." Brian started to get up from the bench. "I got to get home."

Juan pushed him back down. "Lemme finish my beer then I'll drive you home."

"No," Brian knocked Juan's hand away. "I got to go. If I don't drive my car home, she'll know."

"Brian, you're talking crazy now. That's the beer talking not you. You're not driving home."

With a flash of anger, Brian said, "Juan!" Brian sank his head between his hands. "I promised. God, I promised. She can't find out."

Juan said, "MacKay, give me your phone." As MacKay reached into his pocket to pull out his cell phone, he turned to Brian. "I just got to take a piss. Then I'm going to follow you home. I'll stop at the end of your street. Your mom won't know. Sit here till I get back."

Juan got up from the bench and stood behind Brian. He motioned to MacKay and the others, "Keep him here."

Shit, man. Look at that time." Leroy pretended to study his Rolex wristwatch. "It's almost midnight." He looked at the other Hens hunched over the wooden table. "I got to get my sorry ass home before my bitch falls asleep." He laughed, stood up from the bench and made of show of cupping his groin. "What I got for her ain't going to wait for the morning." The other Hens laughed as Leroy swung his legs over the bench.

"Leroy, you're the man!" shouted Dixon the right fielder.

"Leroy!" shouted a half dozen Hens as they hoisted their mugs.

Leroy paused at the door and looked back into the bar. Brian sat with his elbows on the table, eyes glazed, staring at the half full mug in front of him. Leroy shaped his fingers into a gun and pointed his hand at Brian. "Got'cha!" He burst out laughing. He was still laughing as he pushed his shoulder against the door and strolled out into the night.

Leroy spun the red Spider Ferrari out of the handicapped parking spot. He saw Brian's jeep parked at the rear of the lot.

He shifted into first and the car jetted forward. He pulled into the street and went down half a block. He checked his mirrors then quickly spun the car around. He shut off his headlights and the car silently glided back toward the Dugout. He parked in the shadows. He lifted his tiny cell phone and flipped it between the fingers of his right hand like a deck of cards. His eyes drifted from the Dugout's front door across the lighted parking lot to Brian's Jeep. As the door opened, he saw Brian and Juan. Brian staggered as he fumbled with his front pants' pocket to pull out his car keys. Leroy could hear Juan's voice rising but he couldn't make out the words.

"Brian, Brian," mumbled Leroy. "Where have all the heroes gone?" He watched Brian stumble across the parking lot to his Jeep. He snickered. "Let's see if you're still the golden boy in the morning. See if you make the front page of the paper again tomorrow only this time it'll be a mug shot. You think your fans are still going to chant your name? And how 'bout your dad. Is he going to be proud of you or what?" He flipped open his cell phone between his fingers. "Hey, at least you don't have any endorsements to lose." He laughed, "Look at the bright side, they can't send you back to the minors like they did me." Leroy flipped his phone on and started keying in the numbers. He laughed again. "Where are the police when you need them?"

Brian blocked out Juan's voice as he concentrated on fitting his car key into the door lock. He didn't notice the Taurus pull up and park on the other side of his Jeep. As he felt the hand on his shoulder start to spin him around, Brian brought his hand up to slap Juan's hand away. The hand caught and gripped Brian's hand, quickly followed by a forearm that smashed Brian backwards pinning him against his Jeep. Brian felt the wind knocked from his chest. It took him a moment to realize the angry, twisted face in front of him wasn't Juan's but his father's. The pressure increased on his chest as Brian fought to catch a breath.

"What are you doing?" demanded Kevin. Brian felt the hot breath sear his face. Never in his eighteen years had he ever seen that look in his dad's eyes.

His face turning red, Brian tried to force the words out, "I . . . can't . . ."

"Damn!" Kevin pulled his elbow back from Brian. He smashed his fist on top of Brian's Jeep. Brian staggered forward. He bent over and rested his hands on his knees trying to suck air into his lungs. Kevin shouted, "What the hell are you doing, Brian!"

Juan slowly edged backwards. He looked over his shoulder and saw some of the Hens standing outside the Dugout's door. The Ferrari's headlights caught both figures, Brian hunched over and Kevin rubbing his right fist. The tires squealed as the Ferrari zoomed from the lot. Like a punch, Kevin shot out his left hand and yanked Brian's shirt top. He pulled him upright and shoved him towards his Taurus. He screamed, "Get in the car!"

"What's going on?" asked Kern as he and MacKay raced to Juan followed by a couple of the other Hens.

"It's okay," said Juan. "That's Brian's dad."

MacKay pointed his finger at Kevin yanking Brian to the Taurus. "You call that okay?"

Juan yelled at MacKay. "It's his dad. Just let him handle it."

MacKay screamed. "You called him, didn't you?"

"What were you going to do?" Juan turned and poked MacKay in the chest. "Let him try to drive home like that."

MacKay's right palm pushed Juan away. Kern quickly stepped between Juan and MacKay while shouting, "Enough!"

They turned hearing one car door slam followed by another. The Taurus' headlights came on. They watched the car pull onto Eastgate as a police car pulled into the parking lot. The police car's spotlight drifted over the Hens then locked on Brian's Jeep.

Chapter 34

"After all the talks we've had," Kevin slammed his palm on the dashboard. "Where the hell's your brain at?" In the car it sounded like Kevin was shouting directly into Brian's ear. "You went to Kyle's dad's funeral. You know what can happen."

Brian cringed. He pressed his body against the car door, trying to get as far away from his father as possible. It was the only time he was ever afraid of his father.

All the frustration, all of Kevin's pent up anger against Brian for choosing not to play for the Detroit Tigers and fulfill his dream for him erupted. "Jesus!" Kevin's hand smacking against the dashboard sounded like gunshots in the enclosed car. "What are you going to do? Throw your whole life away?"

Brian lunged forward, his hands on his knees. He knew he was going to throw up. "Stop the car." As his dad ignored him he shouted, "Dad! Stop!"

Kevin steered the car into the parking lot of a strip mall. Brian opened the door and just barely stepped from the car before retching onto the pavement. Kevin stayed behind the wheel watching his son's back spasm as he heaved. The pungent smell of vomit drifted back inside the car. As the spasms subsided Brian turned and anchored himself to the open car door. He rested his head on his forearm. His shaking knees rattled the door. Kevin could hear his son cry, "I screwed up, Dad. I don't know why?" Brian's knees buckled. His hands gripped

219

the top of the door as his body sagged. His head hung down between his arms. "I didn't know what else to do." He sobbed. "I just didn't want you and mom to find out." He hung from the car door.

As he watched Brian slumped against the car door Kevin's only thought was *he's my son*. Kevin opened his car door and walked around the car.

Brian felt his dad's hands under his arms. Kevin said calmly, "Come on, get in the car." Kevin lifted and guided Brian to the car seat.

Kevin shut Brian's door. Brian curled against the door his eyes half closed. He stared vacantly out the front window. Kevin shut his own door, rolled down his window and steered back out to the street.

Kevin drove aimlessly through the side streets of the suburbs. He felt autumn approaching in the air flowing through his open window. He thought, what have I done? The bottom of his right fist throbbed from hitting it against the top of Brian's Jeep. I've spent my life trying to control my temper. Why did I lose it? He glanced over trying to determine if Brian was awake or sleeping. His son's elbow was resting on the door's armrest, his head propped on his palm staring out the side window.

"We're not gods, Brian. We all make mistakes." Kevin heaved a sigh. Brian turned away from the window to look at him. "If you're more frightened of what your mom or I will do if we catch you drinking than you are of drinking and getting behind the wheel of your Jeep, then we're the ones who really screwed up."

"Dad." Brian lifted his hands then let them drop onto his lap. "Everything was spinning. I couldn't think straight. I just wanted to get home."

Kevin stared at Brian and asked, "Everything was spinning, so you were just going to get in your Jeep and drive home?"

Brian whined, "I don't know." He shook his head back and forth, "I'm not lying, Dad, I don't know." An edge of panic crept into his voice, "I couldn't even get the damn key in the lock."

Kevin pulled the car to the side of the road. He jammed the gearshift into park. He turned and faced Brian. "You're going to make mistakes. When I was your age . . . Shit! Brian! I'm still making mistakes." Kevin pointed his hand at Brian. "But there are some mistakes you can't make. You make those mistakes you don't get a second chance."

Brian huddled against the door nodding his head.

"I . . . I shouldn't have yelled." Kevin struggled to put his feelings into words. "I was angry but more than that . . . I was scared, scared that you could have been hurt." Kevin shook his head, "or worse. Being a father, you're always scared. Scared that something you can't control will happen. Scared that you weren't a good enough father, that I didn't give you enough to get through life." Kevin started the car and slowly pulled back into the street.

They sat in a booth by the front windows in Big Boy's Restaurant. Kevin massaged the bottom of his right wrist as he glanced at the menu. He looked up as Brian slid into the booth across from him. Brian had soaked his head in the restroom sink. Water droplets glistened on his short blonde hair. Even at this late hour his light facial hair was more like peach fuzz than a five o'clock shadow. Brian folded his hands on top of the closed menu.

"Do you know what you want?" asked Kevin.

"I'm really not hungry, Dad."

"Get a burger and fries." Kevin closed his menu and slid it across the table. "There are some things I know. The food," Kevin tilted his head towards the kitchen. "The grease will settle your stomach. Wash it down with a Coke. You don't eat, your stomach will churn all night." Kevin waved at the lone waitress behind the counter. "Don't ask me how I know."

Brian sat silently as Kevin ordered two Big Boy platters, a Coke for Brian and a Diet Coke for himself. Brian took the salt and pepper shakers and twirled them between his hands. As Kevin watched the shakers shift back and forth between Brian's hands he thought, never stops, he's always got to be in motion.

Brian's hands froze on the shakers when his cell phone started chirping from his belt. He glanced at his dad then across to the waitress behind the counter. She watched, waiting. He snapped the phone off his belt, flipped it open, then hesitantly brought it to his ear. "Mom?"

Kevin watched the color drain from Brian's face. He couldn't believe how radiantly blue his son's eyes were as they stared imploringly at him from his ashen mask. Kevin lifted his hand and motioned with his fingers, "Give me the phone."

Brian found his voice. "Mom, hold on, Dad wants to talk to you."

"Karen, no, we're fine."

Brian looked down at the table and resumed rotating the salt and pepper shakers.

"I thought you were sleeping," Kevin continued. "Brian called, he . . . he thinks he hit one of our famous potholes on the way to the Dugout." Brian stopped rotating the shakers and looked up at his Dad. "When he was ready to drive home his front tire was flat. He couldn't get the lug nuts off so he called me. I can't get them off either; they're frozen. In fact," Kevin glanced at the purplish swollen bruise on this right hand, "the damn wrench slipped and I smashed my hand. No, it's okay; it's just bruised. We'll wait till morning and call the auto club. I got hungry so we swung over to Big Boy's. We're just sitting." Kevin glanced at Brian. "Talking, waiting for our burgers . . . No, we're fine. You just go to sleep . . . we'll be home later . . . love you, too."

Brian watched as Kevin closed the cell phone. He saw his dad stare at the phone while rubbing his lower lip with his other hand. Kevin met Brian's eyes as he extended the cell phone. As Brian reached for the phone, Kevin said, "It stays at this table." Kevin pointed his index finger at Brian, "You learn from it." He pointed back to himself, "I learn from it." Kevin emphatically tapped his finger against the table, "It stays here." Brian swallowed and took the phone.

The side streets were deserted as Kevin drove home at two in the morning. He rolled up his window against the night's chill air and said, "It all comes down to Monday." Brian glanced over at his dad and waited for him to continue. Kevin shook his head. "One hundred forty-four games spread out over the entire summer and now we're looking at Labor Day and one game. One game for the pennant. Damn. Savor it, Brian. Savor every moment. There are so few times that life gives you more than it takes away."

Kevin steered with one hand as he massaged the back of his neck. "God, I miss the game, Brian. Being on the mound," he laughed more to himself than to Brian. "I was never that good but there were times, when the game was on the line and the ball was in my hands. I'd rub the ball and look across the old Lucas County Stadium at the spectators sitting in the metal bleachers staring at me. Then I'd turn and look at each one of the Hens to see if they were in position, checking with my catcher Hills last. And then it was just the three. Me, the ball and the batter." Kevin lifted his right hand to hold an imaginary ball. "God, I was alive, Brian. That's what you miss, that incredible feeling of being there with the ball in your hands."

The tires hummed along the pavement as streetlights alternately bathed them in light and then darkness. Brian spoke quietly from the shadows. "There's this research they're working on at the university, nanotechnology." Kevin turned and looked at his son. "Part of the study involves a way to kill cancer cells." Brian lifted his hands; they looked like a steeple as he pressed his fingers together. "Watching Grandpa . . ." Brian looked away from his father and stared out the side window. "The way he suffered . . . the way cancer destroyed his body." Brian shook his head trying to drive the image of his grandfather's deathbed away. "I promised him. I don't know if he ever heard me 'cause he never woke up but I promised him that I would try to find a way to destroy what destroyed him."

Kevin saw his son bite his lower lip.

"Baseball's a great game, Dad, but it's just a game."

They both fell silent lost in their own thoughts. Kevin shut the headlights off as he turned into the driveway. He used his remote control to open the garage door. Brian watched him turn off the car. His dad seemed to slump into the car seat.

"You okay, Dad?" asked Brian.

Kevin didn't answer. He just sat there.

"Dad?"

"I'm just tired, Brian. Why don't you head inside? I'm going to sit on the porch for a while."

Brian's hand hovered above the door handle. "Dad . . ."

"I'll be along, Brian."

Brian opened his car door, slid outside then quietly shut the door in the still night.

Kevin waited until his son walked into the house then he slowly walked from the garage to the driveway. He passed by the front door. He shuffled along the front porch. The swing groaned as he sat down heavily. He put his left foot over his right knee then pushed the swing with his right foot. He stared at the empty driveway. He was still sitting there when the sun rose.

Chapter 35

Karen stood under her trees in the front yard. She fingered the brittle leaves dried out from the long heat of August, the leaves starting to burst with color in the cooler, shorter days of September. She glanced down at the dry, barren earth under her feet at the base of her trees. Every year Kevin put down new grass seed. Every spring it sprouted fresh and green and soft under her bare feet. Come August when the heat and the drought combined, the trees sucked all the moisture from the surface. The grass withered, died and was carried away by the wind. "Such a short season," she whispered.

The screech of bicycle tires sent the black birds fluttering from the branches. "Aunt Karen," Kyle yelled from the driveway. He dropped his bike on the pavement, ran up to her and jabbered, "Today's the day, today's the day," while dancing around the base of the tree.

Karen grabbed his shoulders. "You're making me dizzy." Looking into the smiling, beaming face under the green and gold St. John's baseball cap she laughed and hugged Kyle to her chest. "Oh, give me some of your youth, that boundless energy. I need it." She tousled his curly hair behind his ears.

Kyle broke away and looked around the porch expectantly. "Where's Brian?"

"He went to get Ali." Seeing Kyle's look of semi-panic Karen added, "He'll be right back."

"We got to get going."

"I have some chocolate chip cookies inside."

Kyle stuck his hands on his hips and said in his most serious young voice, "Aunt Karen, how can you even think about eating at a time like this." Kyle spun around hearing the Jeep's honk. He skipped to the driveway, grabbed the bike's handle bar and dragged it onto the grass. Racing back to the Jeep he clutched the side door and peered in the open window at Ali. "Today's the day, Ali."

"Your birthday," joked Ali.

"Noooo!" shouted Kyle. He shimmied along the door so he could see Brian behind the steering wheel. "The day we win the pennant!" Kyle stood on his tiptoes and leaned in the window. "Ain't that right, Brian?"

"Gees, Kyle, we lost the last three times we played the Clippers."

"That's 'cause you weren't there. Remember, you stayed home because of your grandpa's funeral. Today's different. You're playing today. Come on, we got to go." Kyle opened the door to climb in the back seat."

"Kyle." Brian laughed. "Hold on, the game doesn't start for three hours. Besides, I've got to get my bat bag."

"I'll get it." Kyle ran up the porch and into the house.

Taking Ali's hand, Brian led her up the sidewalk to the porch. As Ali saw Kyle jump up the steps and race into the house, she laughed while asking, "Are you that excited?"

Brian stopped. He pushed Ali's wavy hair to the side of her face. "Yeah." He laughed. "I am that excited." Brian's fingers lingered on Ali's cheek. "This is the game, Ali. We win. We win the pennant." Brian motioned to the front door. "He's contagious."

"Kyle?"

"Dad always says, the game's played on the field, but especially these last couple of games, when I'm out on the field, I can feel the fans' energy. They're driving me. They want it. They want this pennant and you know what, Ali? They deserve it. Twenty years sitting in those bleachers, cheering and wait-ing. They deserve the pennant."

"Got it." Kyle stood at Brian's upstairs bedroom window lifting Brian's bat bag.

Brian waved.

Ali said, "He's your number one fan."

Brian watched Kyle disappear from the window. "He is the game, Ali. Baseball's a kid's game. For Kyle baseball has noth-ing to do with money, filling seats, contracts, egos, drugs . . . all Kyle sees is the game, just putting the bat on the ball."

Brian glanced at his mother coming out the front door car-rying a cup of coffee. "Where's Dad?"

Karen walked over to the green porch swing. She cocked her head towards the inside of the house. "In front of the TV watching the Weather Channel."

Brian laughed, shook his head then made a show of walk-ing into the yard and pivoting 360 degrees while looking up at the sky. "Sunny and clear and not a cloud in sight. We're not going to lose this game because of a storm."

"You sure?" asked Kevin as he crossed the porch and sat next to Karen. "There's a front moving in from Chicago."

Studying his dad's face, Brian walked onto the porch and stood next to Ali.

Kevin teased, "But the only way it will affect the game is if you guys are still playing at three o'clock tomorrow morning."

Brian exhaled. He sat on one of the green plastic chairs while Ali took the other. Brian reached over and tucked a stray strand of hair behind Ali's ear. His hand flowed down her arm and held her hand.

Brian snapped his fingers. "The tickets. Let me give them to you now before I forget them like last time. Come on, Ali, let's get them."

As Ali followed Brian into the house, Kevin stood and straightened their chairs. He glanced back at his wife. "They've got it pretty bad."

Karen pushed her foot and sent the swing gently swaying. "I can remember another young suitor who had that look in his eyes."

Kevin straightened, leaned against the porch pillar and studied his wife. "You can, huh?"

Holding his gaze Karen said, "He still does."

The screen door slammed as Kyle burst out onto the porch and yelled, "We got to go!"

Not taking his eyes from his wife, Kevin said, "You've got to work on your timing."

Karen threw her head back as laughter sprang from her chest. Lifting her hand she waved Kevin away while laughing, "Go. Go to your game."

Kyle turned as Brian, followed by Ali, came outside. Brian glanced at his mother laughing on the swing. Kyle turned his back to Karen. He stepped in front of Brian and Ali and said in a conspiratorial voice, "Old people are so weird."

Still looking at Karen, Kevin said, "Later."

Karen laughed as she shook her head. As Kevin turned away, Karen caught her breath and called, "Ali."

Ali took a few steps away from Brian, moving closer to Karen.

Karen continued, "Why don't you stay with me. Unless you want to go and sit in the bleachers and bake for an extra couple hours."

"I'd like that."

"Good," replied Karen. "We've got a lot to talk about."

"Mom," Brian cut in. "You're not going to be late."

Smiling, Karen chided, "When have I ever been late?"

Kevin glanced at Karen and threw his hands up. As he stalked off the porch he said, "I'm out of here."

"Mom," said Brian his voice rising on the last "m".

"Brian, Ali and I will be there to see you take batting practice."

Brian didn't respond, just kept staring at his mom.

"Promise." Karen's finger traced a cross on her chest.

Kyle picked up the bat bag at Brian's feet. "We got to go!" He leaned to one side, the bag bouncing off his knee as he wobbled to the porch step.

"I'll get that, Kyle."

Kyle looked over his shoulder. "No, Brian, you save it for the game." Not looking, he tripped going down the step. He barely managed to catch his balance before his feet hit the sidewalk. The bag swung out, then back and banged against his leg. He let out an involuntary, "Ouch," then limped to Kevin's car.

Brian glanced at the car backing out of the garage then back to his mom. "Batting practice."

"I won't be late, Brian. I promise."

Brian turned, raced down the steps then stopped. As if pulled back by a magnet, he jumped up the steps to Ali. He kissed her lips and gave her a quick hug. He turned and threw his arms around his mother.

Surprised by the sudden display of emotion, Karen just held her son. When he slowly pulled away she said, "We'll be there."

Chapter 36

"The party's going to be at Stanley's house," Kyle said excitedly from the back seat of the Taurus as they drove to Hens stadium. "Stanley said his dad is ordering ten, extra large pizzas from Marco's. Food is not a problem." Kyle leaned as far forward as his seatbelt would allow. "I'm bringing the pop. Don't worry, Brian. I've already got a twelve pack of Mountain Dew with your name on it. No one touches it but you." Kyle continued picking up steam, "Chris' older sister Nicole is making six dozen chocolate chip cookies. I told Chris I don't like nuts. He said Nicole would make two dozen with no nuts . . . ."

Brian swiveled in the front seat. He glanced from Kyle to his dad. "I was never like that."

Kevin laughed, "You were worse."

"No way." Brian shook his head.

"Hey, Kyle." Kevin met Kyle's stare in his rear view mirror. "We need to talk strategy."

"Right, Coach." Kyle pantomimed taking his finger and zipping his lips closed.

Kevin looked back to the road. "They'll probably start Audette." Kevin shook his head back and forth. "He's not the problem. You've been hitting him all year. When he misses, he misses high. His fastball is really all he's got. He can't get his curve ball to break over the plate. You know he's going to come at you; you know he'll use his fastball and it'll probably be up in the strike zone. Just pull the trigger."

Kevin checked his side view mirror, flicked his turn signal then passed a slower car. "Wilson's the problem. He's their ace relief pitcher right now. He's tough. The Yankees sent him down to the minors when he pulled a groin muscle. He's back. I'd say he's one hundred per cent. The guy led the majors in saves last year. If the Clippers had clinched the pennant, he'd be in a New York uniform right now." Kevin glanced over at Brian. "Don't kid yourself, Brian, the Yankees kept him down here for this game. The Yankees want this pennant for their farm team."

As they stopped at a red light, Kevin took off his sunglasses. He bit on the stem while staring at the new stadium nestled in the old warehouse district. "I can't get a handle on Wilson. The Clippers brought him in for all three games when they swept the Hens down in Columbus. He shut them down. In the final game he came in with the bases loaded and no outs. Struck out the side."

The light turned green. Kevin slipped his sunglasses back on and made a right turn. He shrugged his shoulders. "We weren't there. We were home for Marty's funeral. I've never seen Wilson up close. I've caught him on TV, but it's just not the same. He's dominating. His fastball is probably the best in the majors." Kevin waved his arm. "He'll blow you away. You got to start swinging soon as it leaves his hand." Kevin snapped his fingers. "Then he'll slip in his change up. I've seen batters twist like tops falling for his change up."

Kevin parked in Brian's reserved stadium spot. He put his arm on the back of the front seat and looked at Brian. "Any pitcher can throw a change-up." He glanced at his nephew in the back seat. "Right, Kyle?"

Smiling, Kyle nodded.

"Wilson's change up is devastating because he knows when to throw it."

Kyle's eyes darted back and forth from Brian's face to Kevin's profile.

Kevin finished, "I'll see what I can pick up." They both opened their car doors as Kyle jerked his backdoor open and sprang from the back seat. Kevin opened the trunk and Kyle reached in to lift out Brian's bat bag.

"Kyle, I'll . . ." Brian started but stopped as he caught the look from his dad that seemed to say, "no, let him get it."

Kevin helped Kyle lift Brian's bag from the trunk. "I'll catch up with you guys inside."

Kyle hefted the strap up covering one of his small, bony shoulders. He looked at Brian. "What were you saying, Brian?"

"Nothing, come on."

Kyle wobbled like a duck with the bag hanging from one shoulder. He looked at Brian as the bag bounced off his right leg. "You know, Brian, I can't stay. I promised the guys I'd sit with them with the tickets you got."

"That's cool, Kyle."

A look of sheer wonder on his face, Kyle asked, "You know where we're sitting?"

Brian laughed. "I bought the tickets."

Kyle spun in a circle almost knocking Brian's leg as the bat bag swung out from his arm. He shouted, "I can't believe we're sitting in "The Roost."

Kyle lurched to a stop just before the gates leading into the stadium. "Wait." He reached into his front pocket and pulled out an unopened packet of sunflower seeds. "For the game, Brian." As Brian took the seeds Kyle looked confidently at him. "We're going to win right, Brian?"

The way Kyle looked up at him, his boyish face so full of determination made Brian feel as if he could do anything. Brian ruffled Kyle's curly hair sticking out from under his baseball cap. "Yeah. We're going to win, Kyle." Brian put his hand on Kyle's shoulder and together they walked into the stadium.

Karen didn't have to look at the baseball field to know where Brian was; all she had to do was follow Ali's eyes. To be so in love, she thought. It wasn't the words that gave you away but the way you looked at someone. What were they going to do, she wondered? Brian said Ali's going with him to UW.

Sensing Karen's eyes on her, Ali turned and smiled.

Karen noticed the slight flush of sunburn on Ali's freckled cheeks. "You bring any sun block?"

Ali shook her head.

Karen rooted around in her purse for her sun block. "Here."

"Thanks."

"Do you ever tan?"

"No." Ali smiled. "But I burn and peel very well."

Karen laughed as she observed Ali gaze at Brian who was crossing the infield towards them. Brian stopped at the rail separating the seats from the field. He waved his mitt at the aisles filled with spectators streaming to their seats. "See, Mom, you didn't have to fight the traffic."

"Right," said Karen sarcastically. She looked at her watch, "And only another hour in the sun before the game starts."

Brian cocked his head to the wall behind their bleachers. "Sun's going down. You'll be in the shade in another fifteen minutes. He pointed across the field to "The Roost." "Now Kyle and his buddies," Brian laughed, "will be in the sun for a lot longer than that."

"Brian!"

Brian looked up as a fan called his name. He waved. He could hear his name pass through the box seat section. Some of the fans especially the kids got up from their seats and moved down the aisle coming closer to him. A few more fans shouted his name. He looked back at Ali and raising his eyebrows joked, "Don't be jealous." The fans edged closer. "I better go."

"Wait." Ali reached behind her head and pulled the scrunchie from her hair. Her red, wavy golden hair cascaded down upon her shoulders. "Give me your hand, Brian."

Brian extended his right hand over the rail. Ali spread the dark green elastic scrunchie apart and slipped it over his hand.

She released the scrunchie and it tightened like a sweatband around Brian's wrist.

"Wearing your lady's colors," said Karen.

Brian looked at his mother without a clue to what she meant.

"For luck, Brian," Ali said.

Looking at Ali, he backed away from the bleachers, smiled, then jogged to the dugout.

Ali's eyes follow Brian as he drifted away. Karen wondered what their life will be like? Is love enough? She looked across the field to the lone figure by the fence. Would she have followed Kevin?

"Now remember, guys, we wait till the third inning for popcorn and the sixth inning for hot dogs, except for Chris who wants a brat instead," said Kyle while standing at the rail of "The Roost" in the upper deck of the right field corner of the stadium. His St. John's teammates surrounded him. All the boys wore their St. John's uniform jerseys with Hens 'Pennant' baseball caps a gift Red's sister surprised them with before the game. Kyle continued, "We've got plenty of money left over from our car wash so if we want, we can start the game with peanuts and pop."

"What about programs?" asked Stanley. "We've got to have souvenir programs."

Kyle winked at Red. He motioned his teammates to gather in a tight circle. Red pulled a program out of his back pocket and showed it to the team. "We got one just so we know who's on the other team." Kyle eyed each face in the circle. "Brian bought fourteen from Red's sister before the game. He's got 'em down in the locker room. He's going have all the Hens sign 'em for us."

"No way," screeched Josh.

Red said, "I was there when Brian picked them up."

"Wow! Autographed by the whole team. Man, oh, man,"

whistled Stanley. "My brother James is going to be sooo jealous." He lifted his right hand and slapped Kyle's hand.

Coach Bruno stood at the head of the dugout and looked at his team. He rolled his ever-present toothpick from one side of his mouth to the other with his tongue. The bushy hair from his mustache concealed his upper lip. He lifted his Hens cap and scratched his balding forehead.

"Five minutes, Coach," said assistant coach Toby.

Coach Bruno planted his cap back on his head. He rocked on his heels, looked from the dugout to the stadium then back to his team. The Hens sat on the benches or stood staring at their coach, waiting. Coach Bruno finally started, "If you're waiting for a Knute Rockne speech, you're not going to get it." He shook his head. "I ain't that type of coach. You know what this game means. Now, let's go play ball."

The players filed past Coach Bruno to the diamond. Brian waited with Juan as Juan finished strapping on his catcher's gear. When Leroy brushed past, Coach Bruno held up his hand, "Hold on a second, Leroy." Leroy waited as other players walked around him.

"I'm making you DH today," Coach Bruno said.

"I'm not playing center?"

"Russell's been hot at the plate lately and he covers a lot of ground in centerfield."

"You saying I don't?"

"No, I'm saying Russell covers a lot of ground in center field." Coach Bruno stared up into Leroy's coal black eyes. "I need your bat in the lineup, Leroy."

Leroy turned away from Coach Bruno and looked out to the stands. "Shit, man," he mumbled. He turned back, "Whatever."

It felt like just another game until Brian's foot crossed the top step of the dugout. The boisterous crowd in the standing room only stadium was decked out in Hens colors. They were on their feet cheering the Hens lined up on the third base side of the diamond. Brian remembered the first time he walked onto the field as a Hens. On that day the stadium was not even half full. As he stood in line next to Juan and the other Hens, he took off his cap and placed it across his heart. He was dwarfed by his feelings. He glanced left and right to the players who had shared this incandescent summer. He felt a twinge grip his heart as he knew this day would pass and never return.

Looking across the stadium, as the crowd grew silent for the National Anthem, he felt the energy. They were always there, the fans, always the background. Baseball for him was just a game he played. Throughout his life there had always been fans watching, but not until this summer did he realize that baseball was as much their game as his own. He shivered as the feelings of ten thousand fans passed through him.

Juan's elbow nudging his arm caused Brian to look down. He saw the goosebumps covering his forearm. He rolled his eyes at Juan, shrugged his shoulders and gave a look that said, nothing new.

Juan reached down and tugged the green scrunchie on Brian's wrist. "What's that? You hurt your wrist?"

"It's Ali's," Brian smiled. "For luck."

"Where's mine?" asked Juan. "I need luck, too, you know."

Brian looked at Juan. Without thinking he reached under his jersey and lifted off his silver chain. The St. Christopher medal dangled in the sunlight. He swung the chain towards Juan.

Studying the medal hanging on the chain Juan said, "No way."

Brian said, "Juan," and just looked at him.

Juan took the chain and slipped it over his bare head as the National Anthem started.

Kevin stood at attention by the fence listening to the final notes of the National Anthem. He glanced up to "The Roost."

He could barely make out Kyle and his young teammates gazing skyward, as the air was rent by the shriek of F-16's thundering over the stadium. The jets from the Northwest Ohio Air National Guard crossed the sky like silver bullets then zoomed back. Glancing across the field, he saw Karen and Ali in their front row seats. As he followed their eyes to his son standing with the other players on the third base line by the Hens dugout, he whispered, "God, I wish I was out there with them."

Chapter 37

Brian tapped the fat end of his bat against his helmet in his unconscious ritual as he stood next to the batter's box. He yanked up his batting gloves. The top of his right glove touched the edge of Ali's green scrunchie. He rubbed the scrunchie with his left index finger the same way he would rub his finger along Ali's wrist. Stepping into the box, he dug his feet into the gravel and lifted the bat, high and back, above his right shoulder. As he looked out, it was like looking at an unfocused picture only the pitcher stood out, starkly. Everything else was unfocused, blurred. He watched the pitcher's arm come up, the release of the ball and the rotations of the stitches. He swung driving his hips and weight through the ball.

Soon as he rounded first Brian spotted the centerfielder racing after the ball far back on the warning track. The center fielder snatched up the ball then set his feet to make the throw. In that split second Brian saw what he needed. He knew the throw would go to the second baseman and not to third. Like an F-16 pulling out of a steep bank, Brian's toes brushed second base then accelerated for third. The second baseman waited for the throw as Brian's toes dug towards third. Catching the centerfielder's throw the second baseman pivoted. He didn't care if he hit Brian; he threw the ball hard towards third.

The third base coach frantically waved his hands down. Brian slid with his left foot tucked under his right knee, his right toes streaking towards the base. He felt his toes jam into third base as the ball whooshed above his head into the mitt.

Brian instinctively rolled to his side and signaled "time" to the umpire. Lying on the ground, he tried to catch his breath as his pounding heart sought to return to its natural rhythm. He couldn't help smiling as he heard the crowd roar. He slowly stood and brushed dust from his pants.

Kevin grinned and shook his head. Every time the pitcher, Audette would get set to go into his windup, Brian would lead off from third base daring Audette to try and pick him off. Audette had no choice but to throw over to third to try to keep Brian from getting to big of a lead off. As a pitcher, Kevin knew the last thing you wanted was a player who could steal at will on base. Most pitchers couldn't concentrate on the base runner and the batter at the same time.

Kevin glanced at Russell in the batter's box. He thought Coach Bruno still had some tricks up his sleeve, putting Russell in Leroy Brown's spot and making Leroy the designated hitter. Going for speed today, Coach, play a lot of hit and run. Maybe that's the way to beat these Clippers. You don't lose much by having Brown bat last with Brian coming up behind him as the lead off hitter. They're not going to be able to pitch around Leroy.

Completely flustered, Audette gave up on Brian and threw to the batter. Russell swung and popped the ball over the second baseman's head in the gap of centerfield. Brian clapped his hands as he jogged down the third baseline towards home.

"Come on, Juan!" Brian shouted from the dugout's rail.

Juan set the top edge of the bat against home plate. He made a quick sign of the cross then touched the medal under his shirt. Audette checked the runners on first and second then hurled his fastball towards the inside corner of the plate. All with his wrists, Juan snapped the bat. The ball darted just out of the grasp of the diving third baseman. Brian laughed watching Juan run towards first. MacKay's right, Brian thought, Juan runs like a duck. Russell crossed the plate quickly followed by Kern. Juan rapidly waddled towards second. He saw the throw from the left fielder, and dove head first to the bag. As the dust settled and the umpire flashed the safe sign, Juan pushed up from the ground and stood on the base. He looked to the dugout where Brian and his Hens teammates were on their feet cheering and hooting with laughter. Juan took off his cap and smacked dust from the front of his uniform ignoring the trickle of blood from the scrape on his chin from the gravel.

Brian nudged Parker standing next to him by the dugout rail, "Look at that smile on Juan's face."

In "The Roost" Chris flipped popcorn in the air, stuck his tongue out and tried to catch the kernels in his mouth. The missed kernels crunched under his sneakers as he weaved back and forth. A gust of wind blew one of the kernels towards the rail. Chris lurched and bounced into Kyle.

"Chris, watch what you're doing," shouted Kyle as he just managed to keep his Coke in a large Hens cup from spilling all over his clothes.

"Sorry, Kyle," laughed Chris. He tapped Kyle on the shoulder, "Hey lighten up. Look." He pointed to the scoreboard. "We're up by six going into the fourth inning."

Looking at the flags flying over the stadium, Kyle shook his head. He watched the flags flutter and snap as the wind shifted off Lake Erie.

Ali shuddered. She rubbed the palms of her hands rapidly on her forearms.

"Cold?" asked Karen.

Ali nodded as she watched Brian jog across the field to second base.

"I bet 'cha the temperature dropped ten degrees in the last ten minutes," said Karen as she reached into her tote bag. "The wind's coming off the lake now." She pulled out of the bag a green sweatshirt embroidered with gold letters that proclaimed, *I'm a St. Patrick's Mom* and handed it to Ali.

"No, Karen, you wear it."

"Don't worry I've got another one." Like a magician Karen pulled out and displayed a gold sweatshirt embroidered with green letters that said, *I'm a St. John's Mom.*

Ali did a double take as she looked from one sweatshirt to the other.

Karen looked at Ali. "What? You don't have these sweatshirts at McCauley?"

Ali laughed and sputtered, "Blue and Gold."

"Catholics," said Karen, "You got to love 'em. Practical yes, original no." Karen held the green sweatshirt by Ali's face. "Wait, let's see." She dropped the green sweatshirt and held up the gold. "With your hair, definitely green."

Kevin watched the flags snap in one direction, flutter, then snap another way. He looked into the stairwell and watched an empty paper cup spin like it was caught in a mini tornado. Looking at the lengthening shadows on the field then to the stadium lights slowly coming up, he wished he could ease the pressure in his chest. Up by six runs but he couldn't relax. He'd been in too many games with the Hens where he saw a big lead crumble in the middle innings. He stared down into the Clippers bullpen. Wilson had finished stretching and now was casually tossing a ball back and forth with a catcher. Kevin looked to Brian, poised in his defensive stance, as MacKay hurled the first ball of the fourth inning.

"Come on, MacKay concentrate," Kevin shouted as the pitcher walked the second batter in a row. He eyed Kimmet, the Clippers clean up hitter poised at the plate. "Damn it!" Kevin slapped the top of the fence as the ball took flight. "That one hit, MacKay, is going to cost you three runs."

MacKay was rubbing the new ball so hard that the stitches felt like sandpaper scraping against his skin. He tried to avoid Coach Bruno's stare from the top step of the dugout.

Brian and Juan stood next to MacKay on the mound. "Wind took it," said Brian. "It's swirling in from the lake."

"It wasn't a bad pitch, MacKay," added Juan. "The guy can hit."

"We're still up by three," Brian said. "Let's just get this next batter."

"Damn wind," muttered MacKay as a gust kicked up dust in the infield.

"Don't look for a sign," said Juan. "All I want is your fastball. Just look for my glove."

Brian studied Audette's delivery as the pitcher took his final warm up throws. He settled in the batter's box and checked the infield. They were playing him deep in the pockets expecting him to pull the ball. Brian laughed. It was almost like his dad was standing behind him. He could hear Kevin say, "Take what they give you." As Audette went into his wind-up and hurled the ball, Brian pivoted and brought the bat up across his body. He was gone before the bunt hit the ground. By the time Audette reacted, the catcher had already flung off his mask and scurried forward on his hands and knees. He snatched the ball and looked to the first baseman. He flopped back on his feet, kneeled on the ground, the ball clenched in his fist as Brian grinned from first base.

"Brian! Brian! Brian!" The chant started in the upper decks then grew in volume as it spread contagiously through the stadium. The pitcher Audette kept pulling out the ball and tossing it back into his mitt while he watched the fans stand and sway with the chant. He eyed Brian standing nonchalantly on the bag at first. As Audette turned his back, Brian edged off from the bag. Audette made the perfunctory throw to first. Brian skipped back to the bag then felt the first baseman's mitt brush his leg. Audette caught the ball from the first baseman and with a shrug that seemed to say *the hell with it*, turned his back to Brian and faced Kern.

Edging into his crouch by first base and staring at the pitcher's back, Brian thought, God, it's not even going to be a challenge. He was off with the pitch. Kern swung and missed at the high curve ball. Brian easily slid into second. He called time to dust off himself. Audette refused to look at Brian as he caught the throw from the second baseman. The pitcher seemed to shrink into his uniform as the crowd roared.

Kern took the sign from the third base coach. He got the fat of the bat just where he wanted it on the ball. As the hard bunt squiggled down the third base line, the third baseman had no choice but to go after it. By the time the third baseman got his bare hand on the ball, he could make no play at either first or third.

Russell ripped the inside fastball. The second baseman jumped and gloved the line drive. Kern was halfway to second base. As he tried to change his momentum, the second baseman wheeled and threw the ball to first base to complete the double play and end the inning. Kern slipped on the base path. He looked up at the first baseman holding the ball and pounded his fist into the dirt.

Brian waited by third base for Kern to get up and cross the infield. He caught up with Kern who looked dejectedly at the ground. Brian lightly smacked Kern's shoulder. "Hey, there was nothing you could do. The second baseman made a hell of a play." When Kern wouldn't respond Brian tugged his shoulder. "Hey, come on, we need you. Get back in the game." Kern looked up and nodded.

"Pull him!" Kevin pushed away from the fence. He jammed his hands into his back pockets and paced glancing from the pitcher's mound to the dugout. There were Clippers runners on first and second with one out. MacKay threw another high pitch for a ball. "What are you waiting for Coach, yank him!" MacKay walked the batter to load the bases. As Coach Bruno walked to the mound he tapped his left hand.

"You should have pulled him two batters ago. You're bringing the lefty Wojciechowski in *now* with the bases loaded. You're putting too much pressure on the Wojo. He's just a kid. This is for the pennant for Christ sake."

Kevin clenched his hands jammed in his back pockets into fists as Wojo's threw four pitches that weren't even close to the strike zone. The Clippers runner jogged across home plate then high-fived his teammates standing at the rail of the visitors' dugout.

"Damn son of a bitch." Kevin kicked the fence. Another Clipper jogged home. Kevin glared at the scoreboard as it changed to Hens six Clippers five.

Brian walked to the pitchers mound from one side of the diamond, Juan from the other. As Brian approached Wojo, he could see the ball shaking in Wojo's hand inside his glove.

Wojo looked up at the scoreboard then at the fans sitting or standing eerily silent in the bleachers like a jury waiting to pass judgment. Brian followed Wojo's gaze to the fans then to the scoreboard. Looking at Wojo's face, he knew the young pitcher was scared to death.

"They're not there," said Brian.

Wojo looked away from the fans to Brian. He clenched the glove next to his chest to stop the shaking.

"The game's here on the field." Brian pointed at the batter. It's just you and him. That's all."

Coach Bruno forced his way into the huddle. "You hurt, Wojo?"

"No," Wojo said hesitantly. "No, Coach."

With his index finger, Coach Bruno poked Wojo in the chest. "Then put the damn ball over the plate!"

Anger flashed across Wojo's face. He pulled the ball from his mitt, his knuckles turning white from gripping the ball so tight.

Coach Bruno turned and stormed off the mound as Brian and Juan backed away.

Parker charged from third base. He scooped the ball up between hops and fired it to Juan who was standing on home plate. Juan shouted "Down Wojo!" The pitcher dropped to the ground. Brian jumped and caught the high throw from Juan. His foot landed on second base. When the Clippers runner slid into second Brian was already jogging to the dugout after completing the double play.

Kevin released his breath, pushed his cap up and leaned against the fence.

"Hot dog time," cried Stanley. He stood and waved his arms at one of the roving vendors. How many should we get, Kyle?"

"I . . . don't know. I'm not really hungry right now," Kyle said as he crossed his arms against his stomach and leaned forward in his seat. He stared at the scoreboard willing the numbers to change.

"Me either," said Red

Chris asked, "Why don't we wait till after this inning?"

"What's the matter with you guys," whined Stanley. "We're winning this game."

"By one run," snapped Red.

"And Wojo's pitching." Kyle shook his head back and forth forlornly as he watched Wojo toss his warm up throws. On the other side of the field he saw Wilson warming up by the visiting teams' dugout. "And they're going to bring in Wilson." As his eyes pivoted between the two pitchers, Kyle rubbed his stomach and mumbled, "Gees, I got to go to the bathroom." He pushed his way through his friends and raced up the aisle hearing Stanley shout, "But we've got Brian."

Brian stood in the on-deck circle. He couldn't help thinking that at one time the Hens were up by six, now only by one. As he watched Wilson warm up, he flashed back to his try-out with the Hens. He remembered facing the pitcher, Tim "The Cannon" Lipinski. He remembered how long it took to pick up the rotations, how many swings he took before he could just make contact with the ball. Man, this guy throws faster. Stretching the bat over his shoulder, Brian searched for his father. He must have moved. He couldn't see him anywhere. Brian looked back to the pitcher. He tried to gauge Wilson's fastball but the angle was wrong.

"Strike three!" screamed the umpire.

Brian flipped his bat and tapped the rim against his batting helmet. He stretched his batting gloves on his wrists and rubbed Ali's green scrunchie. A scowl on his face, Leroy barged passed him without a word. As Brian walked to the batter's box, he heard Leroy's bat and then his helmet crash against the wall in the Hens dugout.

Wilson seemed to ignore the batter coming to the plate. He kicked at the dirt in front of the pitching rubber trying to notch an indentation for his heel. With his right hand he took off his hat, rubbed his brown hair back from his forehead, then planted the cap with the visor's band digging into his skin. He put his right foot on the rubber, leaned out over his left foot and gazed past Brian to the catcher to check the sign for the next pitch. He shook off the first sign then nodded for the second. He rubbed his right hand along his thigh, touched the brim of his cap, lifted his glove in front of his chest, fingered the stitches on the league ball and then, in one fluid movement, went into his wind-up and hurled the ball.

Watching the pitcher go through his ritual, Brian thought, this guy's all business. As Wilson got set to go into his windup, the image of Lipinski blurred into the image of Wilson. Brian felt a moment of panic as the feeling returned that he couldn't hit this guy. Brian quickly raised his hand and called time. He backed out of the batter's box as the ball thumped into the catcher's mitt. Walking away from the plate, Brian pretended dust had blown into his eye. He knew he wasn't the same kid who faced Lipinski. He could hit any pitcher. It's simply a matter of picking up the rotations. Concentrate. See the ball. Brian walked back to the batter's box. He twisted his fists around the bat's handle as he lifted it up behind his shoulder.

Wilson made him wait. His back turned to Brian, he rubbed the ball between his hands. Finally he faced Brian, nodded to the signal from his catcher and went into his windup.

Only the ball, Brian would see nothing else. Brian picked up the rotations as the ball left Wilson's hand. He swung, a fraction of a fraction of a second too late.

Like a jack-in-the-box Kyle sprang up on the rail. He followed the flight of the ball over the skyline of the stadium. He lost the ball in the artificial lights then found it as the wind pushed the ball foul over the fence. "No!" he screamed as he pounded his hand on the rail. He looked at the swirling clouds and shook his fist at the sky. "You stupid wind! Whose side are you on anyways?"

Wilson lifted his cap and scratched the back of his head as he watched the ball drift foul. He shrugged his shoulders, set the cap back on his head and peered forward to take the next sign from his catcher.

Brian slowly walked back from first base. As always he was gone as soon as the bat touched the ball. He picked up the bat, flipped it and tapped the rim against his helmet. He stretched his gloves, rubbed Ali's green scrunchie, brought the bat back high behind his shoulder and waited on Wilson. Brian knew he was smiling at the pitcher, but he didn't care. He felt he could hit this guy. He didn't care what he threw. He could hit him.

In flight from Wilson's hand, he saw the ball drift just enough that it would fall out of the strike zone. He stepped back out of the batter's box. He looked to the scoreboard, then at Wilson's face, then back to the scoreboard. Always moving his eyes until he was ready to concentrate on the ball coming from Wilson's hand. He planted his feet. He swung.

Kevin pressed against the fence. He came up on his toes. "Come on, come on, don't drift, come on!" As if someone had just pulled the release valve on a hot air balloon the collective air whooshed out of the stadium. Kevin sank back down to his heels. He watched Brian stroll back from first. "Come on, Brian. You've got to be faster than that. You've got to start your swing before the ball leaves his hand. If you don't he'll keep you fouling them off all day."

Brian shifted the gravel under his cleats. He brought the bat back, once again, and tucked his chin down by his left shoulder. Wilson rubbed his right hand along his thigh touched the brim of his hat then lifted the glove in front of his chest. The rotations of the ball spun downwards. Brian stood immobile taking the called ball below his knees. He stayed in the batter's box; the bat poised above his shoulder as the pitcher repeated his ritual. Brian knew it was a strike and at the same second knew he couldn't drive it. He chopped down with the bat. The ball sliced off the top of the bat and careened high in the air behind the catcher, out of play.

Wilson stepped off the pitcher's rubber. He turned his back to Brian, took his mitt off and slipped it under his left armpit. Rubbing the ball between his hands, he stared vacantly at the grass in centerfield.

Brian stepped out of the batter's box. He glanced at Wilson then swung around and searched for the figure by the fence. Brian exhaled and smiled as he met his dad's eyes. He swung the bat lazily a couple of times then stepped back into the box.

Brian watched Wilson's ritual, rub the thigh, touch the brim of the hat, mitt in front of the chest. As the ball hurtled towards him it seemed to take forever to get the bat around. Clank! The ball bounced off the wall, well to the right of first base.

Brian backed out of the box. Holding the bat between his legs, he made stretching circles with his left then his right hand. He yanked his gloves taut. As he walked back into the box, Wilson stepped away from the rubber. Brian waited. He let the end of his bat rest on home plate. When Wilson stepped back on the rubber, Brian lifted his bat.

He saw the ball snap forward from Wilson's fingers. He flicked his wrists. The ball torpedoed from the end of his bat. It sent up a geyser of dust on the wrong side of third base. Brian rounded first and watched the left fielder jog to the outfield corner to retrieve the foul ball.

As he picked up the bat, his heart rate slowed back to normal. Brian held the bat out in front then tapped the end against home plate. He waited for Wilson to acknowledge him, but he wouldn't. It seemed like Wilson was looking right through him to his catcher. Brian knew this was the best pitcher he faced. He tried to convey his feelings by the look on his face, to say, "Hey, you're good. I'll give you that. But I'm good, too. I'm here. Come on, let's play ball."

Focusing on Wilson, Brian watched the ritual, rub his thigh, touch the brim of his hat, wipe the sweat from his upper lip with the back of his wrist then bring the mitt in front of his chest, the hand comes up, the fingers open, the ball's spinning. Brian swung. Standing at the plate he was shocked when he heard the ball smack into the catcher's mitt. How could he have completely missed it? He glanced back as the catcher tossed the ball down by his feet. Brian searched for Wilson on the pitcher's mound, but he was already gone, jogging to the dugout.

"Shit! He got Brian with his change-up." Kevin replayed Wilson's last five pitches. It was there. He knew it was there, something that he saw, some quirk. All pitchers had them. Most didn't even realize their quirks until a good pitching coach pointed them out. Kevin remembered his days with the Hens. For a while it seemed every opposing batter knew before

Kevin did when he was going to throw his curve ball. The pitching coach McClain filmed him. They poured over the film together and, sure enough, every time he went to throw a curve ball he would rub his thumb over his middle and index fingers before he placed his hand into his glove to take the ball. Kevin found himself unconsciously rubbing his thumb over those two fingers. McClain never could get him to break the habit, that's why Kevin always kept his hand hidden by his glove. As the next batter came into the box, Kevin intently studied Wilson.

Brian turned and watched the ball sail over the left field wall. The Clippers' outfielder, Kimmet quickly jogged around the bases after hitting his second home run and tying the game at six. Coach Bruno sprang from the dugout tapping his right arm. Brian and Juan approached the pitcher's mound. Brian hoped his face didn't look like Juan's. They both knew the Hens had blown a six run lead and the momentum now was all with the Clippers.

Coach Bruno took the ball from Wojo, patted him on the back and sent him to the dugout. As he watched his lanky black relief pitcher, Gibson, walk from the bullpen he said without smiling, "Looks like we got ourselves a new ballgame."

After falling behind in the count Gibson threw three straight strikes. Juan just managed to snag a pop-up behind the plate for the second out. Brian dived knocking down a line drive halfway between first and second. Scrambling to his feet, he waved away the first baseman then easily outraced the batter to first base for the third out. As he made his turn by the visitor's dugout he saw it out of the corner of his eye. It was so out of place, probably the only one in the whole stadium, the cowboy hat. Slowly he walked back to the bleachers. He nodded to Tim O'Connell then looked at Bobby. He tried to make his lips smile as his eyes took in the gaunt pale young boy. Bobby still had the same Hens cap on. He reminded Brian so much of his grandfather.

Bobby said, "I thought you had it, Brian. I thought you had that home run."

Brian stood there not knowing what to say. He looked down at the ball still in his glove. He took the ball and held it out to Bobby.

The small hand clenched the ball. As the boy's smile spread from his eyes to his mouth, Brian covered Bobby's hand with his. Brian eased back from the rail remembering his grandpa's words, "You'll be carrying a lot of kids' dreams out there, Brian. Don't let them down." Jogging to the dugout Brian thought, but what are Bobby's dreams?

Between pitches Kevin glanced at the scoreboard. Bottom of the eighth the game tied at six. Wilson struck out the first Hens batter of the inning. He had a two balls one-strike count on the third baseman Parker. Kevin rubbed the back of his neck trying to ease the tension creeping up his spine. Parker missed Wilson's fastball. Kevin's eyes hurt from staring so intently at Wilson. He tried to take apart every aspect of Wilson's windup and delivery. Parker stood there and took the called third strike.

Brian leaned against the dugout rail. Juan walked to the batter's box as Parker, looking at the ground and mumbling to himself, walked back to the dugout. Glancing around the somber stadium, Brian thought these aren't the same fans that were dancing in the aisles in the third inning. Brian felt like shouting, "It's just a Game!"

Juan swung before the ball left Wilson's hand. Kevin saw the quick smirk on Wilson's face as he caught the ball from his catcher. Kevin focused solely on Wilson. The pitched rubbed his right hand along his thigh, touched the brim of his cap, wiped the sweat from his upper lip with the back of his wrist then brought the mitt in front of his chest. Juan almost fell to the ground missing the change-up. Kevin looked down as he rubbed his fingers against his right temple, his mind replaying Wilson's last delivery. He snapped his eyes to Wilson. The pitcher started his windup. Juan swung late behind Wilson's streaking fastball for the third strike. Kevin pushed off from the fence. "Got 'cha." He ran towards the Hens dugout.

Kevin shouted, "Brian!" to stop his son before he ran onto the field for the start of the ninth inning.

Brian hesitated and turned back to the dugout. He saw his father quickly waving his hand motioning him over to the Hens on deck circle. Now what's he want, thought Brian as he walked over to his dad.

"Wilson." Kevin waited until Brian looked at his face then wiped the back of his wrist over his upper lip.

Brian just stared then finally said with a touch of annoyance in his voice. "What, Dad?"

"The change up. He telegraphs it. That's what he does."

"Wilson?"

"Just before he throws it." Kevin again flicked the back of his right wrist over his upper lip.

"You sure?"

"Bet on it."

"Brian!" Juan shouted then pointed to the empty spot by second base.

Brian looked at his teammates already on the field. He turned back to his dad. "You're sure?"

As Kevin nodded, a smile spread across Brian's face. Brian jogged to second base glancing at Wilson who was wearing a Clippers warm up jacket standing with his arms folded over his chest at the end of the visiting teams' dugout. Gees, if he does telegraph his pitch.

The Hens pitcher Gibson did a double take as Brian jogged past. He couldn't believe that Brian was smiling.

The Clippers leadoff batter hit a line drive just off the shortstop's glove. Brian covered second base holding the runner at first. He smacked his glove against his thigh as he told himself, get in the game. Forget about Wilson. We've got to get through this half inning first.

"NO!" Kevin shouted as the Clippers batter connected with a hanging curve ball. As soon as the bat made contact with the ball, the Hens centerfielder was racing back to the outfield fence. Russell timed his jump and just caught the ball with the top of his mitt. He quickly fired the ball to Brian on second holding the lead off runner on first base.

Kevin opened his hands that had a vice grip on the fence. He started pacing, his eyes shifting from the scoreboard to the field. He charged back up to the fence as the next batter sliced the ball into right field.

Sitting in his seat, Kyle squeezed his hands together while his feet bounced like pistons in an engine, up and down, against the stadium floor. He glanced at the scoreboard, then at the runners. He jumped out of his seat, hugged the rail and screamed, "Come on, Hens, hold'em!"

Brian checked the runners on first and third base. He raced through what he would do if the ball came to him. There was no force at home. So if he threw to Juan, the runner could stay at third then they'd have the bases loaded with one out, but if he could turn a double play he could get the Hens out of the inning without a run being scored. Brian watched the Clippers best hitter Kimmet move into the batter's box, or, he thought, Kimmet could hit another home run.

As Kimmet swung, everything seemed to happen in slow motion. The bat broke. The top half flew against the side of the visitor's dugout. The ball hopped twice on the infield then died in the grass. The third base runner took off for home. Brian moved to cover second as the shortstop Kern raced in, bent and one handed the ball. Pivoting, Kern threw the ball before falling on the infield. Brian could feel the runner charging from first base. He caught the ball not with his mitt but his throwing hand. His right foot touched the bag then pushed off and up. He was airborne. He threw the ball to first base. As the runner slid into second base, he caught the bottom of Brian's right foot. Brian couldn't see the first baseman as he cart wheeled through the air. As soon as Brian landed he knew something was wrong. Trying to ignore the sharp pain in his ankle, he grimaced as he pushed up into a sitting position. The roaring crowd let him know he got the double play. The base runner, his face dazed, pressed his hand against his cheek. Brian pushed up to go towards him. As he took a step, the pain was so intense he collapsed. His left leg stretched out in front of him, Brian sat on the infield and stared dumbfounded at his ankle.

Jamal dropped down on his knees and bent over Brian. Looking at Brian's face the trainer said, "You look pretty pale, Brian. Is it your leg?"

Brian bit his lower lip and nodded his head.

"Where abouts?" asked Jamal.

"My ankle," Brian took a breath and pointed to his left foot.

Jamal ran his ebony hands gently down Brian's lower leg. He traced the tibia, the main bone in the lower leg, with his palms; then checked the fibula, the supporting connecting bone, that ran parallel to the tibia on the outside of the leg. His hands flowed down and checked Brian's ankle. "It's swelling already." Jamal lifted Brian's leg and pushed back against the ball of Brian's foot. Brian winced. "Sorry, Brian." Jamal's hands continued checking the top and sides of Brian's ankle and foot then he sat back on his feet, glanced at the other trainer Tom and said, "I need an air cast." Tom got up and ran across the infield.

Propped up on his elbows, his face reflecting pain, Brian asked, "Is it broken?"

Jamal rested Brian's ankle on his leg. "Brian there are like twenty six bones in your foot. There's no way I can tell if one of them is broken without an x-ray."

Tom, breathing heavily, flopped down next to Jamal. Reaching into the first aid bag, Jamal pulled out a plastic air cast. He untied Brian's left shoe and carefully removed it. He slid the bottom of the air cast under Brian's heel. The two plastic sides covered Brian's lower leg. "It doesn't matter if it's broken or sprained." Jamal wiped his hands on his pants then adjusted the velcro straps around the plastic supports. "We need to immobilize your ankle and get some ice on it to try and keep the swelling down."

Brian watched as Jamal tightened the straps. He looked up into his dad's concerned eyes, then to Coach Bruno. Juan was standing next to the coach with his catcher's helmet pushed up and resting on top of his head.

"Can I walk?" asked Brian.

Jamal loosened the laces on Brian's cleats then slid his shoe back on his foot. He glanced at Brian. "What are you trying to do, put me out of a job?" Jamal flashed a smile at Brian. "Tom and I will get you off the field. Then we'll take some x-rays."

"After the game," said Brian.

Jamal looked firmly at Brian. "We keep it iced."

Brian nodded.

Jamal stood on one side of Brian, Tom on the other. They bent over. Brian reached up and put his arms around their shoulders. As Tom and Jamal straightened, Brian shifted his weight onto his right leg. They waited as Brian got his bearings then half-carried Brian off the field. Kevin reached down and picked up Brian's glove from the infield. Completely bewildered, Kevin thought this can't be happening. Not now! He smacked Brian's glove against his leg. He watched his son hobbling between the two trainers then slowly followed them to the dugout.

"He'll be okay," asserted Stanley.

"What are they doing to his leg?" asked Red.

"Looks like they're putting some sort of cast on it," Chris said.

"They're probably just being . . . careful, you know," continued Stanley.

"Brian just needs to get up and walk it off," said Red.

"Yeah. There he goes," said Chris. "Brian's getting up now."

Kyle held the rail like he was holding onto a life buoy. His friends kept stealing glances at him, but Kyle's eyes only focused on Brian sitting in the infield. He bit his lower lip as his foot tapped against the pavement. As he saw the trainers help Brian from the field he said forlornly, "Aw, Gees." He sank down onto his seat, put his elbows on his knees and dropped his head between his hands.

Ali felt the hand on her arm pulling her back. She turned to Karen, wiped the tears from her cheeks. "I've got to go to him."

"He'll be okay, Ali."

"I need to see him."

"Kevin's there."

"But he's hurt."

Karen fought to keep the tremor from her voice. All she wanted to do was run down to the dugout and make sure her son was okay, to take him into her arms and somehow take away his pain. Karen saw the panic in Ali's eyes. She took Ali's hand and said as much to herself as to Ali. "Let's sit down. Kevin's with him. Brian will be fine. The game's almost over."

Brian sat on the bench while Jamal taped an ice bag around his ankle. He looked down at the ground to avoid the stares from his somber teammates.

Juan sat on a bench next to him and asked," You okay, Brian?"

Still in a daze, Brian tried to think of something to say, but nothing came to him so he just shrugged his shoulders. As the ice numbed the throbbing pain in his ankle, Brian closed his eyes and leaned back against the dugout wall. He was overcome with the feeling that he let everyone down. He remembered the look on his father's face as he leaned over him in the infield. Brian could see the care and concern but underneath, it was like his dad was screaming, "Not now! How could you do this to me!"

From his spot on the steps leading to the field Coach Bruno looked up at the scoreboard then back at his despondent players in the dugout. He mumbled, "Shit," then charged into the dugout. "Miller, get your bat, get out there." As the eighth-place hitter grabbed his bat from the rack, Coach Bruno looked around the dugout, "Hey! We've got a game to finish. One run. Any sort of run and we've got the pennant. Come'n, bottom of ninth, it's our game to win. I don't want any extra innings. Let's end it now." He walked across the dugout and stood in front of Leroy Brown. "You ready Leroy. You gonna knock one out of here? Keep me from getting any more gray hair?"

"Yeah, Coach. I can do that."

Coach Bruno smacked his hands together. "Let's do it then." He faced Brian who sat by the rail, his foot propped up on the bench covered by an ice bag. "Rally cap time, Brian?"

Brian managed to smile. "Yeah, Coach." Brian took off his Hens cap and put it on backwards.

"Yeah! Rally cap time!" Juan shouted as he reversed his cap then stood by the rail looking out to the field.

Brian sat alone on the bench in the dugout. His view of the field was blocked by his teammates standing at the rail. The ice bag deadened the throbbing pain in his ankle. He pounded his fist against the bench in sheer frustration. His dad was standing by Coach Bruno near the steps leading to the field. He gave me the key to the game. Wilson telegraphs it. He telegraphs his change up. He heard the announcer, "Strike one." Brian lifted his left leg off the bench. He grimaced as his foot touched the ground. Pushing up from the bench he tried to keep most of his weight on his right foot. Edging his left foot out, he took a baby step forward. Sharp pain shot up his leg. He shifted more weight onto his swollen ankle and felt the air cast tighten around his calf. "Strike two." Another step forward.

"Brian, you got to keep your leg elevated," shouted Jamal as he raced across the dugout. Hearing the shout, the Hens players turned from the rail. They saw Brian wave Jamal away and hobble another step towards them. Juan pushed his teammates aside, making a spot for Brian. "Strike three." Brian grabbed the rail. Miller was coming back to the dugout. Leroy stood in the on deck circle staring at Wilson. Brian could hear Juan mumbling a prayer. Brian glanced to the scoreboard then surveyed the thousands of standing fans, each one seeming to hold his breath. One run. We need one run for the pennant. We have to get that run. Brian shifted his eyes from the fans to the on deck circle and shouted, "Leroy!"

Leroy Brown snapped his head to the dugout his face conveying: What the hell do you want? Don't bother me.

"Leroy!" Brian's hands quickly motioned Brown to come to him.

A scowl creasing his face, Leroy swung his bat up on his shoulder and slowly walked to the dugout. Looming over Brian, his brow contracted in anger he said, "What?"

"Wilson." Brian nodded in the direction of the pitcher's mound but he couldn't see Wilson with Leroy towering before him. "His change up. He telegraphs it." Brian flicked the back of his wrist over his upper lip. "That's what he does just before he throws his change up."

Leroy Brown's coal black eyes questioned Brian. "You sure?"

Brian nodded.

Leroy leaned forward, his hot breath steaming Brian's face. "You best not be setting me up!"

Brian angrily swiped the back of his fist across his mouth. "That's what he does before he throws his change-up."

Leroy looked over his shoulder at Wilson then back to Brian. When Brian met and held his stare, Leroy swung around and walked to the batter's box.

Leroy lifted the bat above his head and flexed his immense shoulder muscles. He squared off in the batter's box and stared at Wilson. The pitcher didn't stare back, just concentrated on the catcher's mitt. Leroy watched the first pitch all the way. The fastball cut right across his chest for strike one. Stepping out of the batter's box, Leroy took a couple of practice swings. He glanced at Brian, then settled back in the box. Wilson shook off the catcher's flashed hand sign. Leroy focused on Wilson's wind-up. When he didn't see Wilson swipe his fist on his mouth, he looked for Wilson's fastball all the way. He swung. The fans exhaled cheering the ball on. Leroy jogged down the first base line his hands pushing against the air trying to keep the ball from drifting foul. He stopped, his hands dropping to his side as the ball landed in "The Roost" on the right side of the yellow foul ball pole.

Leroy scooped up his bat and glanced at the scoreboard: no balls, two strikes. He told himself, the pitcher will waste a pitch.

Wilson shook off one sign and then another. He finally nodded his head.

When Leroy didn't see Wilson swipe his lip he knew Wilson would waste a pitch. Wilson would throw a pitch close but out of the strike zone. He sat on it watching the ball streak to the plate, a spec of white flashing past on the inside corner of the plate right above his knees.

"Strike three! You're out!"

Leroy spun and glared at the home plate umpire screaming, "IT WAS A BALL!"

"YOU'RE OUT!" The umpire pointed his finger at Leroy then to the Hens dugout.

Lifting his bat, Leroy charged forward. The umpire backpedaled. Coach Bruno raced from the dugout, grabbed Leroy's sleeve and spun him around. Leroy stared down at the short stocky coach. The coach's head didn't even come to his shoulders, but it was Coach Bruno's glaring eyes that stopped Leroy.

"Get on the bench!" screamed Coach Bruno.

Leroy looked around the stadium at the crowd watching him. He ripped off his batting helmet and hurled it against the wall behind home plate then stomped to the dugout. He barged past the Hens players to the locker room.

As Brian stood at the rail watching Leroy Brown walk to the batter's box, he shifted more weight onto his swollen ankle to find out how much weight his leg could bear. He glanced at Wilson as he took the sign from the catcher. The guy's all business. Watching Leroy take the first strike, Brian glanced around the stadium feeling the collective heart pounding of ten thousand Hens fans. He gazed to "The Roost." Kyle and his friends in their St. John's baseball jerseys were staring intently as Leroy stepped back into the batter's box. Brian rocked from one foot to the other. He looked across to the bleachers by the visitor's dugout. He saw the cowboy hat and then Bobby, but the boy wasn't staring at Leroy Brown, he was looking at Brian.

Hearing the crack of the bat, Brian snapped his head back to the batter's box. He was barely able to catch the flight of the ball. Juan was screaming, "Go! Get out of here!" He saw Leroy jogging down the baseline trying to will the ball fair.

When the ball landed foul, Brian felt the whole stadium was on a roller coaster at Cedar Point that just plunged into a dive. He saw Leroy pick up his bat then glance at the scoreboard. Brian knew Wilson wouldn't throw his change up. Not now. Not with two strikes and no balls on Leroy. He wouldn't give Leroy anything to hit. The pitcher would try to cut a corner. You've got two strikes, Leroy. You've got to protect the plate. You've got to watch for a strike on the corner.

Brian watched Leroy throw his helmet against the backstop after being called out on strikes. When Leroy stomped to the dugout Brian limped away from the rail and collapsed on the bench.

Kyle looked from the scoreboard to the empty on-deck circle. Rising up on his toes, Kyle pressed his hands against his cap and said, "It's Brian's turn." He fought the twelve-year-old tears building in his eyes willing Brian to appear in the on-deck circle. "It's Brian's turn to bat."

Kyle glanced at Stanley on his left, then to Chris and Red on his right. He fought the rising panic that spread through his young chest. "Brian's got to bat. It's his turn." He wiped the tears overflowing his eyes and streaking his cheeks. He jumped up on the rail and yelled, "BRIAN!"

His friends stared at Kyle suspended above them. Kyle screamed again, "BRIAN!" They looked at each other and as Kyle began to scream again, they joined in. "BRIAN!"

Hens fans in the bleachers turned and looked in the direction of the young screams. Some fans pointed to the boy standing on the rail.

Kyle's scream turned into a chant. "BRIAN! BRIAN! BRIAN!"

Brian sat on the bench hearing his name chanted by the thousand of Hens fans. He wondered if Bobby was still there. He couldn't see "The Roost" but he could picture Kyle and his friends standing at the rail. Turning his head he saw his father, by the steps of the dugout, watching him. He wondered, whose dream was he carrying?

Brian bent and ripped the tape holding the ice bag on his ankle. The ice bag fell to the floor. He sat up and saw Juan watching him with a look that said, what are you doing? Brian held out his hand to his friend. When Juan came forward, Brian clasped his strong forearm. He pulled himself up from the bench, wincing as he put his weight on his left foot. He wobbled on his good leg then grabbed Juan's shoulder to regain his balance. Looking at Juan, he tried to smile but it came out more as a grimace. He pushed off from Juan's shoulder and shuffled forward.

The Hens players watched Brian limp forward as the chant from the spectators drifted down the dugout steps.

As Brian walked to Coach Bruno, assistant coach Meyers cut in front of him and said, "Brian, what are you doing? Get back on the bench. Evans, get your bat."

Brian ignored Coach Meyers. He kept shuffling forward, forcing Meyers to the side. He stopped in front of Coach Bruno. "Coach."

Meyers shouted, "He can't bat. Put Evans in."

Coach Bruno chewed on the toothpick half buried by his thick mustache. His eyes shifted from Brian to Jamal. The trainer lifted his hands and shrugged his shoulders. Coach Bruno glanced around at the Hens faces watching him then stopped at Kevin. He remembered the look on Kevin's face when he cut him from the team and what happened to his team that year. He flicked his toothpick to the dugout's floor, swung around to Meyers and said, "I'm not making that mistake again." Facing Brian, he asked, "You want to bat?"

Brian nodded.

Coach Bruno dug another toothpick out of his top pocket. "Go bat."

"Brian," said Juan. Brian turned and took his bat from Juan. He ambled to the steps and stood next to his father. Handing the bat to his dad, he took his batting gloves from his back pocket.

"You've got to make him think you're anxious," said Kevin. "When you get up there, swing at that first pitch. I don't care where it's at. You just swing fast. He'll come back with it. It may not be the next pitch, but he'll come back with his change up."

Brian took the bat from his father's hands. He held it in his left hand as his right hand grabbed the rail. He used his hand to help pull his body up the steps while keeping the weight off his left leg. Brian stopped. He took a breath then turned and faced his father and said, "Dad."

It was the same smile, thought Kevin, the six-year-old kid with the large, orange plastic bat on his small shoulder and the Hens cap falling down over his eyes. Brian's smile. Kevin could feel his throat tighten as he swallowed. He nodded his head towards the field. "They're waiting."

Brian turned and took the last step out into the harsh, bright lights of the stadium. Kevin put his foot on the step, leaned forward and rested his arm on his knee in the shadow of the dugout.

Brian stepped from the dugout. The fans grew silent as they watched him limp with the air cast on his leg across the on-deck circle. The only sound Brian heard was the fluttering of the flags high above the stadium. He ignored the throbbing in his ankle. He glanced at the visitor's dugout and saw the Clippers standing at the rail watching him, then looked back to his solemn teammates with their rally caps. It was so quiet Brian felt he was in church.

Wilson wouldn't look at him. He kept pawing the dirt in front of the pitching rubber with his heel. The ball was hidden in his mitt resting on his hip. Brian settled in the batter's box. He shifted his body trying to keep all of his weight on his back, right leg. He brought his bat back, high above his right shoulder, lowered his chin to his left shoulder and focused on Wilson.

Wilson looked past Brian to his catcher. He took the sign. He suddenly reared back and turned to the Clippers dugout. The Clippers Coach nodded his head at Wilson. The pitcher squeezed the ball in his hand. He turned and shook his head.

Out of the corner of his eye, Brian saw the catcher move a couple of steps towards first base. It took him a second before Brian realized what was happening. Wilson lofted the ball to the catcher. *No! You can't do this*, Brian wanted to scream as the

Clippers catcher threw the ball back to the pitcher. *You can't walk me.* Brian let the tip of his bat fall down and rest on home plate. Using the bat like a cane he pivoted, faced the pitcher and shouted, "Wilson. Look at me!"

Wilson caught the ball. He slowly looked from his catcher to Brian.

Brian screamed, "You're not going to walk me! They didn't keep you down here to walk me!" Brian jammed his bat into home plate and pushed upright. He lifted the bat behind his shoulder. "Pitch to me!"

Fingering the ball in his mitt, Wilson returned Brian's stare. It was just the two of them, the pitcher and the batter. Wilson lifted the ball from his glove. "New ball, Ump." He tossed the ball to his catcher.

His weight settled on his right leg, Brian watched as Wilson rubbed his right hand along his thigh touched the brim of his hat then lifted the glove in front of his chest. He quickly went into his wind-up. Brian swung as soon as the ball left Wilson's fingers. It felt like a dentist's drill hitting an exposed nerve in his ankle. The sharp, needle pain shot up Brian's leg. He jammed the top of his bat into the ground to keep from falling. A white light flashed across his eyes. His teeth clicked as his jaw snapped shut.

"You okay, kid?"

Brian heard the catcher's voice behind him. Not trusting himself to speak he just nodded. He used his bat for support as he stood in the batter's box.

Wilson saw the look of pain on Brian's pale face. He turned his back to Brian, shoved his glove under his armpit then rubbed the ball between his hands. He peered up into the stadium lights, wiped the back of his wrist over his upper lip, snapped the ball into his glove and turned towards Brian.

Brian watched as Wilson ran his hand along his thigh, touched the brim of his hat and brought the glove in front of his chest. As the ball shot forward from Wilson's fist, Brian started his swing. He stopped. The ball streaked below his knees. The umpire behind the plate pointed to the first base umpire who signaled "no." Brian didn't go around. Ball two signaled the umpire.

Brian stayed in the batter's box, waiting for Wilson's next pitch. He centered his weight on his right foot. He watched Wilson, thigh, cap, chest. He saw the ball heading straight down the center of the plate. He swung. Late. The ball careened off the bat into the netting high behind the catcher. The umpire held his hands up. Two fingers raised on each hand.

Brian limped out of the box. He let the top of the bat fall to the ground. His left fist pressed against it like a cane. In the chill September night air his face was bathed in sweat. He took off his Hens cap and wiped his right sleeve along his forehead. He looked up at the flags swirling in the breeze. As he shifted the bat to his right hand, he closed his eyes and blew out a breath. He opened his eyes and lifted the bat in front of his chest with both hands. Twisting his fists on the handle, he stared at the bat. He felt as if someone was standing right behind him. Brian glanced back over his shoulder, shook his head then went back into the batter's box. When he looked at Wilson, the pitcher wasn't looking at his catcher's mitt but staring at Brian.

Brian lifted the bat high behind his head. He lowered his chin to his shoulder. He took a shallow breath and entered the zone, just himself and the pitcher. Wilson rubbed his hand along his thigh, touched the brim of his cap, and wiped the sweat from his upper lip with the back of his wrist, and brought his mitt in front of his chest. He quickly went into his wind-up.

A split second of disbelief as Brian watched the back of Wilson's hand swipe his upper lip then, like being hit with a jolt of electricity, his whole body tingled. He whispered, "Grandpa." Brian smiled and waited and swung.

As soon as the bat made contact, Brian pivoted his right foot and pushed off. He tossed his bat. As he took the first step, it felt like a knife jabbed into the side of his ankle. He pulled up and dragged his left foot behind him down the baseline, watching the ball streak towards "The Roost."

Kevin jerked like he was hit as Brian's bat hit the ball. His breath whooshed from his chest. His eyes were pinpoints as they saw the ball take flight. No breath. The drumming of his heart filled his ears. The pinpoints expanded to pen points as the ball sailed from the infield. No breath. The infielders turned and watched the ball fly to the outfield. Kevin lost it in the artificial lights. He found it, like a falling star streaking down from the heavens. The right fielder backed up against the wall. Kevin's eyes widened as he watched the ball sail over Kyle's outstretched arms. He screamed, "YESSSSS! YESSSSS!" He punched the air with his fist. "BRIAN!"

Kevin stood on the top step of the dugout. He watched his son limp from first to second. The fireworks exploded behind the scoreboard. Like an answering salvo, the Labor Day Citifest fireworks display ignited above the air over the Maumee River. Blinded by the lights, Kevin looked back to the field. He saw the Hens players run out to the diamond and surround Brian, Juan's arm supporting his son as they circled the bases. Wilson walked from the pitcher's mound to the Clippers dugout. Kevin saw him look back at his son. The pitcher shrugged, then Kevin swore he saw him smile.

Chapter 38

In the empty Hens dugout after the game, Jamal taped a new ice bag to Brian's calf. "I want you to head over to St. V's. They'll probably want to take x-rays." Jamal cut the tape holding the ice bag then looked up at Kevin sitting on the bench next to Brian. When Kevin nodded, Jamal turned and smiled at Brian. "Hey, you're young. Couple of weeks from now you'll be back doing cartwheels." Jamal lifted Brian's leg and slid a stool under the air cast. "Here, take these." Jamal reached into the first aid bag by his side. He shook out a couple extra strength Tylenols. "Let them know at St. V's I gave you two here." He handed Brian one of the bottled waters from the bottom of his bag. "I've got to check on MacKay's shoulder. He said it was tightening up on him." Jamal patted Brian's thigh then pushed up and left the dugout.

Brian nodded at Jamal's retreating figure, popped the Tylenols in his mouth and took a gulp of water. He leaned back on the bench and rested his shoulders against the dugout wall trying to ignore the throbbing in his ankle. Shouts and shrieks of laughter came from the Hens locker room. He remembered his teammates carrying him off the field. He looked to the empty baseball diamond suddenly realizing he would never play there again. The image of his grandfather on his deathbed, and seeing Bobby in the locker room kept his life spinning in a different direction, a direction he knew he had to follow. Looking to second base he was overwhelmed with a sense of loss, with a sense that he was leaving the game behind.

"I knew we had a set around here somewhere," said Coach Bruno as he propped the crutches on the wall next to Brian.

Brian blinked his eyes and stared at his coach. He watched the ever-present toothpick bob under the mustache as Coach Bruno cocked his head towards the locker room and continued, "You'd think those boys never won a game before. How 'bout we go join them?"

"Nah," said Brian. "I'm kind a beat right now."

Kevin said, "Jamal wants him to go to St. V's for some x-rays."

Coach Bruno nodded and looked down at Brian. He touched Brian's shoulder gently. "Your locker, Brian, it'll be here. For as long as I'm here, it'll be waiting." He lifted his hand and extended it to Kevin. "You ever want a job as a pitching coach . . ."

Kevin shook his hand. "Thanks, Coach." Kevin glanced up to "The Roost." "I've got my own team."

Coach Bruno held on to Kevin's hand as he grinned at Brian. "Let me know if you got any more Brian's coming up." Coach Bruno released Kevin's hand, "You two, don't be strangers around here."

"I got your mitt," said Juan as the locker door closed on the celebration behind him. "But I have no idea where your bat bag is hiding."

Looking at Juan, Brian couldn't help but laugh. Juan's jet-black hair was pasted flat on his forehead. His uniform top was splattered with champagne while the ends of his shirt hung out over his pants.

"Gees, it's a mad house in there, Brian." As Juan came forward he asked, "You okay, compadre?"

"I'm good, Juan."

Juan wiped his damp hair back from his forehead. "We showed them out there today."

Brian smiled. "Your head first slide into second was more than worth the price of the ticket."

Juan rubbed the scratches under his chin. "You got that right. Come on in, the guys are waiting."

"Nah." Brian motioned to his leg. "They want to take some pictures."

"You're okay, right?" Juan asked.

"I'll be fine. You know Jamal, he's just covering his ass."

Juan glanced at the crutches then to Brian's glove. "Well . . ."

Kevin stood and took the glove from Juan with his left hand as he held his right hand out. Juan shook his hand. Kevin wondered, how do I thank him? What can I say in front of Brian? "Juan . . ."

Seeing Kevin's face Juan knew what he was trying to say. Juan cut him off. "Mr. McBride, no problem." He swiftly glanced to Brian. "Hey, next time we hit Loma Linda's, you're buying." Juan looked at Brian's left leg. "I guess I'll have to drive."

"Nah," said Brian. "Ali will drive."

"You did good out there, Brian," said Juan.

"We all did good."

Juan turned and reluctantly started to walk away. "Oh," he stopped. His hand rubbed his chest. "Your medal."

"Juan, it's yours," said Brian.

Juan started to say something but stopped. He waved at Brian, "Later."

Kevin reached down and picked up Brian's bat. He slid the handle of the bat through the open end of the glove's wrist strap. Brian watched his father swing the bat up on his shoulder with his glove dangling from the end.

Brian asked, "Where'd you learn how to do that?"

Kevin replied, "When I was a kid, no one had a bat bag." Kevin extended his free hand. Brian clutched the hand while his dad pulled him to his feet. Kevin handed Brian the crutches.

Brian slid them under his armpits and looked at the closed locker room door. Kevin sensed his son didn't want to leave through the lockers. "We can cut across the diamond and go out the main entrance."

Brian nodded.

The stadium was empty. The artificial, overhead lights were dimming. Kevin walked slowly with Brian's glove and bat slung over his shoulder. His son hobbled next to him on his crutches. Kevin's eyes kept glancing to the pitcher's mound.

Brian looked up and spotted two figures by the entrance. One broke away and ran towards him. He saw long, wavy reddish blonde hair streaming backwards and laughing emerald eyes. Ali squeezed him so tightly his ribs hurt. Her damp cheek pressed against his face. When he breathed in he could smell the forest in her hair.

As he opened his eyes, he saw his mother walking towards him carrying a shoebox in her hands. Brian watched as she stopped and slid the string off the box. Karen opened the shoebox and slid the lid under the box. Brian stared at the mitt.

When Karen lifted the mitt from the box and held it out to their son Kevin said, "Brian." He waited for his son to look at him. "Take it with you to college." Looking at his father, Brian remembered the photo in his dad's office, the photo with his dad's arm around his shoulder.

Brian leaned on his crutches. He reached out and held the mitt in his hands. His thumb rubbed circles on the smooth, oily surface. As he caressed the mitt, he heard his mother say, "It was your grandfather's. He wanted you to have it. He said it would bring you home."

Brian and the author